LAVENDER HAZE

HARTMAN SISTERS

BOOK TWO

A.N. LEE

This book was written entirely by the author without the use of artificial intelligence tools.

First Edition: July 2026

ISBN: 979-8-9944304-1-5 [digital]

979-8-9944304-4-6 [paperback]

Editing: Amy Pritt

Cover Design: A.N. Lee

Visit the author's website at www.authoranlee.com

To my little flowers,
It has been my greatest gift in life to be able to watch the two of you grow and bloom.
I love you both with all of my heart.

AUTHOR'S NOTE

Lavender Haze contains explicit language, a panic attack, several explicit sexual scenes, and scenes dealing with past trauma (car accident). *Lavender Haze* is not suitable for readers under the age of eighteen. Happy reading!

CHAPTER ONE

LINDSAY

"Oh, I know. There have been so many changes recently, but I am really excited for a more flexible work schedule." As Stephanie continues discussing all of the new work-life balance *improvements* to our company, I can't help but internally laugh at the concept.

Work-life balance. Yeah, I have none of that. I've always excelled with my work life, but my personal? Not so much.

The most recent example being me canceling last minute on a trip overseas with my sisters. I felt like shit, but a client called with a wedding emergency that required me to stay behind. And next thing I knew, I was canceling my Barcelona extended-weekend getaway.

But I love my job. It's the one thing I feel truly in control of. I've worked hard to prepare myself for anything that can and could go wrong, making it easy for me to step in and fix the problem before it ruins what should be the bride and groom's best day of their lives. It's why I've gotten promoted time and time again. And if my personal life pays the cost of that? So be it. It's not like I had much of one to begin with.

Stephanie taps my arm, bringing me back to the conversation. "Lindsay, you have a meeting with Fran later today, yeah?"

"Yes, it's at four-thirty, so I'll be pulling another late night to make up for it."

"Lindsay, it's not called 'another late night' if you've made those your regular hours," Rick jokes, making everyone else laugh at my expense. I can't really be mad since the statement is painfully accurate.

Most of my meals are eaten in my office, whether ordered out or made by me, though I can't remember the last time I took the time to cook, let alone prepare meals for myself.

Hell, I'm so attached to being at my office that I even have one of those under the desk treadmills because there's no way I'm able to squeeze in time at the gym with the hours I keep. But even with the convenience of an in-office workout, I still cannot find time to use it.

My phone rings, providing the perfect excuse for me to leave the conversation and step inside my office.

"Hello, you've reached Lindsay."

"Lindsay." I sigh at my mother's disapproving tone on the line. I've seen her missed calls but haven't taken the time to call her back. "I hate having to resort to calling you on your office phone."

With the current workload I'm carrying, I really don't have time to talk to her right now, but if I don't, she'll just keep calling. I know she means well. I know it's out of love. I just don't have the time or energy to explain why I've been so absent recently.

Relenting, I take a seat at my desk. "Hi, Mom. How are you and Dad doing?"

"It's been almost a month since I've heard from you, Linds. If you hadn't texted your sisters, I would have thought you were dead. I miss you. You work yourself to the bone."

And this, this *exact* conversation, is why I put off calling or texting her. She's always giving me a hard time about work or not taking time for myself. It comes from a good place. I know she doesn't want me to work my life away, but I enjoy what I do. I can't help that it's my passion, plus it's not like I have much of a social life anyway.

"I'm fine, Mom. Just busy as always. I'm sorry I haven't reached out."

And I truly am. It's not like I don't get along with my family; I do. I absolutely adore them, and when I *am* with them, I'm able to relax and joke around.

My sisters and I try our best to do a boozy brunch every month, even though I've missed the last two. Shit, now that I think about it, maybe it's been more like four. I should really make it a point to go to the next one.

"I was wondering if you were going to be at Sunday lunch, seeing how you've been missing. And from what I've heard from your sisters, you've skipped a few brunches, too." Busted.

"I'll do my best, Mom."

"Emma's in town for the next few days and I'm sure she'd *love* to see you."

"Way to lay the guilt on thick, Mom."

Emma, my baby sister, has been in Barcelona for the last few months. She's been busy with her job as well as her new beau. From what I hear, he's a great guy. I'm hoping to meet him at Taylor's—my twin sister—wedding in a couple of months.

"Well . . . I won't keep you any longer. I love and miss you dearly."

"Love you too, Mom. I'll talk to you later."

After a few hours filled with work calls and emails, a chime rings my computer telling me it's time for my meeting with Fran. Four-thirty came around sooner than I anticipated. After a quick desk clean, I make my way down the hallway to the corner office.

"Lindsay, hi. Thanks for coming in today," Fran greets with a sincere smile as she waves to the chair in front of her.

Fran's a relatively new face around here. She's been shaking things up and the rest of my coworkers love her for it.

She believes that having a low-stress work environment not

only equates to happier employees but better work performance. Which in turn creates a more successful business. It's easy to understand the logic, I personally just have never put it in practice.

Ever since college graduation, I've kept my nose to my desk. Worked all hours of the day, including weekends. Holidays even. I've gone as far as canceled trips to help with client emergencies. I can't even remember the last time I went out with friends or on a date. Hell, or even had decent sex.

Taking a seat in front of Fran's desk, I find myself a bit nervous, not quite sure what this meeting is about.

"I called you here today because I am trying to check in with everyone at the firm. Making sure all of the changes we recently implemented have been having their desired effect."

"Oh, sure. The changes are great. Everyone seems to like them around the office," I respond anxiously, attempting to confirm what I think she wants to hear.

"That seems to be the common consensus. But I want to specifically hear what *you* think about them." She looks pointedly at me like I'm a student in the principal's office being caught after skipping class.

"You are a hard worker, Lindsay. From what I can tell from your time here at the firm, you've given everything to this company for almost a decade. You're always the first to be here and the last to leave. You happily sacrifice your weekends, while also taking on all the difficult clients without complaining. Taking a deeper look into your file—" That wakes me up. Since when do I have a work file? "—you haven't taken a single sick day or vacation since you've started here."

Is that right? Surely, I must've taken at least *one* day off. I mean the office is closed for all the major, and some not so major, holidays.

"That's *eight* years of nonstop working. All work and no play makes Lindsay a stressed woman."

I huff out a pity laugh. I get the reference she's trying to make, after all I grew-up watching that movie every Halloween with my sisters. I just don't appreciate her relating that character to me. Though the thought of being alone in a hotel, surrounded by nature, actually sounds like it could be a good time.

"I think it's time for you to take some time for yourself and go on a vacation."

"Oh, I'm fine. Truly," I rush out.

I *so* do not have time to take a vacation right now. But if I could find a way to duplicate myself, maybe I could have a little more "me" time.

"Fran, if I can be frank." She nods for me to continue. "I don't have a need or *desire* to take a break right now. I have so many upcoming events, and there's always a bunch of clients to work through—"

"Let me rephrase that. We are placing you on a paid sabbatical for a minimum of two weeks." Surely I didn't hear that right.

"Oh no, that's not necessary." My voice becomes shrill as I start to freak out.

A sabbatical? Me? What would I even do?

"Like I said, there is so much work I have to do. I have clients and—"

"And as you said, there's always a bunch of clients." Her voice is stern as she speaks, leaving no room for argument. "They'll be here when you come back, and I'll have Stephanie and Rick pick up any you may have scheduled for the next few weeks."

"Wait. Are you putting me on leave *now*? At least let me organize my files so they are available for anyone to pick up where I left off."

"You'll have the rest of today if you feel the need. Otherwise, your paid leave starts on Monday, but I don't want you in the office this weekend either."

I sit frozen, completely stunned by the last ten minutes. She's basically giving me a couple of hours to prepare for at least two weeks worth of events and meetings.

"Oh and I forgot the most important part." I look up and see a giddy smile on Fran's face. "Sunday evening, you leave for an all-expenses-paid trip to France!"

What the fuck?

My face turns more confused as I see her smile grow even bigger. I have a terrible poker face and have never done a great job at hiding my facial expressions.

"Isn't that great? You'll be staying in this adorable hotel that has everything you need to relax and unwind. All of your meals will be provided, and they even have some activities you can participate in if you so choose." She taps a manila folder on her desk. "Everything you need is in this, and an email should be in your *personal* inbox with all of the details. The firm takes work-life balance very seriously and we hope this can jumpstart yours."

I'm utterly shocked as I look at Fran. I have no words for what just happened.

Fran stands up from her spot behind her desk. "Lindsay, you really do deserve a break. I hope you enjoy this time away and come back refreshed. *Bon voyage*!"

And with that she ushers me out of her office.

What the fuck just happened?

"Hi, Darling! Oh, I'm so happy you came!" Mom pulls me right into a warm hug. My sisters and niece are already sitting on the couch talking with each other. Dad's out on the patio barbecuing his famous ribs by the smell of it.

"Hi, Mom." I smile and step out of the hug. "Hey ladies." Waving, I step over to the girls.

"Hey, sis!"

"Hi, Linds."

"Hi there, Auntie L."

"Hey, hey!"

I take a seat in Dad's chair while I look around the living room, finding everyone's eyes on me. "How's everyone been?"

"Well, Haylee and I just booked our flights to Greece for her gap year," Tory says while squeezing Haylee's leg. Haylee's a smart kid. She deserves a break from school, and I'm glad she and my sister are taking that quality time together.

"That sounds like a fun time. I'm sure you'll eat a ton of great food and make some great memories with each other," I reply, internally figuring out how to bring up my own trip I'm leaving for tonight.

"And a great tan," Taylor chirps.

"Or even a man!" I turn to Emma and see her shit-eating grin.

"Emma!" Tory bites out.

"Men are just made different over there. Must be something in the water," Emma adds with a smirk.

I know the "men" she's referencing is really just the man she met a couple months back. Everything seemed so sudden when she decided to move to Barcelona full time, but all in all, I'm happy she's happy.

"Speaking of men . . . how are wedding plans coming along Taylor?" Same ol' Mom, always so subtle.

Taylor fidgets with her skirt while gazing out the window. "It's been going good. You know how Jess' Mom is. She's handling everything. I just show up whenever and wherever she tells me. Less stress that way."

Taylor has been in a relationship for five years. None of us really have a relationship with her fiancé, Jess, but then again it's hard to have bonding time when someone is always working.

Pot, meet kettle.

My relationship with Taylor hasn't been the same since she's been with Jess. There was an argument that happened a few Christmases back that resulted in us becoming distant.

We both had a little too much of Mom's "adult" eggnog and

said some things that could've used some filtering. Ever since then, our relationship hasn't been what it was . . . or what I'd like it to be.

"Ladies! Ribs are done!" Dad shouts from the kitchen.

"Come on. Let's get some food girls." Mom leads us into the kitchen.

Looking at all the homemade food, I realize it's been too long since I've had a home cooked meal. Mashed potatoes, summer salad, and Dad's ribs. Everything smells divine. We all dish up and take our seats around the table.

"So it's been a minute, Linds. How's work going?" Taylor asks before diving straight into her plate.

I guess now's as good of a time as any to bring up my news.

"Funny you should ask." I look down at my plate to avoid any eye contact. "I was put on a sabbatical starting, well"—I clear my throat—"immediately."

"What?!"

I hear someone drop their fork and can just *feel* the multiple sets of eyes staring at me.

"What happened, Lindsay?" Dad asks with a concerned tone.

"Nothing *happened*. We have a new regional manager and she's big on making sure we don't over stress ourselves." The table goes quiet, so I just continue rambling. "She may have mentioned I haven't taken a sick day since I've been at this job. So she put me on leave in the hopes I'll come back 'refreshed.' Whatever the hell that means."

"Well, we know you love your job, and take pride in doing it so well. That must've been hard to hear, " Dad consoles as he gives me a pitying look. He's always been our biggest cheerleader, so I'm sure he's just as bummed as I am.

"How long's the sabbatical?" Tory asks.

"She said at least two weeks." I shake my head. "Oh and get this." I chuckle as I continue to share the news I'm still having a hard time accepting. "They're sending me to some small boutique hotel in Provence. All expenses paid and everything."

"Provence? You mean France?" Mom pipes in.

"Yeah. I looked it up and the hotel looks nice and quiet. There seems to be a small lavender field surrounding one side of the property. Real pretty."

"When do you leave?" I hear Emma ask.

An awkward laugh bursts out of me. "In a few hours actually. My flight takes off around six tonight."

"Way to bury the lead, Linds," Taylor scoffs under her breath.

"Sorry." The word comes out frazzled. "I'm still adjusting to the news myself. Fran just told me Friday afternoon. I spent all day yesterday packing and making sure I have everything I need."

Luckily, I have a valid passport and this hotel doesn't seem like it requires much in terms of wardrobe, making it relatively easy to pack my bag on such short notice.

"Well that will definitely be an adventure for you. Do you need anything else? How are you getting to the airport? You probably need to leave soon then." Mom starts to clear the table, but Tory steps in, taking the dirty dishes from her.

I stand, clearing my end of the table. "Fran seems to have organized everything for the trip already, so I basically just needed to pack and show up at the airport later today."

"Oh, and make sure your e-reader is stuffed with some good books," Haylee adds. Which gets me thinking, when was the last time I used it? Is it even charged? Maybe I can finally read those books I have loaded. I'm sure it needs to be updated too.

"Good idea, Haylee."

I hand the dishes off to Emma as she starts washing them, then she hands them to Haylee who adds them to the dishwasher.

"And yes, I should leave soon, but not without stealing a plate of your blackberry pie, Mom."

"Oh, I guess I can wrap a piece up for you," she says as she sneaks in a kiss on my cheek. I really do need to make time to come to these Sunday lunches.

I clean my hands, grab my pie, and say my goodbyes. "Love y'all. I'll send a text on the group chat when I've landed."

A bunch of "love yous" and "safe travels" get tossed my way as I head out the door and to my car.

France, here I come I guess.

CHAPTER TWO

THEO

Won't be long until this house is finished. If all goes according to plan, I should be able to sell it in about a month's time. Meaning, I need to find a new place soon because it's not only the way I make my income, but it's where I lay my head, too. While I could just move into one of the other projects I have at the moment, all of them are close to being listed as well.

While my way of living isn't for everyone, I'm currently unattached, and live a very nomadic lifestyle, hopping from one project to the next. I never need more than running water, working electrical, and a place to sleep. Thankfully, all the properties I flip check all those boxes. Most times.

The summer's been a doozy so far this year. It's barely July and the humidity is already making me instantly crave a cold shower whenever I walk outside. Not even the air conditioning is providing much relief from the July heat.

I pull the fabric from my shirt up to wipe the sweat off my brow as I finish securing the new bathroom vanity to the wall.

"Hey, Theo?" I hear Mark's voice from down the hall. "You over here?"

"In the bathroom," I shout.

"Hey," he says, appearing in the doorway. "I'm gonna call it a night. But I'll be here at the same time tomorrow, yeah?"

"Yeah, sounds good. Have a great night." Mark nods his thanks. "Tell your wife I'm still dreaming of her sweet rolls," I tease as he heads down the stairs, flipping me off as he nears the door.

Now that I'm alone, I strip off my sweat-drenched cotton tee and head downstairs to see what dinner I can make with whatever is in the fridge.

Opening up my mini-fridge, I find eggs, a bell pepper, turkey deli-meat, and oh, what's this? Leftover steak nachos. Yup, that'll do.

Now if I was at a finished house, I'd just pop the nachos in the oven. But since this property is about a week or so out from getting major appliance installation, I pull out my trusty air fryer.

I learned pretty quickly from bouncing around properties, that an air fryer works pretty damn well. Better than a microwave that's for sure. Have you ever tried reheating nachos in a microwave? Or fries for that matter. They get all gross and soggy, practically making them inedible.

Come to think of it, I haven't found a thing I *can't* cook or reheat in an air fryer. Hell, I even baked a small batch of homemade cinnamon rolls in it just last week. Mark's wife was kind enough to send some my way in an air fryer safe container. She even gave me a little ramekin of cream cheese frosting.

While putting my dinner in the air fryer, my phone rings. It's Dad.

"Hey, there," I greet.

"Hey Son, how are ya doing over there?" Dad hardly ever calls, so something must be wrong.

Sure I talk to him, but Ma is always the one calling, while Dad just hops on at some point during the call. We video call most of the time, but with me living in the States, I don't get to see them as much as I'd like. Though I am thankful for our little chats throughout the week.

"I'm doing okay, Dad. What's going on?" I take a seat as I try to coax him to get right to the point.

"Your grandfather took another fall, and this time it's pretty serious. He's going to have to stay at the hospital for a bit. Your mom and I think it's a good idea for us to go and stay with him."

He must've really done it this time. My grandfather has always been a pretty active man. He started a hotel back when Grandma was still alive, and together they did everything there.

Throughout the years, they got older and the jobs on the property started becoming a little too much. After Grandma passed away, he finally hired more help. But in all honesty, Grandpa should've retired a long time ago, however that little hotel is his pride and joy. Well the hotel, and Ma of course.

When I was younger, we moved around a lot because of Dad's position in the military. We never stayed in one place for more than a year or so. But regardless of where we lived, Ma would make it a point to fly her and me out every summer to help with the influx of guests. After Dad retired, and after I moved out of my parents house, Ma and Dad moved into the family house on the estate in France full time.

"I'm sorry to hear that. I'm sure Ma is a mess. Are you going to shut down the hotel for a bit?"

It wouldn't be the first time the hotel's had to close because of Grandpa getting injured. They did it a few years back when he got his first hip-replacement, and then a couple years before that when he fell and busted his knee.

"Actually, we have a wedding coming up this weekend, so we don't have the luxury of doing that this time." It's clear Dad's tired from his sigh. "We were wondering if you could fly over for the rest of the summer, like you used to. Only for the first week or two, you'll be in charge of the place while we're away."

It's a small hotel, only five rooms, so the wedding can't be *that* big. And it's not like I haven't helped with weddings hosted there before.

"Then you could help with the slack once Grandpa is back home. I'm sure Mom will have her hands full with helping him get back to normal, and the last thing she needs is to be worrying about the hotel. While we're gone, we'd be available by phone, plus we're only going to be a couple hours away if you have any emergencies."

"Would you need me immediately? How full are the reservations for the next couple of weeks? Is there much I need to know about the wedding?" As I pull out my nachos, I rattle off questions but honestly, it doesn't matter. I'd take the first plane out if I needed to.

"It *was* vacant this week, but a couple nights ago we got a reservation for the week. It's just for one person, so it should be an easy time."

Okay, one guest isn't so bad.

"And the wedding party booked out all five rooms, but only for two nights. The wedding is on Sunday so they're checking in on Saturday and leaving Monday morning."

Again, not so bad. This all sounds super manageable.

"Everything for the wedding is already taken care of." Dad tries to convince me but I'm already on board to help out. "We just need someone there to make sure everything goes according to plan while we're gone. If all goes well at the hospital, we'll be back a few days after the wedding."

"Are Mateo and Ettie still going to be there?" I ask before burning my tongue as I attempt my first bite.

Mateo is the hotel's chef, and resident grouch. He's been working there for years, and I never get tired of his cooking. And looking at my mini-fridge, I could surely use some of his gourmet cooking right now.

Colette, or Ettie as everyone calls her, takes care of all the cleaning and housekeeping. She's a nosy one, but I love her. She's been around since I was a toddler waddling the grounds, messing everything up while she cleaned.

"Yes, they aren't going anywhere. Jean is also going to be around to tend to the grounds. So," he pauses. "Can I count on you to take charge while we're gone?"

Like he doesn't already know my answer.

"Of course. I'll take the first flight out I can get. You can give me all the details I need when I get there."

"Thanks, Son. Fly safe."

"Bye, Dad." I hang up and bring my nachos upstairs so I can eat and pack my bag for France.

CHAPTER THREE

LINDSAY

I receive my driver's text, and thirty minutes later, I'm at the airport. When checking in on the app last night, I saw that Fran booked me in business class, which is a pleasant surprise. Especially when the first leg of the trip is supposed to be eight hours.

Arriving three and a half hours earlier than my scheduled take-off time, I walk into the airport with confidence that I have enough time for check-in and security since I'm flying internationally.

I'm quick to check my bag, which fell right under the fifty-pound limit, avoiding an oversized fee. Luckily, there's not a long line at TSA and I go through without any issues. I haven't flown in a while, so last night I did a quick search to double check the liquid size limitations for carry-ons so my bag hopefully wouldn't get flagged for inspection.

Walking straight to my gate, I make sure it's really there, helping to ease my travel anxiety, before I redirect my focus. With that out of the way, it frees my mind to think about other potential issues. Like how I'm taking a long flight, and what happens if the flight takes longer than scheduled? Do I have enough time to go through customs during my layover in Paris? Is three hours enough of a layover to do customs and get back to my gate in time? What if I miss my flight to Marseille and have to sleep in the airport? I packed a spare outfit in my bag, but what if I spill something and need another one?

Stop. *Breathe in.*

One thing at a time. *Breathe out.*

Anxiety has always been a struggle of mine. One that can be tracked back to when I was eleven, when I was involved in a car accident with my mom and sisters. All of us girls saw therapists when we were younger, but as I got busier with school, and then building a career, therapy sort of took a backseat.

Okay, *fine*. I chucked it out the window.

Before our fight, Taylor always tried to be subtle in suggesting I go back—which is ironic because she stopped going around the time I did, though for different reasons. But even if I *wanted* to pick therapy up again, I don't have time for it. I'm so busy with events that I'm barely at my apartment. And even when I am, if I'm not eating or sleeping, I'm on my laptop or phone, busy with work I've taken home with me.

After using the bathroom and stocking up on some airport snacks, I find a bench to sit down on and wait. I have a solid two hours until they start the boarding process.

Checking my emails on my phone, I realize I have one from Fran that was sent earlier today.

> Lindsay,
>
> I should've known better that you would be tempted to check your work emails. However, I thought one step ahead just in case.
>
> At five tonight, your login information will be changed and you will not have access to your emails until you are back, in office that is. But I did transfer your company phone

plan to international for the next month, so you can keep in touch with friends and family during your trip.

Other than that, I want you to unplug and unwind during this trip, and then continue to do so when you get home for the remainder of your sabbatical.

We appreciate all that you have done for the firm and are looking forward to your return whenever you deem fit.

Warmly,

Fran

What the actual fuck? She's taking away my email access?

It's fine. *Deep breath in.*

You know what? *Deep breath out.*

This is actually better. She said everything will be handled while I'm gone, so I need to trust that she can handle it. I can do that. I just need to . . . *let go.* Or at least attempt to.

After all, she is technically my boss and—

I get jolted from behind and gasp as something cold and wet runs down my back.

"Oh, shit! I am so sorry," a man behind me blurts out. "I lost my balance and tripped, and well, now you have iced coffee all over your back."

I slowly turn around, trying my best not to make this worse, but at this point, the coffee has spread through my shirt, drenching my bra as it trails down my back, cold liquid now hurrying toward the waistline of my pants.

Trying my best to remain calm, I put my palm up. "It's okay. Accidents happen."

I attempt reaching behind me and brushing off as much of the coffee as possible, but really, it's no use. This outfit is trashed. I just need to gather my things and head to the nearest bathroom to change. As I start to walk away, the man comes up beside me and I get my first look at said coffee-spiller.

Work boots of some kind peek out from under his worn blue jeans. A plain white tee is semi-tucked in, the fabric so tight I can confidently say he definitely works out. The sleeves are stretched so tight around his biceps, it looks like he's one flex away bursting those helpless seams. Fuck. He even has veiny forearms. Why do veins always make me so feral?

I raise my head and am met with piercing green eyes. I gaze lower at his jawline covered in scruff that hasn't been trimmed in a few days. A little dimple is definitely hiding behind that facial hair and a smile that—a smile. Shit. He's staring.

Fuck. No, *I'm* staring.

Scratch that. I'm full on *gawking*, and his cheeky smile tells me that he noticed as well.

"Hi, there," he greets with a familiar southern accent, waving his free hand at me and smiling even bigger. "Like I said, I'm really sorry about spilling my coffee all over you. Can I buy you a new shirt over at the gift shop so you're not flying all wet?"

My eyes bulge causing his grin to grow even bigger.

"Wet from the coffee that is," he clarifies then winks. He fucking *winks* as he runs his fingers through his warm caramel hair giving it that freshly tousled look.

I wave him off. "No, I'm good. I have a change of clothes. Thanks, though."

As I'm nearing the bathroom, I hear him shout out, "I truly am sorry about the coffee!"

Head down, I walk right into the bathroom and find the first stall available to get this sticky mess off of me. What a great start to what's supposed to be a relaxing vacation.

CHAPTER FOUR

THEO

God, that bench came out of nowhere. That's what I get for trying to text and walk. And that poor woman.

Though the blush that covered her cheeks after our interaction was adorable. She was pretty cute too. And a short little thing, barely reached my chest. Perfect height in my opinion, especially mixed with her rich auburn hair that reached just under her shoulders with stunning eyes. Glacier blue eyes to be exact. The kind of eyes that leave you haunted.

I definitely ruined her shirt. She looked very professional with her white button down tucked into black dress pants that hugged the subtle curve of her ass. I'm sure those are ruined too. She rushed off so quickly and I didn't even get her name.

I look at my phone and realize I have around an hour and a half before boarding. Because I'm flying so last minute, there wasn't much for flight selection. My options were to either use more of my miles for business class from Raleigh to Paris and Paris to Marseille, or save some miles and suck it up in economy but have three long ass layovers.

Since time was of the essence, I chose the business class. I have a ton of miles saved up so what the hell. Plus, I'll probably sleep the whole flight anyway, and with my height, it's nice to have the extra leg room.

Whenever I fly out to visit Ma and Dad, I always try to get a seat in the exit row or bulkhead. Fitting my six-foot-four self in one of those tiny rows, especially for an eight to nine hour flight, is not preferable.

I type out a quick text to Ma letting her know I'm at the airport and share my flight information. They won't be available to pick me up at the airport this time, so I'm just going to grab a rental car once I get there.

"Final boarding call for flight six-nine-three with service from Raleigh-Durham to Paris Charles de Gaulle."

Shit. I startle awake from the announcement.

That was close.

After quickly grabbing my things, I hurry to board. Luckily, there's still a decent line for boarding so I'm not cutting it too close.

I haven't gotten much sleep recently. Plus, I was moving too fast today, doing last minute packing, making sure work was handled, and preparing the house since I'll be gone for the next few weeks, or maybe months. This visit is definitely going to push out the sale of my current flip. Thankfully, the other projects should stay on schedule while I'm gone with all the hired help I have.

I scan my ticket while walking down the humid jet bridge. Small spaces mixed with mid-July humidity, does *not* mix well.

There was only one seat available when I bought my ticket, so I was stuck with a window. Hopefully, I'm not stuck with some dude that snores. Or smells. Or talks really. I just want to lay back and sleep the flight away.

I greet the flight attendant with a smile before I do a double take with my ticket, checking my seat assignment and waiting for the line to move. I peer around the people in front of me to see if the person in the aisle seat next to me has gotten on the plane yet. Sure enough, *she* has.

And fate must be laughing at me because the auburn beauty from earlier is going to be sitting right beside me.

This is going to be a fun flight.

CHAPTER FIVE

LINDSAY

After sanitizing my seat, I grab my e-reader out of my purse as I sit down in my assigned seat, trying to not get too comfortable yet because I know I'll have to stand to let my seatmate in.

I get a couple chapters into my book before I hear a familiar voice.

"Well, isn't this fun?"

I look up from my book to see the guy who spilled his coffee on me earlier. *Of course* he's on my flight.

Wait. He's taking off his backpack and staring at the empty seat next to me. No, not staring, motioning.

I look around and see there are no other empty seats around me except for the one next to me. Fuck my life. Of course he's sitting next to me. Because this trip is already going *so* well.

"Looks like we're going to be neighbors for the next eight hours. Do you mind if I squeeze in there?" He gives me a roguish smile while I stand to let him in. "Pardon me," he says as his hand lightly grazes against my hip while moving toward his seat.

I can't help the shivers his touch creates. I haven't been

touched by a man in . . . well, I truly don't know. I mean who really keeps track of these things.

He takes his seat as I take mine. We both buckle our seatbelts while the flight attendant up front shuts the airplane door. I grab my phone and switch on airplane mode, following suit with my e-reader immediately after.

"So, you come often or is it your first time?"

I choke on air while my eyes go wide, turning to face him. "Excuse me?"

"First time flying? Or to Paris? Unless that's not your final destination. I myself have another flight after this." He sets his hand out, clearly offering to shake mine. "I'm Theo. And who do I have the pleasure of sitting next to?"

I reach out my hand and shake. "Lindsay. And yes, it is my first time flying to France, but not flying. And Paris isn't my final destination either."

"Lindsay," he repeats my name like he's just won a prize. "I can finally put a name to the unlucky woman I spilled my coffee on. Again, I'm so sorry about that."

I shake my head. "It's fine. Thankfully I had a change of clothes," I emphasize with a not-so-subtle look at my fresh blouse.

The screens on the back of the seats light up to share the information necessary should there be any emergencies. I make a mental note of the nearest exits, as well as the others around the plane. The flight attendants do their final checks and the captain calls for them to take their seats as we are ready for takeoff.

As the plane gains speed, my death-grip on the armrest gets tighter and tighter. My eyes are closed as I try to focus on taking deep breaths.

"Don't like flyin'?"

I peek open my eyes the slightest amount, clearly unamused. "No." My breathing becomes more intentional when the plane tips up as we start our ascent. "Something about the whole 'suspended in air' thing always gets me."

"I get that," Theo chirps as I turn my gaze outside the window.

We're low enough that I can still see the city below us. Or not so much city as little square lots of land, creating a patchwork of greens and tans below us lit by the sun that has yet to set on this summer night.

I turn my focus back to the screen before me but catch Theo subtly closing the plastic window cover. Not sure if he's doing it for my benefit or not, but the gesture doesn't go unnoticed.

"Plus, it doesn't help that I am completely and hopelessly helpless up here. I have to give control to the pilots and flight crew for the next eight or so hours. I've never been on a flight this long and I'm starting to doubt that my book will be enough of a distraction." I sigh before adding, "Sorry for the word vomit."

"Please," Theo scoffs playfully. "We've barely just met and I'm sure you can already see how much I like to talk." I chuckle at that. "How about this," he starts as he turns to face me. "I promise to try and be the distraction you need to get you through this flight. When you're not reading of course," he clarifies with a chuckle.

My grip lessens as we start to level out. "Thanks, Theo." I send a genuine smile his way before opening my e-reader. "I appreciate the offer."

Once we get to cruising altitude, the drink service starts. The flight attendant hands a napkin and snack to both of us.

"Good evening. Can I get you folks something to drink? Coffee, tea, or maybe an alcoholic beverage?"

"Could I get some sparkling water by chance?" I read somewhere that the flavor of carbonated drinks actually changes because of altitude. Many claim it makes them better because of it.

"Absolutely! And for you sir?"

"Can I just get some hot water?" he asks with a smile. "Oh, and a spoon please." Strange.

"Sure can do! I'll be back in a minute with those."

She walks away and I open my book back up. The last book I read was a fun cowboy romance, but that was years ago. I was feeling a little more mysterious when prepping my e-reader, so I purchased a few stalker and mafia romances to enjoy during my trip.

Out of the corner of my eye, I see Theo start reaching for something in his bag. He pulls out a little bag of—I crank my head to look over the edge of my device—what looks like a tiny jar of syrup maybe.

Our flight attendant comes back with both of our drinks. Grabbing them from her, we both say our thanks before she walks away.

I watch as Theo pours a small amount of the jar's contents into the paper cup filled with hot water, giving it a little stir before he tears open what I'm thinking is a teabag. From the relaxing floral smell that just flooded my senses, I'm assuming it's some type of lavender tea. He catches me staring and I quickly avert my gaze. Attempting to act busy, I pour my can of sparkling water into my ice cup and take a sip.

"Want to get me wet?"

"What?" I question, almost spitting out my drink. Is it just me or does this man have a knack for making everything sound dirty?

"You know, to even the score because I spilled my coffee all over you earlier? I don't have iced coffee, but I'm sure your soda will work just fine."

"No," I chuckle. "I'm good, but thanks for the offer. If you feel so inclined, you can pour that hot tea all over yourself though."

Maybe that was a tad bitchy, but I just really want to read. I should've brought my noise canceling headphones. That would've definitely sent a "do not disturb" vibe to anyone looking.

"Nah, can't waste this stuff. This is topnotch, homegrown lavender tea with honey I harvested myself."

Okay so maybe that's a *little* impressive. I guess I wouldn't want to waste that either.

"It helps me wind down, especially right before bed."

"Well that does sound relaxing. I could use some unwinding." And I truly mean that. I guess I should take full advantage of this "break" even if it was forced upon me. What person complains about a free trip to France?

"I know a few things you could try to unwind." I spin toward him with my mouth open like a fish. And he's smirking that damn smirk with the dimple again.

"Jesus. How do you turn everything so dirty? I've only had a couple of interactions with you, but all of them have included some type of innuendo," I say while shaking my head with a slight chuckle.

"I haven't the slightest clue what you're talking about, Lindsay." A weird thrill rushes through me as my name comes out of his mouth. "Your mind seems to be rolling around in the gutter." He places his hands over his heart. "I only have the purest intentions," Theo says, all while I can't stop staring at that dimple. This man is *trouble*.

"Yeah, I'm sure you do," I mutter under my breath.

A sudden jolt of turbulence causes me to slam my hand down on the arm of my chair. The jostling causes my drink to spill, the turbulence lasting for what feels like ten minutes, though it was probably not even a fraction of that.

I start taking deep breaths, in through my nose and out through my mouth, trying to calm my racing heart down. That's when I feel a gentle pat on my hand that is now completely white from me gripping the armrest so tightly. And apparently Theo's hand.

"Oh my god! I'm so sorry." During my momentary freakout, I must've latched onto Theo's hand like a bear trap. But even knowing it's highly inappropriate, I still don't move my hand off of his.

"You okay?" he asks but doesn't attempt to pull back the hand I crushed. "It's just a bit of turbulence. Everything's okay now. You're safe."

I startle hearing those words as I shift my hand back to my lap. "Yeah, I'm good. Just really hate turbulence. And really flying altogether." I take another deep breath. "Sorry about your hand."

"Don't worry about it. I have another." He winks before lifting his cup. "You want some of my tea?"

I eye him suspiciously. I'm not about to take some stranger's drink no matter how much I need to calm down. That's one of the top rules for safety.

He huffs. "I promise it's not poisoned. I haven't even had a sip yet," he says, offering the cup over to me.

"Thanks, but I think I'm good now."

"No problem. If you want a teabag, you know who to ask." He fails at holding in his chuckle as he takes a sip from his tea while I go back to my book, attempting to ignore his immature innuendos. But if I'm being honest, his distracting jokes are a much needed comic relief to the tornado of anxiety I'm experiencing right now.

CHAPTER SIX

THEO

I doze off a bit after finishing my tea; it works like a charm every time. I make a mental note to bag more once I get to the estate.

Growing up, I was spoiled having it whenever I wanted at the hotel. That and by having so many great memories at that place. It was the only place I truly felt like I belonged.

Collecting lavender with Ma, and helping Grandpa collect the honey from our bees, are some of my most favorite core memories. Each time, Mateo always made it a point to create his special dessert showcasing the lavender and honey we harvested. The lick-the-plate kind of dessert.

Grandpa and Ma have always been good at teaching me the ins and outs of running a hotel and taking care of an estate that big. Luckily, the skills I've learned have paid off in my line of work. These days, I've been pretty busy going from property to property, making sure everything is running smoothly and ensuring we meet our timeline and budget. Flipping houses pays the bills and then some but it can be hard work. Thankfully, I've got an incredible team, one that gives me the opportunity to take this time away.

I wake up to the smell of what I'm assuming is the dinner service.

"What would you like for dinner, dear? We have miso chicken with brown rice or glazed pork belly with polenta?"

"I'll take the miso chicken. Please and thank you." I sneak a peek at what Lindsay's reading when she says her dinner order. And shit. *I'm* even blushing.

"And you, sir?"

"Um," clearing my throat, I try to shake away the mental image of the very graphic scene I just read. "I'll take the glazed belly—sorry, I mean the pork. Thanks." I straighten up in my seat and open up my tray table in preparation for dinner. "That's some mighty interesting reading material you got there?"

She startles and quickly closes the cover of her e-reader.

Oh, I got her attention alright, but not the kind I was hoping for. She's embarrassed, which was not my desired effect. In all honesty, that stuff never bothers me and she definitely shouldn't feel any shame from being caught reading it.

"Don't you know it's not polite to ask a lady what she's reading?"

"I can attest that nothing *polite* was happening in that book." I tease with a wink, causing her to blush something fierce and mumble something under her breath.

Something that sounds a lot like, "Fuck me."

"Look, it doesn't bother me. My mom reads romance. Or at least she *does* when she has the time. You won't find any judgement here."

"Why don't you just go back to sleeping?" she chirps, clearly aggravated.

"Not when I have such a delicious dinner heading my way."

She shifts her gaze from me to the window in front of us. I closed ours earlier since I figured someone with a fear of flying probably wouldn't appreciate the glaring reminder of being in the air. But maybe I assumed wrong since she's staring so intently out of one right now. Staring at what, I'm not sure because it's pitch black outside and we're over the ocean without a light source in sight besides the red flicker coming from the plane's wing.

I lightly touch her shoulder and she startles again. This woman is either super skittish or not used to anyone touching her. I'm going to make an educated guess based on our previous interactions and go with the latter.

Or she just doesn't want a stranger touching her, Theo. Not everyone is as affectionate or touch-friendly as you.

"Look, I'm sorry if my comment bothered you. Please,"—I gesture toward her e-reader—"continue. I won't make another comment about your spicy book." She narrows her eyes at me causing me to chuckle. "Last one, I swear."

She shakes her head, but opens it back up and continues to read.

"Good girl."

CHAPTER SEVEN

LINDSAY

Good girl?

Good *girl*?

What the fuck? And why the *fuck* did I get full body chills when he said it to me? What is wrong with me? Theo's a stranger. A stranger who has been talking in ridiculously immature innuendos the few hours I've known him in order to distract me. Which strangely enough, are sort of doing their job.

And I've read enough—prior to becoming consumed with my job that is—to recognize a praise kink when I hear one. I've just never experienced a full-body reaction toward it.

I had this one partner a couple years back, well more like a casual hook up when both of us had time—honestly, it was definitely a booty call type scenario, but it worked both ways. He was a lawyer, and just as much of a workaholic as I was at the time.

Okay, *fine*. Not much has changed in that department for me. I'm still a workaholic.

Anyway, he would always attempt dirty talk while we found our releases, but it always seemed forced. Plus, this one time, he used the word "folds." I'm not sure if any woman wants her labia to be referred to as "her folds." It's bad enough when I read it; I don't need that word in my partner's vocabulary unless he's talking about laundry or cooking.

The other times he used dirty talk or attempted to praise me, I just thought I was never into it. But maybe it's all in the delivery. And Theo just delivered the hell out of it.

And to make matters worse, the character in my book just said "good girl," so now I'm picturing Theo's face for the main love interest.

Wait.

Wait, wait, wait.

Did he say that because he had just read it in my book before this whole interaction happened?

Oh my god! He did, didn't he?

I'm not sure how to feel about that, but I know I shouldn't be feeling all sorts of hot. God, why couldn't I have had a different person sitting next to me? Maybe another woman. Quiet. Doesn't snore or smell. Or even talk really.

Instead, I have Mr. Make-everything-sound-dirty with his sexy as hell smirk, and dimple that wets panties. I bet if I peek over now, I'd see that damned dimple. I'm sure he thinks he's *so* smooth. I roll my eyes just at the thought.

"Here's your dinner, dear. I'll be right back with yours soon, sir."

I thank the attendant and prepare to indulge in what looks like a pretty decent meal. I have low standards when it comes to airplane food, but this looks absolutely delicious.

"That smells great. Hope mine is half as good as yours seems to be," Theo comments as I take my first bite of chicken.

"Actually, I'm pretty impressed with it. I definitely won't be able to finish everything though. I didn't realize it came with all these sides." Seriously, who needs this much food. It all looks so good though.

"And here's your pork belly, sir. Enjoy!" Theo thanks her and she walks off while we're left to enjoy dinner.

"It sure *looks* edible but let's put it to the test shall we?" He takes a bite of his pork and chews it a bit. A questionable look comes across his face, and before I know it, he makes a show of swallowing. "It may look edible, but it definitely doesn't taste it."

I giggle. "Just ask for another meal. I'm sure they have extra," I suggest before I snag another bite of my very edible chicken.

He shrugs. "Nah, I don't want to waste any food. I'll just eat around the pork. Everything else seems good enough."

I set my fork down and wave my hand over my dinner. "Want some of my sides? I haven't eaten from them yet and there's absolutely no way I can finish all of this. Really, I was expecting only chicken and rice."

"Oh no, I couldn't possibly take your food."

"But you offered your precious homemade lavender tea so generously earlier." I flutter my lashes to achieve my desired effect.

"And you *so graciously* turned me *down*," he mocks while fluttering his own lashes.

"*Touché*." I shrug and pick up my fork with the intent of continuing eating. "If you want some, you know where to find me."

"Yes, I do."

After we finish eating, the attendant makes quick work of cleaning up our trays then handing out little individual coffee ice cream containers.

I'm always a sucker for anything coffee flavored, especially ice cream. Bonus points if it's java chip. You know, the coffee ice cream with big chunks of chocolate in it. That got me through some stressful times in high school and college.

Once I hand my garbage off to the attendant, I get up and use the bathroom with the intent of going to sleep as soon as I sit back down.

I forgot how tiny airplane bathrooms are. And is it just me, or are they getting smaller and smaller? I make quick work of doing my nightly routine in the miniature space. I brush my teeth, wash my hands and face, then apply moisturizer to both.

As I sit back down, I steal a glance in Theo's direction for the briefest moment. He's still enjoying his ice cream, and I swear he's putting on a show with how he's licking the spoon. Shit, can't he do anything normal? Why does everything he says and does have to be so sexy?

I recline my chair and lay out the complementary blanket over me. I'm surprised how soft it is. Unfortunately, I forgot my sleep mask, but it's dark enough that I shouldn't have a problem falling asleep without one. Plus, most people should be going down for the night about now anyway.

Taking a few relaxing breaths, I try to calm my mind and before I know it, I'm drifting off to sleep.

CHAPTER EIGHT

THEO

Man, that ice cream hit the spot. Out of all the times I've flown this route, I've never had ice cream before. Must be a business class thing.

Everyone has started winding down for the night and by the looks of it, Lindsay is already asleep. She's all bundled up, or as much as she can be given the seat configuration. She looks so peaceful.

It's a shame I have to use the bathroom.

Maybe I can just stretch my legs over hers without waking her up?

I do just that and am successful on exiting the row. But during my *Cirque du Soleil* routine, someone snuck into the bathroom, so I have to wait patiently next to the galley.

By the time I get back to our row, Lindsay has adjusted her position. It will be a little trickier for me to get to my seat, but I'm up for the challenge.

After drawing a quick mental diagram of how to achieve my goal of getting to my seat without disturbing Lindsay, I attempt to step over her legs, but lose my balance as a small fit of turbulence rocks the plane.

After the shaking is done, I look down and only then do I realize I'm straddling Lindsay. As I pull my head up, I meet a set of narrowed icy blue eyes.

"What the *hell* are you doing?!" she whisper-shouts.

"Well," I chuckle as I adjust myself off of her. "I was *trying* not to wake you while I went to the bathroom."

"Really? Because from here, it looks like you were trying to give me a lap dance while I was sleeping."

I shake my head adamantly. "No, no. I would *never*. My mama taught me better than that. I promise no lap dance." I look up from the corner of my eye. "Unless you want one, then I'm happy to oblige." I send a teasing smirk her way before turning my focus on my seatbelt.

"Nope. I'm all good." Her voice cracks as she replies, clearly frazzled at our little interaction. And yup, I look up and see that blush creeping in again. "Just stay on your side, and we'll be fine. And maybe ask me to move like a normal person next time?"

Yikes. Someone's wound tight. "Sounds good. I really am sorry I woke you."

She fidgets in her seat. "It's fine. It's hard to sleep on planes anyway."

"I hardly ever get lengthy sleep on planes. I believe in the logic that small naps are the way to go with these long flights. It helps with the mild time change, too."

I pull up the window cover and gaze out, the red strobe on the plane's wing temporarily illuminating the sky.

"So," I chirp, turning toward her again. "Since we have a little time . . . and clearly aren't falling asleep anytime soon . . . want to play a game?"

A game? Really, Theo? What happened to just wanting to sleep? Well I *did* say I'd be her distraction this flight so I guess that's what I'm attempting to be.

"Ummm . . ."

"Come on. It'll be fun. What else do we have to do? Or maybe you could read me that book you were reading earlier?"

"God, no." She covers her face with her palm. "Definitely not the book, so game it is if I have to."

"You pick."

"It was your idea," she retorts.

"Right, so *you* should pick."

"Ugh, fine." She leans her head from side to side contemplating her choices. "Two truths and a lie?"

"Great!" I shift to face her fully in my seat, motioning my hand to her. "Ladies first."

"Okay . . ." she draws.

Shifting her body so she's facing more in my direction, she lists off her three statements.

"I'm a twin."

That's interesting. Storing that away for a later time.

"I'm a natural redhead. And . . ." She taps her chin, clearly marking this one as the lie. "I have a pet dog named Spot."

"If we're going to play the game, at least make it a *little* challenging," I complain as I roll my eyes dramatically. "Obviously, the lie was the dog. Though I'm not sure if the lie is that you have a dog or that his name is Spot."

"Okay, Mr. Know-it-all. Do yours then," she huffs.

"I have two brothers." I take a pause to not give any hint of a tell. "I spent my summers growing up in France." I rub my chin in an exaggerated attempt in thinking. "And I flip houses for a living."

"Those all seem very plausible, especially with us currently flying to Paris." She bites her bottom lip thinking about which statement is the lie. The sight of it sends me into a momentary frenzy.

"The brother one." Her voice breaks focus on her plump lips.

"Hmm?"

"You have to be an only child. You seem to be a man who needs all the attention on you." She's clearly proud of herself, and I got to give her credit that she guessed correctly.

"Bingo. You're up, and please try a little on this one, *ma chère*."

Her eyes go big at that little nickname and surprise washes over her face. "I guess you really did spend your summers in France."

"Plus, Ma was born and raised in France. French was actually my first language."

"Interesting." She ponders that for a minute and then continues with our little game. "Okay, I have three sisters. I love strawberry ice cream. And I don't know how to ride a bicycle."

She looks smug with herself, and I have to say, she rattled those off so fast, I don't have the slightest clue which is the lie.

I narrow my eyes as I search her face for a tell but come up empty-handed. "Well, the sister one doesn't seem too far-fetched. I know you have at least one since you said you have a twin."

I don't know a single person who would select strawberry as their favorite ice cream, but then again I also don't know anyone who doesn't know how to ride a bike.

"The bike one?"

"Nope. It was the ice cream one. I'm allergic to strawberries." She looks proud of herself but then her mood changes as she plays with her thumbs. "I was actually never taught how to ride a bike growing up," Lindsay confesses. "And I never needed that skill as an adult, so I never taught myself."

"Well, that's a shame. We'll have to remedy that."

She lifts her head and stares deeply into my eyes. "And how are *you* going to do that while we're on a *plane*? Plus, we'll never see each other after this," she adds, chuckling to herself.

"You never know what fate has in store for us." I stare into her tempting eyes. They look a little more grey than they did earlier. She has a very faint sprinkle of freckles along the bridge of her nose. I wasn't able to see if before, but now that we're so close—

She clears her throat. "Your turn."

"Right," I sigh and take a long pause while I think of what

three things to say. "I wear glasses. I color my hair. And am six-foot-four."

"Well that's obvious. Your height because guys always lie about that."

"Not *this* guy." I motion my thumb toward my chest. "And I'm actually offended that you think I color my hair." I scoff, running my fingers through my shaggy hair. It's getting a little longer than I normally wear; probably time for a haircut. "Nothing but all natural here."

"You're telling me you have natural highlights?" she questions while looking at me incredulously.

"It's summer," I shrug. "And I don't always have a hat on me. Flipping homes isn't always inside work." Truly, my hair has always gotten a little golden in the summer, blurring the line between brunette and blonde.

"So where are these supposed glasses then?" She tuts.

"In my bag. I'm sure they'll make their existence known soon enough."

"Jury's still out on that one, but we can move on . . . *for now*," she adds, playfully narrowing her eyes at me. I don't know if it's the game or that's she is finally comfortable around me, but it's fun seeing this lighthearted side of her.

We go back and forth for a few more rounds before she starts to yawn again.

"I'm going to take that as my body's way of saying I need to try and get some more sleep. Thanks for the . . . entertainment." She starts shifting in her seat and pulls her blanket back up, cocooning herself in its warmth.

"Sweet dreams, *ma chère*," I whisper, though I'm certain she still hears me.

I should attempt to get some sleep as well. Unfolding the complimentary blanket, I close my window shade, and settle into my seat, drifting off shortly after with envious thoughts in my mind, wishing I was that blanket wrapped around Lindsay's body.

CHAPTER NINE

LINDSAY

I hear low voices and start to wake up.

"Sure, I'll have some breakfast. Thank you. Can I also get some orange juice?"

So clearly Theo's awake. I wonder if he slept at all. If he's ordering breakfast, I must've slept a good amount of time.

"Yes, you sure can. Did you want me to make that a mimosa?"

I peek my eyes open and see the attendant standing next to me.

"Oh no, that won't be necessary. Just the juice. Thanks for the offer though."

I start to sit up and wipe the sleep away from my eyes.

"Good morning, dear. Would you care for some breakfast or maybe some coffee?" the attendant says with a cheery smile on her face.

"Oh. Um, yes. Breakfast would be nice. Maybe with some water? Thank you," I rasp out, voice still scratchy from sleep.

"Perfect! I'll be right back with those." She walks away and I take the opening to use the bathroom and wash my face.

Walking back to my seat, Theo greets me with a warm smile. Something looks different about him though.

"Well good morning, sleepy head. You sure slept like the dead."

I cover my face in embarrassment. I wasn't expecting to sleep at all, but I must've really passed out. Maybe it's the seats.

"Oh, please tell me I didn't snore?" I say peeking out at him through the hand covering my face, but drop it entirely when I realize what's changed about him.

He chuckles softly, that dimple making an appearance again. "Maybe a tad," Theo says while raising his thumb and forefinger up in a pinching motion, blocking my view of his glasses. "Looks like you needed the rest though. Glad you got some."

"Thanks. Did you?" I'm surprised I even get words out because of how distracted I am. Somehow Theo just got even hotter. Thin dark frames surround the pair of lenses, fitting perfectly over his—"Sorry." I shake my head before I correct myself. "I mean, did you happen to get any sleep?"

"An hour here and there. That's all I need for now."

The attendant appears along with a savory aroma of breakfast.

"*Bon appetit*!" she cheers and continues to assist the other rows around us.

Breaking my stare away from Theo's slutty little glasses, I look down and check out what's for breakfast. It looks like a frittata over sweet potatoes. A cup of blueberry yogurt. A croissant and butter, because *when in France*, and a side of fruit, which is mixed berries, so I'll have to pass on eating that.

"Want my berries?" I ask holding out the little dish toward Theo.

"You don't want—oh, that's right because you're allergic to strawberries. Yeah, I'll take them off your hands." He grabs the tiny bowl and his fingers linger a second on top of mine.

I quickly turn my attention back to the plate of food in front of me, choosing to take a bite of frittata instead of wondering what his hands feel like on other parts of my—

"Can you touch them?"

I get whiplash from turning so fast. Was he just reading my mind? Am I that transparent?

"The strawberries," he clarifies as he points to the bowl filled with the red fruit. "Is it a touch thing too or only if you ingest them?"

"Oh!" I chuckle as I start opening my yogurt. "It's kind of both. I can handle touching them for short periods of time, but if the juices get on my hands, it starts to burn and sometimes leaves them raw for a few days."

"Yeah, I hate it when juices get on my hands." That smirk I've gotten all too used to seeing makes an appearance. "But in all seriousness, that sucks. I'm sorry."

"It's not all too bad. Plus, growing up, my family did their best to avoid them being in the house."

"Is your twin allergic, too?"

"No, it doesn't really work that way. Plus, we're not identical. But it's generally pretty easy to avoid them, unlike other allergies." I finish and take another bite of breakfast, surprised at how appetizing the frittata is.

"So you have two additional sisters, right?"

"Correct. One older and one younger. My twin and I are the middles."

"Well at least you didn't have to deal with middle child syndrome by yourself then," he says in between bites.

I swallow my last bite of egg. "That's true. But I can attest that even though there were two of us, middle child syndrome is still very much a thing." But he's right, the burden of being a middle-child did get shared between Taylor and me.

"I never had to fight for attention, like you said earlier, since I am an only child. But it did get lonely some days. Especially since I was the only kid during summertime." He looks down like he's recalling those summers. "But at least I got taught how to ride a bike."

I laugh. "You got me there." We both turn our attention to

the meal in front of us, enjoying our breakfast in companionable silence. It's not awkward, just peaceful.

After breakfast gets all cleaned up, I decide to pull out my book again. There's still a couple of hours left and I'm willing to bet I could finish this book by then.

"Sorry to do this after you just opened your book but do you mind if I get up?" Theo asks.

"Oh, sure thing," I note as I close my tray table.

"Unless you prefer me to straddle you again." Humor laces his voice and a small smile tugs at my lips. By now, you'd think I'd find his comments annoying, but I've kind of warmed up to them.

My cheeks instantly start feeling warm from the blush that I'm sure is coloring my face. "No, no. That won't be necessary. I'm happy to get up."

"That's a shame," he quips under his breath.

While holding my book, I stand and allow him space to step into the aisle. Watching him head to the front of the plane, I choose to stay standing. I don't want to sit back down, only to have to get up again in another minute. Leaning my elbow against the headrest of my seat, I open my book and get lost in the pages while I wait.

A few minutes later I feel a light touch on my lower back. I startle, only to quickly relax once I realize it's Theo.

"Sorry, let me get out of your—" I say as I shift out of the way to let him pass.

"Thanks," he adds as he takes his seat, quick to open his window shade to let some of the natural light in.

Which reminds me, I forgot to put sunscreen on after I washed my face. I pull out the pale yellow tube and start rubbing it in.

As I give myself a mini-rubdown, Theo turns and looks at me. "You've got a little . . ." He wipes under his eye in an attempt to show me where the remaining lotion is.

"Oh, thanks." I rub one cheek, apparently missing the spot entirely because he only chuckles.

"No, the other side."

I switch cheeks, but still apparently miss the spot again.

Theo shakes his head, his grin a little wider now. "Do you mind?" he asks, reaching his hand out to my face.

I find I don't, so I shake my head telling him to proceed. He moves his thumb gently under my eye, a ghost of a touch while he rubs in the remaining lotion. Lowering his hand on my cheek, he gently swipes his thumb along my chin. I can't help but inhale sharply at his touch, holding back the sounds my body wants to make from this sudden show of intimacy. I expect him to pull away, but his hand doesn't move.

I clear my throat and pull my head back as he adds, "There. All rubbed in."

"Thanks. I guess I could've rubbed it out in the bathroom."

He stares at me with a glint in his eye as he bites down on his lower lip. It's just then I realize what I said. Here comes the blush again.

"I mean—" I look at the ground and take a breath, attempting to calm my racing heart and thoughts. "I should've rubbed in my *sunscreen* in the bathroom. You know"—I look back up at him with mild panic in my eyes—"where there's a mirror."

"Uh huh. And *I'm* the one who speaks in innuendos," he remarks as he narrows his eyes, but I can tell from the mischievous smile, he's jesting. I can't help but lean my head onto my palms, shaking it. "So sunscreen?" He kindly redirects. "Why? We're inside the plane. The only sun is coming from the window."

"Actually,"—I perk up—"it's widely believed that you are at higher risk of UV exposure when on an airplane. Plus, it never hurts to use protection." I try to be cheeky with the last line and by his laugh, it seems as if I was successful.

"Oh, you're good." His joyous laugh continues and I can't

help but join along. “Well, I’ll let you get back to your reading, but thanks for educating me.”

“Do you want some?” I offer the tube over to him as he swipes it.

“Sure. I don’t want to subject myself to any unnecessary *exposure.*” He winks as he squeezes out a bit of sunscreen before handing the bottle back to me.

“I take protection very seriously,” I mock as I put away the tube. Adjusting myself back into my seat, I open my e-reader and pretend to read while enjoying the view of Theo’s strong hands working the lotion into his skin.

Ugh! Dammit, Lindsay.

Now I have a whole *different* image in my head. One with a creep saying, "It rubs the lotion on its skin.”

“Flight attendants, please do your final checks for landing.”

I fold my blanket and hand my garbage to the attendant as she does her last pass through.

That was a relatively smooth flight. Now I just need to go through customs, collect and recheck my bag, and pass through security one more time for my final flight. I can do all that in under three hours right? If not, I know there are more flights going out. Worst-case, I’m sure there’s a train I could catch.

We land and arrive at the gate in Charles de Gaulle Airport. People start standing up and gathering their things to leave, making me do the same. I reach up and grab my roller, setting my purse right on top. I do a double-check of my seat back to ensure nothing is left behind before heading off the plane.

“It was nice meeting you, Theo.” My genuine smile turns teasing. “I guess you weren’t awful as a seat neighbor.”

He chuckles and shakes his head. "You weren't half bad either, Linds."

My heart freezes and I do a double take at Theo. I've only been called Linds by my family and to hear such a familiar nickname come out of Theo's mouth, who is essentially a stranger, it gives me . . . god, I don't even know what feelings it gives me right now. I mean I don't even know his last name. Or where he lives. Or if he's single.

Wait.

Why is that last one important?

It's not going to happen, Lindsay. You literally just shared an eight-hour flight with him, and you'll never see him again.

The line starts to move and I toss a small wave his way. "Well, I'll see you, probably never again." I awkwardly chuckle. "Safe travels."

"You too, Lindsay." He's still sitting, clearly in no rush to leave. And after sneaking one more look back at him when I reach the door, I walk out and off the plane.

Customs was a breeze, as was rechecking my bag. Airport security was also relatively quick. No huge lines which allows me plenty of time to journey through the huge airport.

Walking around the Paris airport, I'm completely blown away at how enormous it is. Thankfully, I used some of my time on the plane to map out where my next gate is or else I'd be scrambling.

I've only flown domestic, so the only reference I have for European airports are movies. From what I gathered during my small amount of research, a lot of people have lengthy layovers while enjoying eating and shopping at Charles de Gaulle, and I can see why.

This airport easily has more shops than my city's mall, most of them are luxury stores, too. I read that some people fly here just to go shopping in the airport because of the price and tax differences compared to the stores back in the States.

Moving through the labyrinth that is Paris' airport, I find my gate without too much trouble. I will say that the signage is *phenomenal*. Multiple languages and all very clear on where to go.

After double checking the gate's location, I proceed to the nearest bathroom before getting comfortable. I have a little under two hours until boarding starts so I decide to walk around and see what is available for food. I'm not sure when I will be able to get my next meal so I want to buy a few items I can easily bring along with me for the rest of the journey.

Using my time wisely, I mentally review the rest of my day's itinerary. After my final flight lands in Marseille, I have to catch a bus that goes to Provence. Or technically Aix-en-Provence as I found out when googling the train station. From there, the hotel will pick me up, which is great because there is absolutely no way I could manage driving in a foreign country. Plus, aren't all the cars there stick shifts? I have no idea how to drive a stick. And from what I've seen, some of the roads can be *super* narrow. I am more than happy to be a passenger princess during this trip.

Normally, I would be nervous taking the bus, my biggest concern being getting on the wrong bus and going to a completely different destination. Or even getting off on the wrong stop and getting stranded somewhere. But I looked it up right before the flight, and it seems pretty straight forward. The bus I'm taking only has one route, from the station in Aix-en-Provence and then back to the Marseille airport.

Finding an adorably small bakery, I grab a small variety box of macarons and chocolate croissant, because again, *when in France.* I should coin that the phrase for the trip.

I need to find something with protein, too, so I stroll into another shop and quickly find a few options. I pick up a couple protein bars for the journey after the flight and a package of two hard boiled eggs to tide me over for now.

Making my way back to my gate, I see the city on the display changed so I assume my flight has a gate change. While walking over to the board, my phone lights up with a notification from the airline informing me of the gate change.

I get set up at the new location, opening up my eggs and diving into my croissant immediately after.

And oh. My. God.

I literally have to suppress a moan from the delectable chocolate treat. This is the most flakey and buttery croissant I have ever had. It's so warm and fresh. Plus the chocolate-to-dough ratio is absolute perfection. If I lived here, I would easily eat one of these a day. I'm half tempted to go back and buy another but I'm sure there will be plenty of treats at the hotel. Maybe I'll get a box of them on my way back to the States? Maybe even bring some over to Mom and Dad's for a treat at Sunday lunch when I come back?

Speaking of my family . . .

I pull my phone out and send a quick text to my family letting them know I've landed in Paris all safe and sound.

Scrolling through my phone, I check if any clients have reached out during my flight. It's only after the third time I've attempted to refresh my mailbox that I remember Fran blocked me from the company's server. This will definitely take some getting used to.

Since I have so much time, I pull out my e-reader and pick back up where I left off.

I didn't get to read nearly as much as I thought I would on the flight, but I can't really complain. Clearly my body needed the sleep, and Theo was a nice distraction, once I warmed up to him. Funny too. And now that he's not around, I can finally admit how attractive he was.

And a *dangerously* smooth talker.

But he's in the past now, and our paths will never cross again. Oh well. What's that thing they say in movies? *C'est la vie*?

CHAPTER TEN

THEO

I have some time to kill between flights so I decide to call Ma. She picks up on the second ring.

"*Mon fils*. How was your flight?"

Hearing her voice instantly puts a smile on my face. I haven't been able to talk to her since everything happened. It's only been a couple of days since our last call, but it's nice to hear from her.

"It was amusing to say the least," I confess as I think of my time with Lindsay. "But no delays, so that's good. I board my next flight in a couple of hours and should be at the hotel before dinner."

I wonder what Mateo has on the menu tonight. I should probably grab a snack before the next flight, because other than that, I won't be getting a chance to eat until I reach the hotel.

"Any word on Grandpa?"

"He's still resting. No surgery yet." Mom sighs before her tone picks up. "Oh, I meant to tell you. We need you to pick up the guest at the bus station in the city before you arrive. Is that alright with you? They should be arriving at the station by the time you get to Aix."

I've never picked a guest up before, but I know the station

very well. It's the same one Ma and Dad pick me up at, depending on how I get into the city.

"Yup. As long as they don't have a lot of bags. I didn't reserve a large car this time."

"They are here for five nights, so it could go either way depending on how they pack. But if you run into any issues, you can always strap a bag to the top of the car. You're handy. I trust you'll figure it out."

I chuckle. "You're right, it's nothing you need to worry about. I'll take care of it. Just send me their name and phone number in case I can't easily find them. Other than that, I'll see you later today. Love you, Ma."

"I'll text it over. I love you. Have a safe flight and drive over." And with that, she hangs up the phone.

The next few hours move without issue; my flight boards on-time. I wasn't fortunate enough to select my seat for this flight either, landing me in the back of the plane. But luck is on my side today because no one is sitting in the middle seat, giving the stranger in the aisle seat and me a little more room for the ninety minute flight. Perfect amount of time to snag a quick nap.

Once we land and reach our gate, I wait for the rest of the passengers to deplane before I walk over to baggage claim to collect my luggage, which happens to be the first bag out.

I thought I may have seen Lindsay heading to baggage claim, but by the time my bag came out, I still hadn't seen her at our flight's carousel so it couldn't have been her. But it did look like her. At least from the back it did. Same below-the-shoulder auburn hair. Same height. Even the same color shirt she changed into after I spilled my coffee on her.

Great, now I'm just seeing her.

I shake my head as I walk to the car rental area. No. Come on, Theo. What are the chances she traveled to Marseille? And even if she did? What's going to happen then? You awkwardly say hello? Maybe spill another drink on her?

No. Just focus on getting to the estate.

"*Monsieur*?"

"Oh yes. Sorry, I didn't see you open over there." Damn. I've never been lucky enough for a line this short.

"Reservation today?" the woman asks. She reminds me a lot of Ettie. More mature in her years and aged with grace.

"Yes, under Johnson. Theo Johnson?"

"Oh, yes. I see you are reserved in a standard car for twenty-eight days. Is that correct?"

"Yes, that's me." I lean in a little closer to her, like I'm sharing a secret. "But you wouldn't by chance have a larger car available would you? I just found out I'll be needing to pick someone up along the way and I'm not quite sure how much baggage they're bringing."

"Oh, how generous of you."

I bring my palm to my heart and shrug. "I'm only trying to help out when I can."

She types something on her computer. "It seems like we have a few mid-size SUVs, but with how long the length of your rental is . . ." She sighs, making it clear she's not sure she's able to offer me a deal.

"I understand. I know it's quite long." I shake my head, letting my gaze turn up to the ceiling. "*Le pépé*"—my grandfather — "had a fall a couple of nights ago and he and my parents own a small hotel outside of Aix. I took the first flight out so I could look after it during his surgery. We're not entirely sure how long I'll be needed to stay in and help."

"*Quelle tragédie*!" she sympathizes then quickly types something into her computer. She brings the newly printed document up onto the counter. "I am sorry to hear about your family. We have no problem providing you with a complimentary upgrade to the mid-size SUV during this troublesome time."

"Oh, wow." My eyes go wide. I was only word-vomiting my situation. Hopefully she doesn't think I was using my grandfather to get out of paying for the upgrade. "Thank you so much."

She walks me through the rental agreement and charges my card for the original balance.

"And if I need to extend the rental?" I ask as she hands me the keys.

"You can call the toll-free number on the back of your agreement and they'll help you out with the updated cost."

"Perfect! Thank you"—I take a peek at her name tag—"Odette. I appreciate all of your help. You've been a true treasure."

"*Merci, bonne fin de journée!*" She gives her thanks to me and wishes me a good day.

"*Au revoir*!" I wave as I head to the garage to grab my car.

After shooting my parents another text letting them know I arrived and the estimated time I hope to be in Aix, I load up the car and settle in for the drive. It can vary because of traffic, but I should be able to reach the bus stop in forty-five minutes or less.

When I'm finally out of the airport's surrounding area, I take in the familiar scenery. Though I wish it was under different circumstances, it's good to be back in France.

CHAPTER ELEVEN

LINDSAY

Stepping off the jet-bridge, I take a deep breath in and relax as I breathe it out.

You made it Lindsay, and the only drama was a little coffee on your shirt. Really, the air travel went as smooth as it could go. Everything went just as planned and all is well. Now I just need to get my bag and hop on the correct bus.

I quickly use the bathroom, tidying up my hair before making my way to baggage claim. It looks like most of the bags have been retrieved. My bag must've been one of the last ones unloaded. Only my thoughts quickly start to spiral when a beep sounds, signaling the carousel has come to a stop.

I frantically search the conveyor belt but come up empty handed. Walking around the belt once more, I double check that the neon green roller or the hard-shell with a woman's toothy grin face printed all over it didn't mysteriously turn into my sleek black SwissGear suitcase.

Shit. Did the airline lose my bag?

Okay, no need to panic. First thing's first, let's check the app.

It shows my bag has made it to this airport. It even says it has been scanned for this very carousel.

I walk around the circular baggage belt one more time but come up empty handed. I really should have bought one of those tracker-tags before flying. When I fly domestically, it's normally such a quick trip, making it easy to get away with only bringing a carry-on bag. With a trip like this one, I had no choice but to check a bag.

I walk over to my airline's desk finding a line about eight people long. As the line moves at a glacial pace, I look my bus up again.

From the airport map on the app, I'm not too far from the bus station and if I miss this one, there's a bus in another thirty minutes. Not too long of a wait. Inconvenient, sure, but not horrible.

Standing in line, a thought comes to me of a potential problem for one of my events this weekend. So naturally I text Stephanie to let her know.

LINDSAY:

For the Wilson wedding, be sure to double check that the luggage for the honeymoon is loaded into the limo before they leave since they are going straight to the airport after.

STEPHANIE:

Lindsay, it's too early for this shit.

I should've listened to Fran and blocked you until you get back.

But yes. I will make sure to do that.

Thank you.

Now go enjoy France because I'm blocking you.

I roll my eyes. At least she took my advice.

After what feels like forever, it's finally my turn. Stepping up to the counter, I immediately hand over my baggage receipt from when I checked the bag.

"*Bonjour*!" Shit, I definitely butchered that.

"You will need to fill out this form and we will contact you if we find your bag," the woman says with a thick French accent. Apparently my one-word greeting made it clear I'm from the States.

"The app says the bag is here. Is there a chance it got put on the wrong carousel? Should I walk around the other carousels?" I suggest.

"*Madame*, please fill out this form," repeating her previous statement while she taps the paper in front of me. "I assure you, if we find your bag, we will get it to you."

I start filling out the small card. "And when is it normal to receive an update? Or should I call if I haven't heard after a certain amount of hours or days?"

Her tight-lipped smile is telling me all I need to know about her mood today.

"An airline representative will call you on the number you have listed when they have an update. That is all we can do for now." She rips off a claim ticket and hands it to me before waving me off. Kind of rude but whatever.

Maybe I need to take a page from Emma's book and put on some rose-tinted glasses. At least I packed all my toiletries and a spare set of clothes in my carry-on. Wait . . .

Fuuuuck.

Deep breath *in*.

Deep breath *out*.

I groan. Well, I *did* have a spare set until I had to change into it because Theo spilled coffee on it. Thankfully, I had the forethought to wash out the coffee in the airport bathroom, but I'm sure the shirt is stiff and smells like stale coffee since it wasn't washed or dried properly.

At least I have my toiletries. I guess I can't do anything more than I already have. I just need to keep moving forward. Hopefully the airline will find my bag by tomorrow and it won't be too big of an inconvenience.

I walk over to the bus stop and see the sign for Aix-en-Provence. I glance at the bus parked under the sign, finding a paper in the bus's window that says the same thing.

After loading my roller, I triple check again with the bus driver.

"Aix-en-Provence?"

"*Oui*!" he agrees before motioning me onto the bus.

As I take a few steps up, I see another sign about the bus's route. My anxiety eases up a bit knowing I'm as certain as possible that I am on the right bus.

It's a smooth bus ride and once we get out of the city, most of the drive is filled with views of the countryside and lush, green pastures. It's actually very peaceful out on the road and there's not a crazy amount of traffic. It even looks like we passed a basin or little lake on our way into Provence.

As we get closer to another city, no longer being on a highway, I can take in the beautiful architecture surrounding me. Cream, tan, and orange colored buildings. Clean paved streets lined with planter boxes that are filled with flowers, providing a fun pop of color.

The building styles change as we near the city-center. More modern buildings line the streets, some industrial looking and resembling more of a metropolis the closer we get to our stop. At least I *assume* we are getting close based on the people around me gathering their things.

Within five minutes, we reach our destination. It's not what I assumed France would look like. Then again, I'm in the city center . . . at a bus stop.

Stepping out, I thank the bus driver, collect my bag, and head to the nearest bench so I can call the hotel, notifying them I'm waiting at the bus stop.

A kind voiced woman answers the phone and greets me in French. "*Bonjour*" is all I catch before all the words start to blend together.

Shit. Maybe instead of reading my spicy mafia book, I

should've been attempting to learn a few French words for this trip. I can't believe I didn't even *think* about the language barrier. I could've even asked Theo for some help. He sounded like he was *more than* proficient in that department.

And maybe a few others.

Oh my god. This again? Are you kidding me?!

You know what? It's fine. I'm fine. I just haven't had a little male attention in some time and it was . . . nice. But I will forget it in time I'm sure. Maybe I'll even meet someone on this trip. No strings. No real emotions. Plus, I don't plan on coming back, so there'd be no commitment. An expiration date so to speak already in place.

But where exactly am I going to meet this no-strings partner? I'm staying at an all inclusive hotel, known for relaxation. Surrounded by acres of lavender fields and orchards—at least that's what it says in the paperwork Fran gave me. Not exactly a hot pick-up scene.

So maybe this *isn't* the time for that. I guess if I wanted that, I should've gone with the girls to Barcelona. After all, that's where Emma had such great luck.

But then again, what was supposed to be a chance encounter turned into love for Emma. And even more, now she's living full time in Spain. *Spain* of all places! But she's always been a free spirit and goes whenever the wind blows her.

"*Allô*?" I hear and startle back to the present.

"Hello! Yes! Sorry, I don't speak French. My name is Lindsay Hartman. I am a guest staying at your hotel and was told to call when I arrive at the bus station in Aix-en-Provence?" I ask, hoping I sound more confident than I feel.

"*Ah oui*! Lindsay! Yes, my son should be arriving soon. I messaged him your number, and he will call you when he arrives. Hopefully you won't need to wait much longer, but if you haven't heard from him in"—there's a break like she's thinking—"say twenty minutes, please call again and I will track him down. We look forward to greeting you soon." She sounds warm and welcoming, and I'm thankful she'll be there assisting me during my stay.

"Oh, okay. That sounds great. Thank you again," I add before hanging up. I feel myself actually getting a tad giddy, maybe even excited, to see this hotel. I saw some photos on the confirmation, but I have no idea what to expect for my room.

When I looked the place up, they just had a few photos available. I only saw the pictures of the outside of the property, but if the inside is anything like the outside, it will be a perfect place for a peaceful retreat.

Within a few minutes my cell chimes and I'm assuming this is the son from the hotel, but the country code says it's coming from the States.

UNKNOWN NUMBER:

Hello, Lindsay. I'm picking you up today and taking you to Le Château des Lavandes. I should be arriving in less than five minutes in a white midsize SUV.

Perfect. I think the drive is only another thirty minutes from here, so I should be there in time to unpack and get freshened up for dinner.

I text my family, letting them know I should be arriving at the hotel soon. Given the time change, they should all be getting up to start their day.

LINDSAY:

I'm in Provence. Just waiting for the hotel to pick me up.

EMMA:

Hope you have a relaxing time. But maybe not too relaxing ;)

Or actually, maybe some hot French sex is exactly what you need.

MOM:

EMMA!

DAD:

Emma, you do know this is the family chat and not the girls' chat?

EMMA:

Oops! Sorry, Dad.

TAYLOR:

No you're not.

DAD:

Have a safe trip, Lindsay! Take a lot of photos.

MOM:

I can't wait to hear about everything! Call us if you need anything, sweetie!

TORY:

Try to relax a little sis.

EMMA:

Have fun!

LINDSAY:

Thanks, everyone! I'll try to send a pic when I get there.

"Lindsay!" A male voice shouts my name. I look up from my phone and see someone outside of their car waving. My eyes meet his and—

No way.

You have to be shitting me.

It's Theo. My Theo.

Well, not *my* Theo, but the Theo from the plane. Theo, who I thought I would never see again. *That* Theo.

He works at the hotel? Wait, she said her son was picking me up.

Shit. Is he staying at the hotel with me?
He *did* say he spent his summers in France. And it is summer.
This is definitely going to make for an interesting week.

CHAPTER TWELVE

THEO

"*Bonjour, madame*," I say grinning wide because of course it would be Lindsay I was picking up. I knew I saw her at baggage claim. Well, maybe I didn't *know* know, because *had* I known, I would've just driven with her from the start.

I didn't receive Ma's text until I was already on the road and had this gut feeling that the "Lindsay" that I was supposed to be picking up would end up being *my* Lindsay. And fuck if I'm not excited to have another shot at . . . whatever this is.

She's going to be at my family's hotel for five nights. And she is the only guest. Meaning, I get her alone for five whole nights. Maybe not *alone* alone since Mateo and Ettie will be there, doing their own thing. And sometimes Jean, but really he only comes a few hours a week. And he's outside for the majority of his time working on the estate.

This has to be a sign.

"Of course, it would be you." Lindsay tries to sound aggravated or annoyed, but it's clear in her tone she's fighting off a little hint of excitement. She starts to walk over and I race to the back of the SUV to load her small bag alongside mine in the truck. I turn to face her and see she's tilting her head while pursing her lips.

"I could've done that myself."

"I'm sure you could've, but it's always nice when someone else lends a helping hand." I wink at her and she rolls her eyes as she turns back to get into the car. "Plus, you are officially a *Le Château des Lavandes* guest now," I add rushing over, opening the passenger door for her and waving her inside. "I can't believe you packed everything in a carry-on."

"I didn't," she huffs out. "The airline lost it. And you"—she points at me, clearly pissed off—"spilled coffee on me which caused me to use my one and only backup outfit." She closes her eyes and takes a deep breath before taking her seat. This poor woman. I can't help but feel a little guilty about adding to her unlucky day.

I close the door and hustle around to my side, hop in, and buckle up.

"Ready to go?" I ask looking over to check if her seatbelt is fastened. Working my way up to her face, I find her staring at me, eyes narrowed with a small crease between her eyebrows. I throw my hands up innocently. "I'm just checking you have your seat-belt buckled." I look at her chest pointedly again, out of duty more than anything, and then back to her eyes. "Which obviously you do." Oh yeah. She's fuming. "Safety first and all."

She just scoffs as I start the car.

Only thirty more minutes until I'm back home.

Lindsay seems to relax a little once we get on the open road. We pass the time easily. Warming up with small talk.

"I can't believe we were on the same flight. I must've just walked right past you."

"I was trying to distract myself with reading while everyone was boarding, so I was probably easy to miss."

"Trust me, you're not one to be easily missed, *ma chére*." I turn to face her and find her already looking at me with a glimmer in her eyes. "I was just looking in all the wrong places." She gifts me with a soft smile before turning back to gaze out the passenger's side window.

"So," I clear my throat. "Do you like what you see?" Clearly there's a not-so subtle double meaning. I sneak a look and yup, those cheeks are turning red again. She's bitten her bottom lip so hard in an attempt to not smile, it's a wonder it's not bleeding.

"If you mean France, then yes." She's smug with her answer, a teasing smile sneaking out. "So far, from what I've seen from the bus, it's mostly been pasture or fields of some sorts, but it all looks so peaceful. I didn't see *too* much of the city in both Marseille and Provence. Or Aix-en-Provence—"

"Aix," I correct.

"What?" She turns to face me, clearly confused.

"Aix. Like X. You say Aix if you want to shorten Aix-en-Provence."

"Oh. I thought it was Provence for short."

"Provence is the region while Aix is the specific city. Similar to how Raleigh is the city and North Carolina is the state," I explain.

"Oh, I didn't know that. Thanks for the lesson."

"I'm always willing and able to teach you a lesson, Lindsay." I smirk, still managing to keep my eyes on the road, but out of the corner of my eye I see I have her attention again. "Anyways . . ." I sigh. "Why here? What made you pick our hotel?"

"It wasn't *my* decision," she scoffs while brushing invisible lint off her trousers. "I was sent here by my boss. Apparently I don't know how to have 'work-life balance.'" She motions air quotes over the last part. "So here I am. On a sabbatical. In Provence—or Aix, of all places." She looks around the car, then back to me. "I guess things could be worse, and I really shouldn't be complaining about getting a free trip to France," she sighs. "I just really love my job, and I haven't taken a day off in . . . well, so long that my boss had to get involved I guess," she confesses while softly chuckling to herself.

"It sounds like a few nights away in our little hotel is just the escape you need."

"It does look stunning from the photos," she muses with a bit of awe in voice. "I've seen a lot of beautiful venues as an event planner, but this looks like it could take the cake."

"The photos really don't do it justice. And they're a little outdated." I pinch my fingers together, laughing at my own joke. "I'd know since I took them myself a few summers back. When we arrive, I'll have to give you the grand tour to make sure you get a full grasp on how special of a place it is."

My heart warms just thinking of all the memories I've made throughout the years around the property.

"Each of the five rooms are unique and have their own special identity to them. Since you'll be the only guest, you'll be able to pick which one you stay in."

"Sounds like a drea—" She whips her head back to me. "Wait. What do you mean 'the only guest?'"

What is that emotion in her tone? Confusion? Anxiety? Curiosity?

"There's no one else but you staying during the week. Get used to seeing me because you'll be my sole focus for the next five nights. And Lindsay," I chance a look at her and hold her gaze. "It would be my pleasure to see to your every need."

CHAPTER THIRTEEN

LINDSAY

Holy shit.

I'm currently a puddle in Theo's passenger seat, and according to my math, I still have roughly fifteen minutes left of the drive.

What do I say to *that*? "Thank you" or "I'd like that" or "I'd love to see you on your knees?"

Maybe the last one's a little much.

If there was any doubt in my head that he was flirting with me, that last comment sealed the deal. Because to me, it sounds like he just blew that door wide open. *My pleasure to see to your every need.* If that's not an invitation for more, I don't know what is. But maybe he's just one of those guys who is all talk?

I internally huff. *Please.* Like a guy who looks and talks like that, wouldn't be able to back it up. His smirks and freely given winks prove that Theo knows *exactly* what he's doing. I may be a bit out of practice, but two can play at this game.

"I have a lot of needs, and I'm not sure if you have enough"—I blow out an exaggerated sigh—"*stamina.*"

"Oh trust me, *ma chère*, I would never turn down an opportunity for me to show you just how much *stamina* I have." He looks at me smirking, dimple on full display with a sparkle in his eyes. Oh yeah, he's definitely into whatever this is.

And I think I am too.

But as much as I'd like to think I can continue this hot and sexy banter, I need a few practice rounds before I can go head to head with someone like him.

I release a deep breath to calm whatever is going on in my head and between my legs and attempt a topic change.

"So your mom works at the hotel, huh?" I cringe. Yeah, Lindsay. Bring up his mom. Because that's exactly what he wants to talk about after a crystal clear pass at you.

He clears his throat and returns his focus to the road ahead. "Yeah. Well, technically she's an owner now. My grandparents started it up a couple decades ago. My parents always helped out, but never lived full time at the estate until Grandma passed away. When it was clear Grandpa was in over his head, my parents moved in and started working full time at the hotel." He shrugs. "And I've been visiting ever since I was a baby." His soft smile shifts to one with a touch of sadness. "Though in the past few years, I haven't been able to visit nearly as much. Work's been great, but also keeping me busy, moving from project to project."

"Well, I'm glad you're able to visit them now."

I think about how hard it would be if my family lived a literal ocean away. I know I don't see them as often as I should, but it's nice to know they are only thirty minutes away. I don't think I could be like Emma and live such a faraway distance from everyone. Not that I hold it against her, it's just not the lifestyle I see for myself.

"Actually, it's not going to be too much of a visit this time around. They needed me to fill in because Grandpa broke his hip. He's needing to have an extended visit at the hospital in the city after he gets surgery. Ma didn't want him to stay alone." He lets out a breath, keeping his eyes focused on the road before us. "She's been visiting for now, but once I get to the hotel, she's going to go stay with him. That way she doesn't have to spend as much time on the road driving back and forth. And ever since Dad retired from the military, wherever she goes, he goes too. That's where I come in."

"I'm sorry about your grandpa," I add solemnly. It's sweet hearing how his parents are such a packaged deal though.

"He'll get the surgery and once he recovers, everything will be fine. He might even—"

"Wait. Did you say you'll be running the hotel? Like you *alone*." I cut him off, now fully registering what he said.

"Well not *completely* alone." He stretches out the word. "We have our chef, housekeeper, and groundskeeper that will be in and out. But for the most part, yeah. Just me." He shifts his gaze over to me conspiratorially. And just like that, the car is suddenly an inferno again.

I let out a deep breath and try to calm my heart that's beating a mile a minute.

The whole hotel.

Alone.

With Theo.

The rest of the ten minute car ride is awkwardly silent and filled with an exorbitant amount of tension. Both of us waiting for the other to say something.

We pull onto a long gravel driveway lined with tall cypress trees swaying in the small breeze. There's a stunning lavender field on the right side of the driveway with flowers so vibrant as the sun beams down on the rows of purple. I'm sure one walk through that field would give me the best nap of my life from the aroma coming off of the blooming buds.

I can see the hotel from here and it's a stunning countryside estate. This is much warmer and more welcoming than some of the chateaus I've seen on television. Its creamy white exterior is covered in plenty of windows adorned with smoky blue shutters, some even overlooking the lavender field. I'm hoping one of those windows is a guest room. One that I'll be picking for my stay here.

The estate's landscape is one filled with beauty and color, making it clear someone has put a lot of time and energy into taking care of all this vegetation. Surrounding the property itself, there are olive trees and a variety of shrubbery, a few covered in colorful flowers and some I've never seen before. There are even a few bushes of thyme boarding the house's perimeter. It truly is a dream.

Theo turns off the car, parking us in the gravel parking lot next to the chateau. He gets out and rushes over to my side, opening up the door for me while extending his palm. Placing my hand in his, he assists me out of the car.

"Thank you for the hand." I nod before turning to head to the back of the car, but I stop when I feel Theo's hand on my lower back, instantly giving me goose bumps at his gentle touch.

"Don't worry about your bag. I'll come back and get it after we get you settled," Theo says as he ushers me in the opposite direction toward the entry steps.

The double glass paneled doors are the same shade of blue as the shutters covering the estate exterior walls. We walk in and are immediately greeted by a very petite older woman, one with a welcoming smile that only turns more genuine when Theo walks in. I assume this is his mother. He has her smile and piercing green eyes.

"*Bonjour, madame*! Welcome!" She hurries to greet me with air kisses on each cheek. She steps out of our embrace and turns to her son. "*Mon fils*!" She greets him with a big hug and multiple kisses. "It is so good to have you back. How was the trip?"

"It was," Theo's eyes find mine, lip turning up on one side. "Entertaining. Actually, Lindsay was on both of my flights. Even sat next to me on the flight to Paris."

His mom looks at me curiously. "Is that right? Please tell me Theo here was nothing less than a gentleman."

I smile at her. "Yes. I couldn't have asked for a better neighbor." I look back to Theo. "Well, other than the coffee incident," I scold sarcastically, causing him to grin. I look back to his mom and see her suspiciously eyeing both Theo and me with a twinkle in her eye.

"Well, welcome again, Lindsay. I am Antoinette, but you can call me Annie. My husband, Will, is busy right now finishing up some things before we have to leave." She looks over to Theo. "Can you bring in her luggage while I give her a tour?"

"Actually, Mom, she only has her small roller. The airline lost her checked bag."

"*Quelle tragédie*!" She clicks her tongue while shaking her head. "Then why don't you see if we have any clean clothes that will fit her in the lost-and-found while I give her the tour." She grabs my hand and ushers me down the hall, but pauses to turn her head toward Theo. "Oh, and everything you need while we're gone is in the office including all of the notes and contacts for the wedding."

"Thanks, Ma. I'll go find Dad and catch up before you two leave. And I'll see you at dinner, Lindsay," he shouts as we part ways.

"Now Lindsay," Annie starts while patting my hand. "Since you are the only one staying on property during your time here, I thought you could pick what suite you would like to stay the week in, though I'm confident you will choose the room I brought the key for." She pats her pocket with a knowing smile. Why do I get the feeling like this is some sort of test?

The property really feels more like a home than a hotel. A *huge* home, larger than any house I grew up around, but a home nonetheless. I can just feel all the warmth and love packed in these four walls. There's character in every room we walk through, making it feel different than the sometimes cold and lifeless feel of traditional hotels. And the attention to detail is truly astounding.

There are five suites and so far I've toured four of them. Each one is decorated with its own theme, but not in a kitschy way like you would expect with some of the B&Bs back in the States. No, these all have a modern feel, but with different colors and pieces of furniture.

All have large plush beds, kings if I was guessing, with cozy fireplaces. I adore the abundant amount of windows allowing a generous amount of natural light into each space. There's something to be said about waking up to the sun rising. God, I haven't done that in years. I'm always being jolted out of bed by the ringtone on my phone before the sun is even tempted to rise.

The suites also all come with an oversized jetted tub. Some right next to the bed and others near a window or sliding door leading out to the grounds. I'm sure this would make for a perfect romantic getaway. Or even a wedding! Oh, I definitely should keep this place in mind for future destination weddings.

No!

No working, Lindsay. Just enjoy the beautiful, picture-perfect, hotel. Don't think about how the lavender-covered grounds would make a stunning backdrop while a couple says their vows. Or how the grass would make for a great spot for a sunset reception. Nope. Definitely not thinking about that.

Cozy tables for two are also in all of the suites making it clear I could choose to enjoy my meals in the privacy of my room. Though with what I'm seeing from my quick peek out the windows, I could easily see myself eating all my meals outside in the back, near what looks to be an infinity pool with an orchard behind it.

Damn. I didn't even *think* about bringing my swimsuit. Maybe I can ask Theo if he can run me into town to grab one? No, it's not that big of a deal. I'm only here for a few nights.

But it *does* get hot and humid here. Maybe it wouldn't be such a bad thing to have the option of using the pool.

We walk up the steps to the last suite, and Annie opens the door, pausing to let me in first. I can immediately tell this is the room I'll be choosing for my stay. While all of the other suites were modern with a touch of moody, this one is bright and welcoming.

Each wall is painted pure white, except for an amber yellow accent wall peeking out just behind the bed. The ceiling is pitched with beams running across, and similar to the other suites, there is no shortage of windows. Only in this suite, the white walls reflect the sunlight, giving the space even more warmth.

There's a wall of windows with a balcony door leading out to a flight of stairs to the pool, and what looks to be the rest of the backyard. As I walk deeper inside the suite, I glance up and find a couple of oversized skylights. This room would be an absolute dream during a storm.

Heading to the opposite side of the room, I find myself completely awestruck because of the beautiful view overlooking the lavender field below. As I shake myself from the minor hypnosis the view causes, I realize there's a bathtub right in front of the window. On the nearby ledge, the hotel has provided all ingredients for the most serene experience known to mankind. All I would need is a cup of tea and I'd have it made.

"I take it I assumed correctly?"

I turn toward Annie, who's dangling the keys like a prize to be won. I can't help but nod vigorously, unable to string a sentence together.

She beams. "I'll leave your key on the table here, and send your bag up with Theo. Dinner will be ready in two hours. If you need anything, please call down, and Theo will be happy to assist. Enjoy your stay, Lindsay." She sneaks out of my room, closing the door softly behind her.

I can't believe I get to stay here.

Walking around the room again, I try to commit every detail to memory before remembering to take out my phone, ensuring I have an obnoxious amount of photos and a couple short videos to share with my family.

When I reach the bathroom, I end my photoshoot and rinse

the airplane feel off my face. I want to take a shower, but don't have anything clean to change into yet. Hopefully Theo's hunt for some clothes proves successful. It feels a little weird to wear other people's clothes, but beggars can't be choosers. If my bag doesn't arrive tomorrow, I wonder if they have a washer I can clean my two outfits in. And if not, a bathing suit won't be the only thing I'll need to buy in town.

I grab a water bottle and cup from the dry bar, and pour myself some water. Approaching my bed, I come to the conclusion that even though I don't have a clean outfit to change into, I still don't want my grimy one dirtying up my bed with all its airport germs. So I take all my clothes off, except my panties. Only when I unhook my bra, I find I still have a bit of stickiness leftover from the coffee. I guess I do need a rinse off.

I walk over to the shower and turn it on without much issue once I figure out the mechanism. While it gets to temperature, I pull my hair up and out of the way from the showerhead. I don't have the energy right now to blow dry it afterwards.

Without my carry-on, I'm at the mercy of the hotel's toiletries. I find a wrapped bar of soap on the sink counter and grab it before stepping into the tiny boxed shower. I guess it doesn't need to be a lavish shower since most people probably enjoy the view from the tub.

Unwrapping the soap, I'm overtaken immediately by the smell of lavender, but there's something else. Something warm but complimentary to the lavender. It smells divine. I wonder if they sell these? I'm sure Mom and the girls would all love one.

Stepping out of the shower stall, I throw the soggy soap wrapper away and grab a towel. I pat myself dry, enjoying the lingering floral scent from the soap while I wrap the towel around myself. Sauntering over to the bed, I dive deep into the luxurious sheets, still wrapped in my towel so as to not soak the linens.

I have about an hour and a half until dinner, which gives me about an hour to nap and thirty minutes afterwards to figure out which clothing items are clean enough to put back on and wear to dinner.

Shit. As I'm taking a mental inventory of what's in my carry on, I realize I only have one extra pair of underwear. Thank god, I packed an additional one of those in my carry on. Given the feel of my bra when I took it off, there's no way I'm putting that back on without cleaning it first. The girls will just have to be free tonight. It's not like they are huge, especially not compared to Taylor's perfect surgeon-crafted ones, but they are definitely large enough to tell when I'm not wearing a bra. Too bad I don't have a textured shirt.

You know what? No. If I want to go braless, I'll go braless. It's not like anyone else is here, well besides Theo. And I'm sure he's seen lots of breasts.

Well, I hope not *lots* of breasts. A normal amount of breasts.

God, I don't want to be thinking of Theo ogling some other woman's breasts. I'm just saying I don't care if he ogles my breasts.

Wait.

What am I even saying? Lindsay, you need a nap. Like immediately, the jet-lag is going straight to your head.

I send a text and photo of the room to my family saying I made it safe and sound, place an alarm on my phone for five-thirty, then immediately put my phone on "do not disturb." Shortly after, I fall into easily the best nap I've taken in my adult life.

CHAPTER FOURTEEN

THEO

Walking the grounds outside, it takes no time to find Dad. Of course he's out in the fields; it's his favorite place to be now that they live here full time. I must've missed him out there when we pulled up.

"Hey, Dad!" I shout, attempting to get his attention. He's notorious for getting lost in what he's focused on. He's a hard worker, always has been. I learned almost everything I know from him including what he's doing right now, harvesting lavender. He taught me one of the years he surprised Ma and me by flying over here during the summer.

I take a glance around the field blooming with the purple flowers. Growing up, I called it the "Field of Dreams" because Ma would always take a stroll with me right before bed in summer. Back then, I thought it was magic because I would always have the best sleep, *and* dreams, after a walk in the field. It would never fail to put me to sleep as soon I laid my head on my pillow afterwards.

Whenever we'd return to the States for school, I'd never sleep as well. It wasn't until later that I picked up on the connection of my sleep with the calming properties of lavender. Still, those late night walks with Ma hold a special place in my heart.

"Theo!" I look back up and find Dad walking over to me. "How ya doing, Son?" He hugs me tight, kissing my cheeks before he lets go, patting me on the shoulder as he releases his hold on me. "I've missed you."

Dad's always been affectionate. Growing up being the baby of five kids, four of them being girls, he was the tough one in the family, but there was also no fear in showing emotion.

"Missed you too, Dad." I smile, my heart feeling full being back with family. "I've been good. Busy, but good. How's Ma doing with all of this?"

"She's worried of course, but holding up well. I'm so sorry you had to fly over here, but I'm glad you're here." He pats me again on my back.

"Need any help with the lavender?" There's no doubt he's capable, but there's no need for him to do all the work alone when I'm here.

"Oh no. I'm done for the day. Just checking it and the bees one last time before we leave."

We have a few hives around the property. Of course they help with the lavender, but they also help with all the other plant life around the estate. In addition to helping the plants, we also harvest the honey and beeswax. We use them in all sorts of ways for the hotel. Mostly in the kitchen and bath products used by the guests.

Ma makes all the bath products herself. The bars of soap are her specialty. She even sells them to the guests who want to take them home.

The best one is this honeycomb and lavender soap. I make sure to take a few bars for myself every time I visit. And when I run out, she happily ships me more. Though not without her telling me something along the lines of "If I really wanted more, I should fly out to see her."

"Need help with anything else before you leave?" I turn to ask Dad while we walk back to the front door.

"Nope, but thank you." He smiles that toothy grin of his before adding, "Let's stop by the office though. I'll walk you through everything you need to know for the next couple of weeks."

By now, I know what needs to be done on a daily and weekly basis at the hotel. Plus, with the help from Ettie and Jean around the property, it's a relatively light work load when everything is running smoothly. Most days, I don't even have to cook because Mateo always makes enough for our family too, even though Ma tries to push back saying he doesn't need to be worrying about us. Mateo's cooking is one of my favorite things here and I have yet to find a place that compares to his creations.

Dad and I finish up right before Ma walks in the office. "Ready?" Dad asks her.

"Yes, *mon chéri*." She gives Dad a light kiss, then turns to me. "Theo, don't forget to bring Lindsay's bag to her suite. She's upstairs," she adds, sporting a proud smile.

That suite is the best in the hotel. It's not only a favorite among our guests, but a favorite of mine as well. And I've definitely taken a few baths in that tub. I was raised with an appreciation for them after all. The best time for a soak in that room is when it's storming outside. You can watch the rain coming down over the field while the sound of rain pelts down on the skylights.

I haven't been back during the rainy season for awhile, but that room layout has stuck with me over the years. It has even inspired a few bathroom designs in some of my house flips.

"Well, my Little Flower, we better head out before it gets too late. Call us if you have any trouble, Theo," Dad adds before he hugs me goodbye.

"Will do. Do you need help loading your bags in the car?" I turn to Ma, opening my arms for one of her warm hugs.

She squeezes me tight. "No, we already loaded them. I love you, *mon fils*. I will keep you updated with any news."

"Thank you. I love you both. Please drive safe." I wave as they head out the door.

Heading to the lost and found, I search for clothes for Lindsay but come up empty. We've got to have *something* she could wear.

After brainstorming solutions, I decide to run to our family home and grab a couple of the spare sweats and plain tees I have stored for when I visit. It's nothing fancy, but it'll get her by until the airline can track down her bag. Hopefully, they'll reach out tomorrow with some news.

Running back to the estate, I grab her roller and head upstairs. I knock on the door, but there's no answer. I knock once more, a little harder this time, knowing it's almost time for dinner and if she was napping, she'd probably want to be woken up for food.

There's still no answer. I leave the roller and the folded spare clothes on top of her bag in front of her door. No one is here so it won't go anywhere, and this way she has clean clothes available if she needs them for dinner.

I step back downstairs and head toward the kitchen, excited to see what Mateo is cooking for dinner.

"Mateo!" I greet as I burst through the kitchen doors. "Long time, no see. How's my favorite chef doing these days?"

Mateo barely moves from his spot at the range. In fact, I would've thought he didn't hear me if it hadn't been for his huffing as I walked in.

Making my way closer to him, I wrap an arm around his shoulder. "Good to see you, pal." I take a peek at what he's finishing up. "Is that beef bourguignon? Oh, you really *do* love me, don't you, Mateo?" He just shakes his head and moves over to start plating dinner.

Beef bourguignon is a favorite of mine, and though Mateo likes to play hard to get, he always spoils me by making it for me whenever I visit.

He hands me a plate while I smile cheekily. "Thank you, Mateo."

He just hmphs and turns to start cleaning up.

Dinner comes and goes. Still no Lindsay. Mateo left her a plate in the fridge and gave me instructions for heating before he left for the night. I'm pretty sure it pained Mateo to have to talk to me, but he took one for the team, making sure I didn't do injustice by ruining the beef bourguignon by heating it up wrong. I'm sure I could do the dish justice if I had my air fryer here.

It's about eight at night and still not a sound from Lindsay. I feel like I at least need to *attempt* to offer her dinner before I go back to the family house for the remainder of the night.

After climbing the stairs up to her suite, I call out her name while knocking firmly on her door. I hear her voice and what sounds like an "oh shit" before a loud crashing.

"Lindsay? Is everything okay?" I ask, doing nothing to hide the concern in my voice.

"Umm . . ." She pauses, a little too long for my comfort. "Define 'okay'?"

Shit. "I'm coming in." I announce as I open the door, flip the nearest light switch on, and find Lindsay standing deathly still next to the bed in nothing but a towel.

I freeze. She's naked.

Well, not *technically* naked. She has a towel on. And who knows, she may even have shorts on under too. Or maybe just her underwear. I wonder what I'd find if I pulled back that towel. Maybe a black strappy thon—

I shake my head trying to focus on the task at hand. I don't need to be thinking about what kind of thong she could be wearing. And plus, she very well could be completely naked under there. Not even a hint of fabric covering up her—

Shit. No. Focus, Theo.

I take a look around the room and see nothing out of the ordinary.

"Are you okay? I heard a crashing sound." I hesitantly step closer to her, still searching for the cause of that crash.

"Yeah, that would be the glass cup I just broke." She sighs as her shoulders drop. "After my shower, I thought I'd take a nap. I must've slept through my alarm for dinner, so when you called my name, it startled me out of bed. I tried to grab my phone to get a little light and check the time, but ended up hitting my glass of water."

My eyes roam the rug she's standing on looking for any evidence of the glass.

"So on top of the wet mess, there are now tiny glass shards all around my feet. And of course, I'm barefoot." She slaps her hands down on her thighs; the sound of her hands hitting the soft terry cloth reminds me again of her state of undress.

So she really *is* naked under that towel. I lick my lips but try to keep my mind focused on helping Lindsay. Now is *so* not the time, Theo.

Walking over to her, she crosses her arms over chest, ensuring the towel won't fall down any second. And with the way luck has been mistreating her the last twelve hours, I'd put the odds on the towel doing just that.

"First things first," I take a cautious step toward her, glass crunching under my shoes. "Did any of the glass land on your feet or legs?"

"I don't think so." She looks down at her feet, wiggling her toes a little. "I mean I don't feel any glass."

"Great. Next step," I say, reaching out and preparing to lift her bridal style. "I'm going to get you out of this glass. Is it okay for me to lift you?"

"Oh." She shifts in place still grasping for dear life at that damn towel. "Um, sure. I guess that would be fine."

"Great." As I lift her up, one of my hands sneaks under her arms, resting along what would be her bra line, while the other is wrapped around her thighs. My fingers are pressed tightly into the exposed skin of her thigh while her towel rides up.

I take a few steps over to the dining table, and pull out a chair with my foot. The weight of her in my arms feels so natural, but I reluctantly set her down into the chair, the one furthest from the glass mess. I turn to walk out of the suite to grab the vacuum downstairs, pausing as I get to the door's threshold.

"Now be a good girl and stay there while I go grab the vacuum." I give her a slow and seductive once over. God, she looks like a fucking treat sitting in that towel. "Wouldn't want me to punish you if I return and see that you've moved, would you?" I turn and walk out the door, smirking knowing her cheeks are probably fifty shades of red right now.

CHAPTER FIFTEEN

LINDSAY

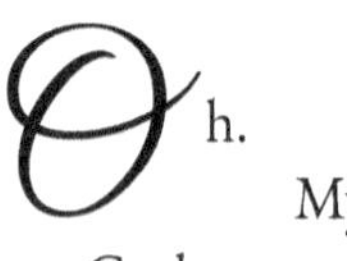

h.

My.

God.

I shake myself out of my horned-out haze, just now realizing I'm in a towel and nothing else. My shirt is on the edge of the bench at the end of the bed, but my pants must've slipped off the side at some point during my little nap this evening because they are now on the floor next to the bed, covered in broken pieces of glass.

I tiptoe over to grab my blouse and switch that out for my towel. Normally, it's tucked in, but by itself it hangs around my upper thigh. I button it up enough so none of my bits are showing, but I'm basically just Winnie the Pooh'n it right now. Still, it's better coverage than the towel I was sporting.

I hear a noise and turn around to find Theo walking through the door, vacuum in one hand and what looks to be a stack of clothes on the other. God, he looks so . . . domesticated. Fuck, and how did I not notice he's wearing those little glasses again.

He's frozen, just staring at me. I look as guilty as a kid getting caught sneaking the last cookie out of the jar.

"Theo?" I ask, trying to wake him from his momentary stupor. His eyes snap to mine. He looks positively feral.

He shakes his head and tsks, going back to his very *thorough* staring, clearly assessing the state of my body.

"Someone's been a naughty girl." He stalks closer, putting the pile of clothes on the table and parking the vacuum up against the chair back. He pulls at the bottom of my blouse, finger tips grazing my upper thigh. "I thought I told you to stay put?"

I bite my bottom lip and attempt to look anywhere but his piercing gaze. "I couldn't stay in just the towel." I tug on the fabric, my hand grazing his while I do it.

"So exchanging a towel for a button down is somehow more" —he tugs again at my shirt—"modest?"

"Well, maybe not *modest*," I say sheepishly, returning my eyes to his. "But at least it won't fall down at any point."

"Believe me, I could pop those buttons open just as easily as I could tug a towel off."

Good god.

I try to step back out of . . . well whatever this is. I'm not nearly as confident as he clearly is. But before I can even take a step, his hand moves from the hem of my blouse to my back right above my ass, the other quickly joining it. Keeping me locked in this spot.

I'm trying to catch my breath. I can't remember a time where a man was this forward with me. Or rather this forward and I actually *enjoyed* it.

He leans down right next to my ear, so close my hair catches in the scruff covering his chin. "Now take a seat and let me clean this mess up," he commands, his breath a warm whisper on my ear and neck.

"Ye—yea—yes," I stutter, trying to gain back at least some of my senses as he ushers me back to the table and chair. I sit down and try to pull at the bottom of my blouse, the fabric not budging a bit to help me cover the surplus of skin on display. My legs are completely exposed and I'm feeling so much more airflow than when I had the towel on. I might as well be in my underwear.

Shit. Underwear.

I just remembered I'm still not wearing any. I move my hands from my pathetic attempt to cover my thighs to shield the lack of coverage between my legs.

He walks over to where the glass is, making quick work of throwing away the larger pieces of glass before vacuuming the rest of the tiny shards. Seeing him with the vacuum makes me think I might need to create another mess for him to clean up.

Theo moves through the space until the clinking of the glass getting sucked up lessens, telling us he's successfully cleaned up the glass, or at least most of it. Why is it that no matter how many times you sweep or vacuum, you still find a random piece weeks later?

Theo wraps the cord back up and walks the vacuum out of the room, apparently trading it with my roller bag.

"I came earlier." My eyes snap to him, clearly my mind is having the time of its life playing in the gutter. "I think you were napping and didn't hear me knocking."

"Oh right." I nod. "Sorry about that. Are these for me?" I gesture toward the clothes on the table.

"Yeah. That's all I could find that would work. If you want, I could wash your other clothes tomorrow?"

"I appreciate that, but if you don't mind showing me where the machines are, I can wash them myself."

"I think I can make that happen," Theo says with his face relaxed and a slight twinkle in his emerald eyes. He walks toward me, stopping when he reaches the table I'm sitting at. "You missed dinner, but I have a meal in the fridge that I can warm up for you. You must be starving."

"Dinner sounds nice. Let me just throw on my trousers and I'll meet you in the dining room?"

"It's just us here. No need to be formal." He pauses, staring down at the exposed skin on my thighs. "Plus I've already seen your impersonation of 'Risky Business.' Just come as you are." He looks back up at me. "If you're comfortable, that is. Otherwise, there are some sweatpants on the table you can slide on."

As tempting as it is to be the super sexy and confident woman who prances around in nothing but a button up, legs on full display, that's something Taylor would do, not me. I'd feel more comfortable with some pants. So after grabbing a pair off the table, I quickly pull them up my legs, making sure not to give Theo a show before motioning to the door. "Lead the way."

His eyes sparkle with amusement as he smiles and guides me out, directing us to the kitchen.

"Take a seat while I warm this up." Theo points to a couple of wooden barstools surrounding the kitchen island, which is more like a rectangular table, definitely used for prep work.

The kitchen is smaller than expected, and not a single inch of it is wasted. It's a little worn down, but clearly loved. There's an eight burner stovetop with dual ovens underneath. The counters are clean without many gadgets on top. And there's a beautiful apron sink with an oversized picture window sitting right above. I can't quite make out the view because it's dark outside, but I do see the walking path and a lit up olive tree just outside. I bet it's beautiful when the sun's out. Golden hour would be a dream as the sun sets over the expansive estate outside. I wouldn't mind washing dishes if that was my view.

"I preheated the oven before I came up thinking you'd be hungry, so it should only take about fifteen minutes to warm up." He steps toward the cabinets, opening the door. "Want anything to drink? Water, juice, wine?"

"Water would be nice. Thanks."

He grabs two glasses from the cabinet, fills them, and heads over to me. He places one in front of me and takes a sip from his. "Breakfast will be served around nine tomorrow, so feel free to sleep in. I can either bring it to your room or set up a spot basically anywhere else on the property."

Nine? I haven't slept-in in almost a decade. "I was actually thinking about sitting outside for breakfast if that's possible."

"I'll set something up outside then." He smiles at me and shifts his position so he's leaning back against the island, hands gripping the wooden edge. With the subtle adjustment, I can't help my eyes from wandering his body. Shit, even his hands are hot. I can just imagine one hand roaming down my body while the other grips my—

"You're staring, *ma chére*." I look up and see the dimple is out and so is a cocky as hell smirk.

CHAPTER SIXTEEN

THEO

I can't help but feel like the kitchen warms up a few degrees while I observe her checking me out. It's almost like she'd rather eat me than the meal in the oven. And by the look on her face, I'd let her do just that. Hell, *I* want to be the one eating *her*. Maybe lift her up on the island. Spread her wide open so I can devour her like the delicious treat she is.

She grabs her water, clearly attempting to break the tension. But I don't want to make her feel too uncomfortable. "What if we take a tour around the grounds tomorrow after breakfast?"

She clears her throat. "Oh, I'd like that. Thanks." She glances around the kitchen. "Are you staying here for the time being or do you stay in the other house I saw on the drive in."

"The one you saw on the drive in. It's my family's house so I'll be staying there," I explain, but an unsure expression overcomes her face. "That is, unless you would feel safer with me staying here?"

"Well not here, meaning my room. But I thought maybe, since no one else is staying in the hotel, you'd be staying in one of the other suites."

It's not like I've never stayed in one of the rooms. In recent years, if the hotel isn't booked out, Ma would place me in one of the suites to give me my space since the family house can get a little cramped.

"But I don't want to put you out or anything. It just feels weird being in such a huge house, alone. Plus—"

I send a smile her way. "If it makes you feel safe, *ma chére*, I can stay here. Truly, it's no issue." I'll just stay in the suite under hers, that way I'm not too far from her if she needs me.

The timer goes off and I grab Lindsay's dinner, plate it up, and place the dish in front of her.

"Make sure to blow." She gives me what I've now dubbed the Lindsay stare down. "What?" I shrug nonchalantly, but my lip creeps up at the corners, giving my intentions away. "The food is hot. You should blow on it."

"Uh huh." She rolls her eyes while picking up a fork full of food, proceeding to blow dramatically over it. When she bites down, her eyes roll back as she moans around the food. Fucking *moans.* I am not going to last long.

"Oh my god. This is *divine*," she says, dragging out the last word then ending the sentence in another moan. It's smaller, but still there.

I drag a hand down my face trying to recite all fifty states in alphabetical order to keep myself calm. Alabama, Alaska, Arizona, Arkansas, California, Colora—

"*Mmm.* This is *really* good."

Fuck. Does she know what she's doing? I doubt it, but it affects me all the same.

"Your chef is amazing," she adds around another mouthful of food. "What is this?"

"It's beef bourguignon. Mateo's is the best I've ever had." She digs deeper in her food. "He tries to make it whenever I visit since it's a favorite of mine."

"That's very sweet of him," she observes while looking up at me with sauce on the corner of her mouth. I reach down to swipe my thumb across her lips, catching all of the rich, flavorful sauce, and pop my thumb into my mouth, sucking off any evidence. All while staring right into her shock-filled eyes. Payback from those taunting sound effects of hers.

We keep up this stare down, tension pulled so tight between us it will snap any second. She breaks the spell by looking down at my lips with nothing but lust in her eyes.

I quickly find out Lindsay is full of surprises as I watch her bring her sauce-covered fork up to her mouth, painting her lips in the delicious red sauce.

Fuck it.

I reach down and weave my fingers through her wavy hair and slam our lips together. It's a messy clash of lips as I reach one hand to her back urging her to stand so I can get her right where I want her. With my height and her sitting on a barstool, the angle isn't the best for what I want to do to her.

She stands, breaking our kiss while gasping, "Are we sure we want to do this?"

I look at her, unclear because I could've sworn she was feeling the same things I was. I mean that move with the fork . . . fuck me. But I step back, moving one of my hands so it cups her face and sliding my other down to grip her waist.

"Do *you* not want to do this?" I ask while attempting to get a read on her face, but all I'm seeing is uncertainty.

"Maybe *want* was the wrong word to use." She turns her head away, biting her lower lip. I grip her chin and shift her face so I can look back into her intense eyes.

"Hey," I feel like a hunter who's trying not to startle the prey that just wandered into his path. "If you say stop, we stop. This doesn't have to go any further," I clarify sincerely and watch as her eyes start to glisten.

Shit, I'm making her cry. I go to drop my hand from her face, but she quickly slaps hers on top to keep it in place. I look to her for some type of permission to continue and find her eyes looking up at me through her long black lashes while shyly nodding her head. That's all the confirmation I need before picking up right where we left off.

CHAPTER SEVENTEEN

LINDSAY

Is this really happening? Yes.

Is it the best idea to do this knowing there is literally no escaping each other for the next five nights? Probably not.

I *attempted* to pull the brakes and mentally list off the multitude of reasons why it's not a good idea to get involved with Theo. But as soon as he slowed down and gave me the choice, I was done keeping my walls up. I'm only here for a little under a week, so I'm going to take advantage of as much time I can get with my hands all over Theo. How's that saying go? Here for a good time, not a long time? I guess now's as good a time as any to try out that mindset.

The kiss is rough at first, but as I relax it turns soft and explorative. I'm suddenly lifted onto the island countertop before Theo spreads my legs with his thigh, stepping between them while kissing down my neck. His lips are like velvet against my skin and his hands take their time roaming my hips and waist. It all feels so overwhelming, not knowing which sensation I should focus on. But it's the best kind of sensory overload.

I shift my hips and that's when I feel it. Yup, he definitely set me on top of my dinner. Well, this blouse is officially destroyed because there's absolutely no way I'm stopping this hot make-out session to go soak my shirt in the hopes of removing the red wine sauce.

He must have sensed my change in focus because he stops his exploration of my body to look up at me, question in his eye.

"You kind of," I say looking to my right hip, "set my ass on my dinner plate."

"Oh shit," he chuckles and pulls me up and off the counter only to turn me around and bend me over the edge. "Well look at this," he comments, grabbing my hips and swiping his thumbs across the fabric covering my ass cheeks. "I do believe we just created my favorite meal." I turn my head looking back at him to see the feral look in his eyes from earlier today framed by his round lenses. Only somehow it's even more wild as he playfully bites his lower lip.

"Are you going to sit there and stare or are you going to take a bite?"

He lifts his eyebrows in pleasant surprise as the corner of his mouth picks up. I've shocked him with my forward comment, and honestly, myself too. I never say shit like this, but something about him makes all of this so easy. So natural.

"Oh, *ma chére*," he tsks while giving a tight squeeze to my hips. "Don't ask for things you can't handle, because I won't simply bite," he looks at me with hunger in his eyes. "I'll devour."

Fuck. He's going to ruin me for all mankind. And he hasn't even gotten my pants off yet.

"Big words coming from a man who's just standing and staring," I taunt before turning my head back to face away from him while leaving my ass in the air.

He clicks his tongue and I don't even need to turn around to know I'd find that damn smirk and dimple.

I feel his fingers slip under the waistband of my sweats, teasing me oh so mind-numbingly slow. But when he reaches my hip and finds nothing there, he stops.

"Lindsay." He rubs his palms up and down my hips, fingers

begging to move to the front of me. "Are you not wearing any underwear?"

"You tell me." Who am I? Apparently, I developed a new persona after landing in France.

He shifts closer so his chest is hovering over my back. One hand deliciously close to where I need him. He leans in close to my ear, breath hot when he says, "Is that what you want, Lindsay?" I close my eyes, leaning my head into him. "For me to *devour* this perfect body."

I nod slowly as his fingers trail southward, pulling my pants down along the way.

"For me to lower my touch."

Once my pants fall past my knees, he wedges his knee in between my legs to widen my stance while kissing my shoulder.

"For me to feel how wet I make you?"

I moan as his fingertips reach my lips and continue to roam lower, finding me drenched from all his teasing.

Theo starts slow, almost taunting me while he continues to pepper kisses on my shoulder, then moving up the column of my neck. He raises one hand to start unbuttoning a few of the top buttons on my blouse. Just enough to pull the shirt down my shoulders so he has better access to my breasts, but not enough to disrupt his other hand's movements.

Repositioning himself, he tucks his head in the junction of my neck while his hand rests on my breast, thumb swirling my nipple, making it peak under his touch.

I breathe in, relaxing into the feel of his hands on my body, only to immediately take a startling breath when his two fingers plunge inside of me.

His hand's rhythm is steady, while the other hand massages my breast. His touch is so gentle yet possessive. He nibbles on my ear and I'm already getting close. He adds another finger while swiping my clit with his thumb.

Fuck. "Theo—" I barely get out. "I'm going—" I thrust my

hips matching the rhythm of his fingers as I chase after what I want.

"Let go, *ma chére*," he whispers in my ear before sucking on my neck.

I moan and curse and buck my hips like a mad woman as my release bursts through me. Waves of pleasure hit without a break in sight. He kisses me through it all, slowing his fingers inside of me but not quite stopping, making my orgasm last even longer.

Theo must feel me relax as he places a kiss on my shoulder as I'm able to finally catch my breath.

He slowly pulls his fingers out before I turn to face him. I'm still in a haze from that mind-blowing orgasm so I don't notice my blouse falling down until it hits the floor, leaving me standing in front of Theo utterly naked.

I stare in bewilderment at him as he puts those very fingers that were inside of me into his mouth. He sucks them clean and then licks his lips with a savage smile afterwards.

Fuck me.

Up until now, I've only read about a man doing that in one of my books. I never really could make up my mind on if I would enjoy seeing my partner do that or not. But now? Hell fucking yes. And I want him to do it again because holy shit was that hot.

I reach down to pull up my shirt, but meet Theo's hand doing the same. He shifts the fabric on the floor to get a view of the huge stain setting in on my white blouse. I'm not sure if I'll be able to salvage this shirt after all.

"I really did make a mess out of you, didn't I?" He chuckles huskily as he helps me out of the shirt that's pooled by my feet. But instead of putting it back on me, he tosses the ruined fabric onto the island.

I'm left standing, awkwardly aware I am completely naked in front of a fully dressed Theo. But before I can ask him what his next move is, he strips off his shirt then pulls it over my head, helping my arms through their respective holes.

The white tee falls to my thigh, a little longer than the blouse I was wearing. It's still white so he's definitely getting some sort of show with how hard my nipples are underneath the thin fabric.

I'm surrounded by his scent. It has a hint of woodsy, but that's not at the forefront. I take a few breaths, inhaling the smell. It reminds me of the soap I used earlier. Definitely floral but with a warm sweetness I can't put my finger on. Now that I think about it, it was the same scent I smelled on the plane but I just chalked it up to being the tea and honey he was enjoying. I brush my hands down the tee out of habit, not sure what to say or do next.

"It's clean. I changed while you were napping," he adds as he mistakes my insecurity as me thinking he gave me a dirty shirt.

"Oh, thanks." I turn to clean up my plate, trying to find something to distract me from how much I want to climb this man like the tree he is.

"You don't have to do that. Just leave it and I'll clean it later." I look back at him. "Really. I'm sure you're still tired, so I'll walk you to your room so you can get some more sleep."

I eye him with suspicion but he puts his hands up innocently.

"I'll be a perfect gentleman. Even say my goodbyes in the hall so I won't step inside your room." I give him a once over making it clear I don't believe him. "Unless you don't want me to." He winks and I roll my eyes, expecting nothing less.

"Alright. I guess I am still a bit tired," I relent.

As we walk up the steps, my exhaustion sets in. That nap did nothing to help my jet-lag because I'm beyond tired at this point.

Theo opens the door, but doesn't step inside, keeping his word. He pulls me close, hands wrapped around my waist. "Sleep well, *ma chére*." Theo kisses me with such warmth and a promise for more, just not tonight, then pulls out of our embrace. "I'll see you in the morning," he adds as he closes the door.

I walk to the sink to wash my face, not locking the door because it's just Theo here. Mentally telling myself it's only because he has a key and can come in even if it's locked, definitely not because I'm hoping that if I leave my door unlocked it will be a sign telling him I'm up for a midnight hookup. Even in the morning, it will only be the staff who occupy the hotel and they all have access to room keys, too.

I take a look in the mirror and find my hair completely disheveled, if anyone else *was* at the hotel and ran into us, there'd be no doubt what Theo and I just did.

While running through my nightly routine, my heart finally calms down and I'm able to think clearly about what just happened.

I just let Theo—a practical stranger—finger the fuck out of me without any thought of the consequences that will come if this doesn't work out.

In all honesty, I did *try* but I was too damn tempted by his lips on mine. Plus, seeing those slutty glasses of his fog up . . . *fuuuck*. It was like catnip. And he didn't even *attempt* to satisfy what looked—and felt—like a very hard dick. No. He was fully focused on me and my pleasure.

What would it be like to be with a man like that? A man who doesn't pressure a woman or claim he's "owed" something because he made her come.

Too bad there's no future with Theo.

Ugh. I'm too tired to go down the spiral of all of that, so instead I cuddle up in bed with the fluffy comforter. Still wearing Theo's tee and wrapped in the subtle scent of honey and lavender.

CHAPTER EIGHTEEN

THEO

I close Lindsay's door and lean my back against it as I slide my palm down my face.

Fuuuuck. I breathe out.

I barely held the restraint to not take things further in the kitchen. When my fingers didn't find any fabric under her pants, I knew I was done for. I was attempting to show a *little* restraint, but even a bucket of the coldest water couldn't turn my dick's attention away from knowing Lindsay was bare while she asked me to do something about it.

Luckily, my upstairs head had enough blood flowing to it to realize I didn't have a condom on me. And I definitely don't have one back at our family house. It's not exactly the place to entertain women. Especially when your parents are down the hall. I'll have to run into town to grab some. Maybe I can ask Jean if he can grab some before heading this way in the morning?

That's not weird right? Just one guy asking another to get condoms. Totally normal.

Either way. I can't have sex with her until I get those, and judging on how quickly things just progressed, I need to get them fast.

I walk myself over to the family house and gather some things so I can stay in the suite below Lindsay. I understand her not wanting to stay in an empty hotel. Alone. In the middle of nowhere. It doesn't bother me to stay in a guest room until she leaves. It actually makes more sense. I'll be closer if she needs me.

But I definitely need to do something about this situation in my pants. I almost lost it as I felt her come around my fingers while moaning my name. I used all my mental strength to not be that guy who comes in his pants, though with how much I was enjoying watching her squirm around my touch, it might have been worth it. Everything just felt so good.

And now my erection is back.

Walking into what will be my room for the next few nights, the first thing I do is turn on the shower. I undress as it warms up then grab the soap before I step in. As I rub myself down and can't help picturing it's Lindsay's hands doing the touching. Imagining her hands working the soap into a lather up and down my body while her breasts glide against my wet skin.

The soap slips out of my hands, waking me from my daydream. Reaching down, I grab the bar and then place it on the shelf, all while hot water pours over me.

My dick remains hard with the image of Lindsay still fresh in my mind. Her ruffled hair from sleep framing her rosy cheeks. Lindsay's perky tits giving me more than a handful to hold. And that smart mouth of hers making an appearance while teasing me. Fuck me, that was hot. And that perfect ass, the kind that is so voluptuous that it makes its own little shelf.

I start to stroke myself from base to tip, but I know I'm not going to last long. Honestly, it was a miracle I held it in for this long. A few more tight strokes and release takes over. It happens so fast, I don't have time to adjust my aim, making a mess all over the shower wall.

I take a few breaths, willing my heart rate back to a normal pace while still floating in that post orgasm haze. I spray down the shower, cleaning up any evidence, before turning the water off and stepping out to wrap a towel around me.

The bed is cool as I get situated under the sheets. One can only hope that the temperature change helps turn off my brain. As I lay down, my mind can't help but replay the image of Lindsay completely stripped down after I made her come. Face flushed with hair sticking to her cheeks. Her perky pink nipples sticking out above her soft stomach, shaping her subtle hourglass figure. A little patch of hair fits between her legs, trimmed but not bare.

Fuck. And I'm hard again.

It's going to be a *long* night.

I wake up from a restless night, losing count after waking up for the third time with a hard-on. I'm pretty sure I rubbed myself raw throughout the night.

Around three in the morning, I gave in and texted Jean to pick up some condoms. I blamed it on late night preparation for the wedding this upcoming weekend, but one look at me this morning and he knew I was full of shit. He just threw the box with the receipt tucked inside at me, smirking as he walked away to start the morning's work.

"I appreciate it, man!" I shout. His only answer is a chuckle with a shake of his head.

After doing all my morning's tasks, I walk into the kitchen.

"Good morning, Mateo. What's on the menu today?" I pat him on the shoulder while he preps whatever dish he feels like making for the day.

"Breakfast." He points over to the counter near the sink and I find fresh fruit, *pain au chocolat*, and tea all set on a serving tray, ready to bring outside for Lindsay's breakfast. "Lunch," he waves his hand to the chicken in front of him, like it's the obvious answer to my question. Mateo walks over to the fridge and does a fine impression of Vanna White to show off the fresh fish in the fridge for dinner. "Dinner."

"Sounds great, Mateo."

We talk for a minute, or rather I talk and he *maybe* listens. I can never tell with him.

"It was great catching up, Mateo," I pat his back. "But as much as you love my company, I should get breakfast ready for our guest, Miss Hartman."

Mateo shakes his head as I stroll out, breakfast tray in hand, in the hopes to set up a table outside for Lindsay.

It's a clear morning, not too hot yet. I decide on the table near the garden. After setting the table, I clip some flowers and put them in the vase I brought out with breakfast.

As I'm walking back, I see her face coming around the corner of the hotel. She must've been exploring this morning. Or she got lost. Really, with how expansive the property is, I could see either of those options being true.

"Good morning," she greets while waving.

I start to smile as I see she's wearing my clothes. But of course she is. She doesn't have any other clean clothes to wear, but it brings a smile to my face nonetheless.

I know she was wearing my sweats last night, and then my tee after our kitchen island "activities" but it feels different knowing she chose to wear these today. I'm half tempted to call the airline to send the bag back to her house when they find it because she could wear my clothes for her whole damn trip as far as I'm concerned. It looks like she's braless too. Oh shit. Does that mean she doesn't have any underwear on either?

Fuck. Now all I'm thinking of is repeating what we did last night. Bet I could clear this table with one swipe of my arm and have her naked on top of it in less than—

"Is this for me?" Her voice shakes me from my intrusive thoughts of her naked and writhing beneath me.

"Good morning. And yes, it is. However, if you prefer coffee I can exchange the teapot for a carafe."

"Tea is fine, thank you. Wanna join me?" she asks with a bubbly smile, but her face drops when she corrects, "I mean you probably have a bunch of work that needs to be done, so no pressure. But you're welcome to sit and eat with me."

I chuckle as I take a seat at the table. "I have a little time to sit and enjoy the view." I wink and with the amount of winks I've given to this woman, someone might think I was developing an eye condition.

I already started brewing the tea with two of the bags Ma makes before I brought the tray outside. "Do you like honey?" I ask, jar in hand.

"Sure, just not too much."

I pour it out, accidentally dripping some on my finger. I look at her and find she's already staring at the sticky mess on my finger. I bring it to my lips and suck it off, ridiculously slow, making sure I put on a good show for her. She's staring at my lips, mouth gaping open. I pour her tea and slide the cup over. "If you want to taste, all you have to do is ask, *ma chére*."

That shakes her from her stupor. She clears her throat and picks up a *pain au chocolat*. Taking a bite, she moans. And now I'm the one gaping.

"And I thought the chocolate croissant in the Paris airport was good. Can I request these every morning or is that too big of an ask?" She wipes her mouth, cleaning off the little crumbs surrounding her lips.

"I will tell Mateo and he'll make it happen."

"You're not eating?" she observes. "I have more than enough to share," she offers and motions to the plates of food before blowing on the tea before taking her first sip.

"Already ate, but thank you. How's the tea?"

"It's nice." The porcelain teacup clinks as she sets it back down. "Lavender, right? The same tea you had on the plane?" she questions before picking her croissant back up, enjoying the remainder of it as flakes of dough rain down on her plate with every bite.

"One in the same. Dad picks the lavender and Ma dries and bags it. The honey is from our bees, too." It's a wonder how I'm even forming a coherent sentence when all I'm doing is staring at her lips and picturing what I could do with them.

"Well, it's great," she praises as she grabs a napkin to wipe her face. "I could see why you would want to bring it back with you." We both go quiet as we get lost in each other's gaze.

"So," I start before I clear my throat and look around the estate. "Want to go on that tour around the property now, or did you want to spend some time relaxing, maybe even by the pool?"

"Actually, do you mind showing me where I do my laundry? I'd love to start it before we take our mini adventure."

I smile. "*Mini adventure*, I like that. Yeah, after you finish, we can get your clothes and start a load. I'm sure Ettie will be able to switch it to the dryer while we're out."

"I'm ready now," she says before taking one more sip from her tea cup, tidying up the space as she stands. She goes to pick up the tray of dishes and I quickly take it from her causing her to huff. "I could've carried a tray to the kitchen." She rolls her eyes, but starts to walk alongside me.

"I know, but you don't have to."

After dropping off the dishes, and starting the laundry, we wander to the side of the property.

I motion toward the bikes we keep for guests. "Care for a ride?" Judging by her face, I'm not sure she saw my gesture at the bikes. I tilt my head, lips turning up. "I meant the bikes, but we can definitely pick up where we left off last night if that's where your mind's at."

She forces a laugh out. "No, it's not that. But it's good to know where *your* mind's at." She relaxes a little more. Then it dawns on me. When we played two truths one lie on the plane, one of the truths was that she didn't know how to ride a bike.

"I can teach you." I step closer to her.

"What?" She shakes her head a little and looks at me. "Oh, no. I won't ask you to do that. It's fine, we can just walk."

"You're not asking. I am." I grab her hands in mine. "Let me." She exhales and I can see no is on the tip of her tongue. "Come on. It's perfect weather. And I'll even put a timer on it. If you can't figure out how to ride it in"—I tap my chin—"let's say twenty minutes? We can abandon the bike idea and just use our legs. Sounds good?"

She takes a minute, clearly contemplating my offer. "Make it fifteen, and you've got yourself a deal."

I bring her hands up to give them a quick kiss and squeeze. "You drive a hard bargain, Miss Hartman, but you've got yourself a deal."

Fifteen minutes later, and a few dozen curses and unnecessary touches on her body, she's riding alongside me like she's been doing this her whole life.

I turn to face her. "See, I knew you could do it."

The sun is shining behind her, illuminating her like she's a gift from heaven. And maybe she is. She catches me staring and sends a bashful smile my way. I smile wide and hers gets even bigger in response.

"Thanks, Theo." She dips her head in appreciation before increasing her speed.

"Oh, so we're racing now?" I match her speed. "What do I get if I win?"

"Who said anything about *you* winning?" she goads, pedaling even faster as she steals a look over her shoulder.

"Oh," I taunt as I lower myself to the handlebar. "You'll pay for that one, *ma chére*."

Her answering giggle is light and carefree, just like her auburn hair flowing in the breeze.

CHAPTER NINETEEN

LINDSAY

He did it. Theo actually taught me how to ride a bike. And in under fifteen minutes. I haven't felt this relaxed for a long time.

The sun warms my back as I ride through the expansive property. There's nothing else on my mind other than making sure I stay balanced on the bike. No planning, no budgeting, no clients. No responsibilities other than relaxing and being in this moment.

Hearing Theo's approach, I look over to my right and find him staring at me like I'm something to be cherished. I feel a slight blush warm my cheeks as I smile.

God, does he have a beautiful smile. It's contagious. One you can't help but grin back to.

This is crazy though, right? It's been, what? Thirty—thirty six hours since I met him. If any of my sisters said they felt feelings as strong as mine about any man they knew for that time, I'd say they were crazy.

Then again, Emma was pretty torn up about what to do with Diego, not wanting to ruin a professional relationship for just a quick overseas hook-up. From the story they shared, she also met him the first night she arrived. I should call her when I get back to the hotel. Out of everyone, she'd understand what I'm feeling.

We spend the next couple of hours riding through the many acres, viewing the orchards and gardens, then concluding our time walking through the lavender field after we park our bikes.

Standing in the middle of the many rows, the scent is so overpowering, but in the best way possible. I feel wrapped in a blanket of lavender. It's warm and floral with a bit of woodsy. It's similar to rosemary but carries its own distinct scent. Ever so calming to my soul.

Theo interrupts my thoughts but I only catch the last word: honey.

"Hmm?" I turn and look at him, confusion clear on my face. My mind finally catches up to what he had said. "Oh!" I softly laugh at myself. "The honey from the bees. Yes." I motion for us to walk. "Let's go see the bees."

Walking over to what looks to be a white wooden box, I'm a little nervous. There are more bees over here than what were in the field. It makes sense since this is their home, but I'm always on my guard around bees.

"We have these all around the property, ensuring the bees are spread out evenly."

"And the honey is inside that box? Along with all the bees?" I stand on my tip-toes trying to get a peek around the box.

"Yup! Maybe later in the week I can show you how to harvest it. But right now," Theo waves at someone behind me. I turn to find who I'm assuming to be Ettie waving us in. "It looks like lunch is ready." He reaches out for my hand and I don't hesitate to take it.

Lunch was delicious. Herb crusted, roasted chicken with vegetables. I ate outside with a view of the pool, alone. Unfortunately, Theo had to tend to some business that came up while we were out.

I walk into my room and see that Ettie has not only cleaned my room, but has also set my cleaned and folded clothes on the bench at the foot of the bed. I could change into the clothes, but I tell myself it's silly to dirty another outfit when the sweats I'm wearing are perfectly acceptable. Plus, the sweats are much more comfortable than the trousers and blouses I currently have.

I grab my phone and decide to video call Emma. Years ago, I would have normally called Taylor, my twin, when asking for advice, but with how things have been these last few years, she's become the last sister I'd call. Plus, I'm not even sure she'd have that much in terms of advice for something like this.

Taylor has been with her fiancé for the last five years. And I don't even think Tory has even had a relationship, let alone sex since having Haylee, so she'd definitely wouldn't have much advice in this particular department.

I sit on the bed and wait for her to pick up the phone. She's still at home for a quick visit with the family, so there's a time difference of six hours. However, it's after two in the afternoon for me so she should be awake by now.

"*Bonjour*, bitch." Her strawberry-blonde hair fills the screen as I watch her plop down on the couch. "How's it going?"

"Hi, Emma. I'm, um, fine." I look at the ceiling in my room. I know I just need to spit it out but I chicken out. "How's your trip going?"

"Good, but I miss Diego. I leave early tomorrow, so I'll be on your time soon!" She cheers. "How's France? Have you found the meaning of *relaxation* yet?"

"Well . . ." I really don't know how to go about this, "I guess it depends on your definition of relaxation . . ."

She's quick to notice my lack of enthusiasm over the screen. "Spit it out, Linds. What's going on?"

Deep breath in.

Deep breath out.

"I met a guy and I may or may not have let him finger fuck me in the kitchen of the hotel," I rush out, speeding through the sentence before I lose my nerve.

Her eyes bulge out in shock. Not by my language. Never by the language. Almost all of us girls curse like sailors thanks to growing up with a father who worked on a nearby ranch. My sisters and I used to visit regularly before Mom's accident. We learned a lot from those visits, including our colorful language.

"Was it good?"

"Emma!" I scold, covering my eyes with one hand and shaking my head. "That *so* isn't the point!"

"So it *was* good . . . interesting," she notes with a mischievous grin.

"The best orgasm in my life," I sigh and drop the hand that was covering my face. "Bar none," I add defeated. Now that I said it out loud, I can't deny it.

"So, does Mr. Magic-fingers have a name or . . ." She wiggles her fingers as she talks, making me chuckle.

"Theo. And he happens to be the grandson of the hotel owner. He actually sat next to me on the plane from Raleigh to Paris."

"Oh, so stalker romance vibes. I love it." She tilts her head like she's putting something together. "Wait, are *you* technically the stalker since you went to *his* family's hotel?"

"Again, not the point," I huff.

"Okay, okay. So what *is* the point, Linds?"

What's the point? What *is* the point?

"I don't know, Em." I stand up and start pacing my room, carrying the phone with me while I cross the space. "I feel like the last few days have turned my life upside down. I've been completely severed from all ties to work. Forced to fly out to a place I've never been before. I met this hot guy only to be staying at his family's hotel, where I'll be staying for the next few nights, with no other guests besides me."

"Had the best orgasm of your life from Mr. Magic-fingers—"

"Theo," I correct. "Oh, and the airline lost my bag." I fall back on the freshly made bed while I list the last one.

"Sis, the only thing I see wrong with all that is the lost suitcase. But if the last twenty-four hours are any indicator of what's to come, you may not need a suitcase full of clothes," she snickers.

I bring the phone back up to my face. "Oh my god! Emma!" I shout, shaking my head again. "I called you to help me, not encourage me to continue this charade. I mean think about what could happen?"

"If you wanted a list of why you shouldn't do something, you should've called Tory."

She's right. Tory is the queen of listing off all the reasons *not* to do something.

"I mean what's the worst that could happen, Linds? You have four more nights filled with killer sex and orgasms, then come home . . . refreshed? I'm not seeing the problem here."

"The *problem* is, what happens after those four nights? What if something goes wrong and things get awkward?"

"You've got a good point, I mean you haven't even seen his penis. It might be ti—"

"Shut your mouth, Emma Lynn Hartman," I scold but we both end up breaking out in a fit of laughter. "And it's definitely not small," I add under my breath.

"I thought you said he just finger fucked you?"

"Yeah, but I could *feel* things." I not-so subtly raise my eyebrows. "*Big* things. *Huge* actually."

"Yeah, yeah. Okay, okay." She holds her hand up. "I get it. This 'Theo' is packing."

I sigh, rolling my neck as I think about all the ways this could go wrong.

"But seriously, Lindsay. You deserve, and definitely need a

break from work. Take advantage of all this place has to offer. And I really do mean *all* it has to offer. I say go for it." She gives me a stern look in response to my eye roll. "What do you have to lose?"

"I guess nothing really." I blow out an exhale while fidgeting with the drawstring on my sweats. My phone vibrates and it's an international number. "Hey Emma, I have to go. This might be the airline with an update on my bag."

"Okay. Love you, Linds."

"Love you, too."

"Don't forget to use protection!" I hear her shout as I switch the call over to the other line.

I'm still laughing as I greet the new caller. "This is Lindsay."

"Hello, Lindsay. My name's Todd. I seem to have accidentally grabbed your bag instead of mine at baggage claim yesterday."

That's frustrating; there's a reason why luggage tags were invented.

"I'm sorry I took so long to call. I've been trying to reach out to the airline, but they wouldn't pass along your number. I double checked for a luggage tag this morning and that's when I found your number on the hidden tag on the back of your bag. I'm so sorry for the mishap. Are you still in Marseille?"

Ugh, now I feel like a bitch. It's been so long since I've used this bag, I forgot the luggage tag was one of those hidden sliders on the back. Mental note, get an obnoxiously flashy luggage tag for next time.

"Oh wow. Okay. Well at least my bag isn't lost," I note before adding, "I'm actually staying right outside of Aix."

"Oh great! I'm staying in Aix, too. The airline said when they drop off my bag, they could pick up yours and deliver it if it wasn't too far. So if you don't mind texting me the name and address of the hotel, I will pass it along to the delivery driver."

I don't know how good I feel about passing my information to a stranger, but Theo *is* staying on property. And this Todd guy *did* explain the location of my luggage tag. *And* got my number off my tag, so he also has my home address. If he wanted to do anything horrific, I guess I can't really stop him now.

"Yeah, I can do that."

We wrap up our conversion and I text him the hotel's information after we hang up.

Finding myself with nothing to do, I run myself a bath with the salts provided and get lost in one of my books. It feels weird not doing anything productive at the moment.

You know what? No. I *am* being productive. I'm literally working on my relaxation techniques. Calming my body in order to calm my mind. Or whatever my childhood therapist would say.

Afterwards, I put on another set of the clothes Theo brought up. I'd rather be wearing these sweats than what I wore on the plane, honestly. They're oversized and super cozy. I should note the brand for a future purchase.

When dinner time comes, I bring my book with me to the dining room. Sitting alone in the room lit by the outside sun, I'm served a mouth-watering fish dinner by Mateo. I feel so spoiled with all of these gourmet meals. I'll definitely have to up my cooking game when I get back home. Maybe I could ask for some recipes to take home to make?

Dinner passes, and still no news on my bag being delivered. I'm not too worried at this point but I'll probably call Todd tomorrow to see if the airline ever picked up my bag. I've saved his number under "bag stealer" just in case.

I'm reading in bed when I hear a knock at the door. Grabbing my phone, I check the time. It's only eight thirty. God, this jet-lag is really messing with me. I walk over to the door, opening it to find Theo there.

"Sorry I missed you at dinner. There was an issue with the wedding for this weekend, but it's handled. At least for now," he adds under his breath. "I wanted to see if you'd like some company and maybe"—he pulls a bottle of wine and two glasses from behind his back—"some red wine?"

"That sounds great." I open the door, stepping aside to give him room to come inside.

"I would ask if you wanted a fire, but it may be a tad too warm for that." He places the glasses on the table and proceeds to use the wine opener that was in his pocket to open the cork. He pours both of us a glass and swirls it around a bit.

"How was dinner?" He takes a seat at the table while I perch myself on the bench at the edge of the bed.

"Delicious. I was actually wondering if the very talented Mateo shares any of his recipes or if they're top secret?"

"You're in luck. We have a few recipe cards ready for when guests ask. I'll make sure to grab some for you next time I'm in the kitchen."

"Oh perfect. Thank you," I say, reaching to grab my glass of wine. "Cheers." I salute him with my glass and take a sip. I may not have a refined palate like Taylor when it comes to wine, but this wine is one of the best I've ever had. "You wouldn't happen to know if my suitcase was dropped off earlier, do you?"

He scratches his chin. "The only cars on the driveway tonight were Ettie, Jean, and Mateo's. Did the airline find your bag?"

"Well, not the airline itself but another passenger."

He purses his lips together, squinting his brows while making a "hmm" sound.

"He said he grabbed my bag instead of his and that the airline was going to deliver my bag after swapping the bags out with each other. He is supposedly staying in Aix and got my number from my luggage tag."

"No suitcase delivery. I'll make sure to leave the gate open and keep an eye out on the cameras in case they drop it off." He takes a sip of his wine.

"Thanks, Theo." Taking another sip I remember I meant to ask about a swimsuit. "Hey, so, weird question." I chuckle nervously while biting my lower lip. "I forgot to pack a swimsuit, and since there isn't much to do except relax in various places around the hotel, I figured it might be nice to have the option to swim. The hotel doesn't happen to have any suits for purchase do they?"

He shakes his head. "Sorry, we don't have too much in terms of clothing. That's why I gave you some of my clothes to wear."

I choke on my wine. "What was that?"

"Those sweats you're wearing," he eyes me up and down appreciatively, spending a little extra time on my breasts. Based on how my nipples harden under his gaze, if there was any doubt I was wearing a bra, there isn't now. My nipples perk up just at the thought of him looking. Those little traitors.

"Those are my spares. I keep extra clothes at the family house for when I visit." I look down at my sweats. Or *his* sweats.

Standing up, I go to reach my actual clothes. "Oh, I'm sorry. Let me go change and I can give them—" He reaches out and grabs my hand, stopping me in my tracks.

"Lindsay, it's fine," he chuckles. "You don't have to change. I *do* have other clothes you know." I turn and sit back down. "But if you wanted to take your clothes off, I wouldn't object," he adds with a roguish grin.

"Oh, I'm sure you wouldn't," I huff while rolling my eyes. Shifting myself to try to calm the heat gathering low in my stomach, and somewhere else, I redirect the conversation. "Back to what I was saying." I clear my throat. "I was wondering if there was any way to get a swimsuit for the pool."

"You could always skinny-dip." My eyes bulge out and I gasp at the suggestion. "Oh come on, Lindsay. You're telling me you've never skinny-dipped?"

I shake my head vehemently. "Never have I ever."

"Now that should've been something you said when we played 'two truths and a lie.' I would've definitely thought that was the lie." He takes another sip of wine before continuing. "It's not that crazy of a concept. Nudity isn't a thing to be shameful about, especially in France. Plus, no one is here at night if you need privacy." He brushes his thumb against his bottom lip and I get the sense he's actually serious with his suggestion. "Well, no one besides me. And I'll have to supervise your pool time. For safety purposes of course." His grin widens, making that damn dimple appear again and fuck me do I want this man.

I tip my wine glass back and down the rest. Before I lose my nerve, I stride toward my balcony door that leads down to the pool.

"I didn't mean *now* but okay," he adds as he scrambles up and follows like an excited puppy, knowing exactly what I'm about to do.

Once we get downstairs, the pool is lit with soft, dim lighting, giving it an ethereal glow in the night. More low lights shine on the olive trees surrounding the pool, but they aren't bright enough to ruin the beautiful night's sky. The stars are the true sight to see out here tonight.

Mustering up all the confidence I can manage, I take a deep breath, and start to do my best impression on a seductive strip tease. I'm in control right now and if I'm going to do this, I'm going to do it to the best of my ability. I'm not going to cower away. No, I'm going to look him right in the eyes while giving him the best show of his life. I may not be the most graceful or sexy, and this *definitely* is the first time I have made a show of taking off my clothes for a man, but here I am.

I start stripping off a very oversized T-shirt and a pair of oversized sweatpants. Not the sexiest clothing items. In fact, I feel about as sexy as Adam Sandler right now, but I make it work. That is until my foot gets stuck in one of the pant legs. Luckily, I save myself from a near faceplant.

Once I reach the point where I'm only in the little triangle and string wrapped around my hips, really the sexiest thing I have on, Theo pounces.

He smothers me in kisses while grabbing my ass to lift and spin me around. I giggle as he smothers me with kisses.

While still being lifted by Theo's muscular arms, I stare at him with a mischievous look in my eyes while tugging on his shirt's neckline.

"Your turn."

CHAPTER TWENTY

THEO

Thank fuck I had enough forethought to put a couple condoms in my pocket before I met back up with Lindsay. I know I was doing some wishful thinking, but that thinking saved me from ruining this fantasy by needing to head back to my room.

I've known Lindsay for about two days now and somehow already feel like I understand her. There are times she overthinks, and it's clear she's wound tightly. But when that little sliver of carefreeness slips out, man does she glow.

It's not that she doesn't know how to have a good time, she has just been consumed by work for so long and needs a little . . . warming up. And I'll happily be the one warming her up, even if it's just for the next few nights. But I can already tell, four more nights won't be nearly enough time with her.

I set Lindsay back down on the ground and though I don't make it a show like she did, I do go a step further and remove my boxers, leaving me bare-ass naked, already sporting a hard-on, because how could I not with the absolute knockout in front of me.

Her eyes roam down my body full of lust as she bites her

lower lip. When her stare reaches my hips, I make my move, wrapping her up in my arms and throwing us both in the pool.

We both pop our heads up and I'm greeted with a huge splash of water. "You asshole!" But she's laughing, a vivacious and joyous laugh.

I swim over to her, grabbing her legs and wrapping them around my waist. "I'm sorry, you were just making me so . . ." I look at her, then pointedly stare down at my hard dick before meeting her wanton gaze. "Hot. I needed to cool off before I made the decision to skip the pool entirely." I squeeze her ass to emphasize my point.

"My strip tease was that good, huh?" She runs her hands up my chest and around my neck.

"I could lie, but I'm pretty sure the evidence is stacked up hard against your stomach right now." I smirk and must be dreaming because she reaches down between us for my dick. She starts in slow, teasing strokes from base to tip, making subtle waves in the pool water. I tip my head up enjoying her movements. "Fuck, Linds."

I somehow manage to swim us over to the pool wall and pin her to it, taking my time kissing her down her neck while one hand makes its way down underwater to her thong.

Lindsay gasps while her legs squeeze my hips tighter as I push the flimsy material to the side so I can slide my fingers up and down her pussy. My mouth moves to her breast and I gently bite down on the nipple. Her moans are a melody to my ears as I soothe her nipples with my tongue afterward.

She starts shifting her hips so I move my thumb over her clit. I lift my head to look into her eyes for some sort of consent but find her head bent back enjoying this moment. "We can stop this at any—"

"Don't stop," she gasps before bringing her head forward, kissing me hard. I lose myself in the feeling of her. Strumming my thumb back and forth over her sensitive clit. "I want this," she pants as she stares right at me, desire clear in her eyes. "I want *you*,

Theo," she says with finality. And fuck, I'm almost coming at those four words.

I lift her up on the ledge, making her ass rest right at the edge, spreading her legs wide open. She reclines back with her palms splayed on the concrete. Without wasting any time, I pull the soaking wet fabric off to the side and take my first taste of her.

"*Fuck*! Theo!"

"Mmm." I lick my lips as I look up at her. "I've never loved my name more than I do right now," I admit before immediately going back to the feast Lindsay has so graciously gifted me, only this time using my thumb to help bring her closer to the edge.

She starts rocking her hips while grabbing hold of my hair in one hand, guiding me right where she wants me. "Yes . . . right there, Theo."

I move the hand on her thigh up to her waist, bringing her even closer. Her legs tighten around my head, letting me know she's about to come.

I suck her clit as I move my fingers inside of her. The new sensation and pressure pushes her over, allowing her to reach her climax with ease. I lick her gently as the waves of her orgasm slow down.

"Fuck *me*, Theo." She's shaking her head as her eyes meet mine, cheeks warm while she grins ear to ear.

"Hold that thought." I wink before hopping out of the pool to grab the condom in my pants.

As I pull on the rubber and turn back to Lindsay, I notice something flying for my face. I catch the black fabric, and it dawns on me that it's her thong. She apparently took the opportunity to take off the one remaining shred of clothing she had left on.

"Oh, you're going to pay for that," I warn as I point to her, stalking back to where she's at in the pool. "And just so we're clear"—I hop into the water—"these are mine now, *ma chére*." I dangle the thong by one of the hip strings and fling them over to our little pile of clothes. She's sporting a shy yet sensual grin on her face, definitely excited for what's to come.

Caging her on the tanning shelf in the pool, I palm the back of her neck under her wet hair while my other hand takes residence on her hip. Our mouths meet and she opens immediately for my prying tongue.

She widens her hips, inviting me to move in between her legs while she grabs my hips, fingers digging into my ass cheeks. Now it's her time to cage me in.

She jumps at the first brush of dick against her clit. Clearly she's still sensitive from the orgasm I just gave her. I pause our kissing and catch her eyes, but before I can make sure she wants to proceed, she thrusts forward, forcing my dick to slide home inside of her. Both of us moan out a curse.

Fucking fuck! She's tight. Like *really* tight. I'm not sure if it's the position, or the fact that I haven't had sex in six months, but she feels glorious.

Okay, maybe it's been a little more than six months.

Fine, it's been two years.

Lindsay reaches up and pulls my head down to her, bringing my focus back to this unbelievable reality. She's biting my lip as I pull out and thrust back inside of her, squeezing her ass to help me get as deep as possible from this position.

Moving one of my hands in between us, I use my fingers to play with her clit.

"Right there—fuck, Theo—that feels," she pants between breaths.

I add a little bit more pressure as I swirl my thumb.

"Oh my—" She interrupts herself with a moan. Yeah, those swipes are definitely her kryptonite.

I kiss and suck on her neck a little, feeling her tighten around my dick. She's close again and thank fuck because I am too, especially after just having her come on my mouth and fingers.

"Theo," she pants. "I—I—"

"Just let go, *ma chére*. I'm right here to catch you." I run my other hand down her back and she does exactly that. It takes two more thrusts for me to finish while she still pulses around me from her climax.

I lean my forehead down to hers as we both take a few steadying breaths. We breath in each others' hot air, both of us not wanting to leave this moment.

But fate has something else in store for us.

A car horn wakes the both of us from our post-sex bliss.

Who the fuck is that? Both of us look at each other with confusion, then recognition dawns on Lindsay's face. "Oh shit," she rushes to untangle herself from me, scurrying out of the pool. "That must be my suitcase."

I follow close behind and throw on my pants. I look at her as she's spinning around in nothing but a tee, looking annoyed.

"Ugh," she groans and leans down, pinching the ball of wet fabric between her fingers. "I forgot," she grumbles. "My underwear is completely soaked."

"And *mine.*" I reach over with a toothy smile, plucking them out of her hands, and stuff them in my pocket. I turn, walking backwards toward the front of the hotel. "I'll handle the suitcase. You just meet me back in your room."

CHAPTER TWENTY-ONE

LINDSAY

I stand in utter disbelief, trying to catch my breath from the turn of events. So much to unpack from such a short amount of time.

The not one, but *two* mind-blowing orgasms.

All in a freaking pool. There may have even been more had we not been cockblocked by my luggage.

Then the panty stealing bit. I don't even know what to think of that one yet.

I haven't let loose like that in . . . actually, I don't know when. Maybe I never had. Can't say that doesn't make me a little sad. But now's not the time for a pity-party.

The shirt's long enough to not have to put my pants on, so I carry them over my shoulder and march back up to my room.

Drying my hair with a towel, I think back to what we did in the pool. Up until tonight, I'd never had sex in a pool. Or really any body of water for that matter. And Theo has quickly turned me into a fan of water play. Whatever the hell that means.

A thudding sound comes from just outside my door, and I hurry over to open it. My eyes meet Theo's topless body, giving me an unobstructed view of his sculpted abs and light trail of hair leading my eyes to the waistline of his jeans.

"Package for a Miss Hartman?"

I reluctantly pull my head up to look at his face, finding him already smirking and lifting his eyebrows in a teasing look. God, is that smirk just permanently painted on his face?

"I'm sorry to disappoint you, *ma chére*, but I wasn't talking about the package in my pants." He wheels my suitcase inside my room. "Though do feel free to unwrap that anytime you want." I roll my eyes at his comment, though if I'm being honest, I can't say my thoughts weren't already doing just that.

"Thank you for saving me from greeting the delivery driver commando," I say as he laughs. "However I do believe it was *your* fault I was put in that position in the first place." I give him a stern look, but I'm not doing well because I can feel the side of my lip creeping up giving away my true feelings.

"If memory serves me right, *you* were the one who left your underwear on after your strip tease." He wraps his arms around me and pinches my ass.

"Hey!" I giggle while swatting his hand away from behind my back. "And *you*"—I poke his chest—"are the one who had the brilliant idea to throw both of us in the pool while I was still wearing said underwear."

He kisses me then pulls his head to my ear, his scruff brushing up against my cheek as he whispers softly. "And a damn brilliant idea it turned out to be."

Theo snags another kiss, melting me into a puddle.

"I was thinking about taking you somewhere tomorrow," he says in between kisses to my neck and jaw. "It's"—kiss—"place"—kiss—"parents"—kiss—"every summer"—kiss—"bloom"—kiss.

I'm trying to concentrate, but failing entirely, catching only every other word or so. He must have noticed because he nibbles on my earlobe.

"Did you hear a single word I just said, *ma chére*?" he questions with a teasing chuckle as he moves his face to look me in the eyes with one eyebrow raised.

"It's not my fault." I playfully shove his chest, but he just crushes me closer. "But sure. A field trip sounds good," I say with a reassuring smile and he grins right back.

"Good."

My phone goes off and we both look over to it. From the sound, I can tell it's just a text, but it's enough to pop our bubble.

"I'll let you get that." He brings a hand up around my cheek. "Breakfast tomorrow? Same time, same table?"

I lean into his touch, not quite ready for him to leave yet, but knowing he should. "Sounds like a dream, Theo." We kiss a little more before I walk him out.

When I return to my bed, I grab my phone and see it's the sister group chat.

TORY:

How's France going, Linds? See any good sights?

EMMA:

Oh, she's seeing the sights alright.

TORY:

What does that mean???

TAYLOR:

OMG!

Did you meet someone??

TORY:

Tell me you didn't pull an Emma?

EMMA:

HEY!

Why do I get the sense you're saying that like it's a bad thing?

TORY:

It's not, but it wasn't surprising when you did it. But Lindsay doing it?

LINDSAY:

Okay and what does THAT mean?

EMMA:

You're alive and all that sex hasn't killed you yet!

TORY:

Hasn't even been 48 hours Lindsay!

How much sex have you had??

LINDSAY:

Technically, it's just been once.

TAYLOR:

What do you mean technically?

EMMA:

Yeah, Linds. Curious ears need to know. • •

LINDSAY:

We just fooled around a little in the kitchen last night is all.

EMMA:

That was yesterday's news.

What happened today?

LINDSAY:

We just had some bonding time in the pool.

All three of my sisters' texts come in at once.

TORY:

IN THE POOL?!?!

EMMA:

GET IT LINDS

TAYLOR:

OMG

LINDSAY:

Well, on that note. Good night ladies.

EMMA:

Are you kidding me? You can't drop a bomb like pool sex and then dip out like that.

TORY:

I think you did something similar a few months ago, Em.

EMMA:

Fine, be a tease.

We still love you.

LINDSAY:

It's late. But I'll update you later.

Night ladies.

EMMA:

Enjoy yourself!

TAYLOR:

Night.

TORY:

Be safe!

Shaking my head reading the last few texts, I finish up my nighttime routine then fall asleep satisfied and giddy for tomorrow's adventure.

CHAPTER TWENTY-TWO

THEO

Just like yesterday, Lindsay walks toward me as I'm cutting flowers for breakfast.

"Morning," she greets me with a wave as I take in what she's wearing, which is unfortunately not the clothes I gave her.

It makes sense. After all, she does have her suitcase back. With her white button-down blouse tucked into her beige trousers, she's the picture of professionalism.

"No sweats this morning?" I tease as I pull out her chair.

"Oh," she says, looking down at her outfit. "Yeah, I figured I should wear the clothes I packed. Though I won't lie, your sweats are more comfortable."

"Mhmm," I murmur as I admire her ass as the fabric pulls tight when she takes her seat.

I plate her breakfast as she pours our tea. "So tell me, what would a normal day look like for you? If you weren't here being wined and dined by a roguishly handsome man, that is."

"Roguishly, hmm?" she questions as she quirks an eyebrow. "Well, normally I'd be in the office for a couple hours by now. Probably in a meeting or assisting with an event in some capacity.

You?" She takes a bite from the chocolate croissant in her hand, flakes of the buttery treat raining down on the plate and table.

"Touring job sites, checking budgets, or checking out potential sites. I spend more time than I'd like in my car, driving from place to place, and less time working on the sites. Though I try to end my day working on the project I call home at the moment." I pause, thinking about the list of things that still need to be done at my current "home."

"Sometimes I miss being able to start and finish a project with my own two hands," I confess before taking a sip of tea. "But work is good, so I can't complain."

"I can understand that. The higher I get at the firm, the less I get to enjoy the complete process of it all. I'm too busy putting out fires or being the one people come to for advice."

"Yes, exactly. You get it."

"I really do." She nods as her finger paints patterns on the white tablecloth. "Though, I have to admit. I do like imparting some of my knowledge to a new generation of event planners." There's a break in conversation before she asks, "So . . . you grew up here?"

"Partially." I look out to the grounds, taking in the beauty I'm surrounded by. "Dad worked in the military and was gone a lot when I was young. During the summers, Ma and I flew over here so she'd have help with raising me. This was all I knew from June to late August."

"Sounds like you have a lot of memories here," she adds thoughtfully.

"More than any other place I've lived that's for sure," I joke before shifting the conversation. "How about you? What were your summers like?"

"Some of my favorite ones were spent on a ranch with my dad. The landscape definitely wasn't as beautiful as this, but I made some core memories during those summers."

"What kind of ranch?" I ask before sneaking another bite of the egg dish Mateo made us.

"It was a horse training ranch. All four of us girls learned to ride fairly early. Though Taylor was the only one who really took to it. I never felt like I belonged on the back of a horse. And Tory," she laughs at the mention of her sister, clearly an inside joke I'm on the outside of. "Poor thing broke out in hives if she didn't take her allergy meds. She's allergic to hay. And Emma," she sighs. "She didn't get too much time on the ranch before . . . well, before things changed."

Clearly there's more to this story, but I sense the need for a topic change.

"And who's where in the birth order?"

"Oh," she startles and shakes her head. "Sorry. It's Tory, then Taylor and me, then Emma. She is the baby."

"And Tory is the one with the daughter?"

"Yes. Haylee. She's eighteen."

"Is she still with the father?"

"Oh, no." She chuckles and shakes her head like it's the silliest idea. "The only boy Tory was ever serious with was Eli. And they were just friends. Eli was practically our brother growing up. Broke her heart when his family vanished one night."

"So this Eli couldn't be the dad?"

"Oh god, no. No, some deadbeat guy from a high school party-gone-wrong is. At least, that's how she explains it. There was so much going on during that time in our lives, I don't really remember how it all went down. But the bio dad got freaked out and said something about him being too young to be a father."

"So he just left your sister to deal with a newborn?" What an asshole.

"Yup," she says, popping the *P*. "Mom and Dad helped out when they could, but she had Haylee while Mom was in the thick of recovery." Recovery from what, I wonder, but Lindsay just continues on. "Tory busted her ass and got into nursing to provide for her daughter. And she's been doing that ever since."

"Damn. Go Tory," I cheer.

That earns a smile with a playful bump of her shoulder into mine as she comments, "I know, right?"

"And what's it like having a twin?"

Lindsay pauses, taking a sip of tea while staring out to the pool.

"When we were at home, it was great. But growing up . . . the kids in high school would always pit us against each other. Taylor was the more popular twin. Always known for being the fun, sassy, or beautiful one while I was known for being the smart and quiet one."

Lindsay pauses and looks down at the teacup in her hand.

"That never really mattered. Not until Taylor lost a lot of that spark after meeting Jess. And one day, after a little too many cups of my mom's special eggnog, I told her exactly that. Obviously that went over like a fart in church."

"And how about Emma" I ask, trying to change the subject to something a little less heavy.

"Emma," she starts as her smile creeps back up her face. "God, is she a firecracker." She chuckles before continuing. "People think Taylor has sass but she's got nothing on Emma. But there's something so freeing about Emma. She goes where the wind takes her and she excels at everything she does. Honestly, I'm so proud to call each of them my sisters."

I've always wanted siblings. The idea of a big family always intrigued me, especially growing up in a quiet house. But I'm fortunate to have had a happy and loving home, even if it was on the quiet side.

"Unfortunately, I have a few things to do around the hotel, but are you still up for our adventure this afternoon?" I ask as I clean up our plates before we get ready to part our ways.

"Absolutely. Just tell me when and where and I'll be there." She smiles as she stands.

"I'll send you a message a little closer to lunch with more precise time." I sling my arm around her waist and bring her close to kiss. "Enjoy your morning, *ma chére*."

"See you later, Theo."

I steal one more kiss before we go our separate ways.

Before I reach the office, I stop by the kitchen, running into Mateo who's already preparing lunch.

"*Bonjour*, Mateo." His haphazard wave is all the greeting I receive. And honestly, that's more than I get most days. "Is it possible for me to raid the fridge and pantry for something that would resemble a dinner for tonight? Something I can pack in a picnic basket?" Before I get Mateo's response, I hear the door creak.

"Theo?" Ettie peeks her head inside the kitchen. "Are you behaving yourself around our one and only guest?" She never misses a thing. Ettie comes into the kitchen and greets me with a warm smile, air kissing both my cheeks while grasping my arms. "You've been so busy these last few days, I've hardly gotten to talk to you at all."

"Oh, Ettie. I'm so sorry."

I catch her up on everything that's been going on in my life back home and she does the same for herself while she helps me pick out things for the picnic.

I've known Ettie since I was little. She helped keep me in line around the estate. When I got a little older, she showed me how to properly clean the rooms and take care of things around the hotel.

Actually, a lot of the skills I learned growing up here, fixing and caring for the estate, are all thanks to the wonderful women in my life.

"Well, I won't keep you from your work *or* a special someone." She winks and starts walking out. "Have fun at the abbey later. I'm sure you'll enjoy the view," she adds with a knowing grin.

Lindsay and I haven't been *too* obvious. At least, not when everyone is around. Then again, I have had breakfast with her both mornings, and intend to do so for the next three mornings. Not nearly enough time in my mind.

"Thanks, Ettie."

After loading up the car, I double check that I have everything I need for our afternoon away from the hotel. Just as I turn around, I spot Lindsay coming out the front door. I left her a note with her lunch earlier, telling her to meet me out in front around three o'clock.

"I didn't know what to wear," she sighs and looks down, brushing her palms down her light blue dress.

It's got buttons running down the front of it, hugging tight around her waist then falling freely down her hips to right below her knees. Her shoulders are already covered, so I won't need Mom's scarf after all. Most religious sites ask visitors to respect a dress code of knees and shoulders being covered.

"Is this okay?" she asks as she does a little spin.

I walk up to her and run my hands down the sides of her perfect silhouette. "Absolutely breathtaking," I observe and punctuate with a kiss. "Now get moving." I smack her ass. "We're on a tight schedule."

Beating Lindsay to her door, I open it for her, only closing it after she's safely inside. After situating myself in the driver's seat, we head out to our picnic spot. It's a bit of a drive to get to our destination.

The beginning of the drive is quiet, especially as Lindsay takes in the scenic drive up to the abbey. This drive is always a pretty one. Surrounded by fields and farms, beautiful buildings, some centuries old. Don't get me wrong, there are some beautiful drives back in North Carolina, but you just don't see spots like this over there.

"We've talked about what you do for work now, but what do you *want* to do? What's Lindsay's *dream* job?" I turn to take a peek at her reaction. She's leaning up against the window, peering out at the approaching hills.

"I don't really know," she confesses as her shoulders sag before she turns to face me. "I really do love planning events and helping people on what should be the happiest day of their life. So maybe my own event business? But on a much smaller scale. I've always loved planning smaller, more intimate weddings and events. What about you?"

"I've always dreamed of opening my own B&B stateside. Something on the smaller scale, like you said. Preferably a property I get to fix up myself. Really put my mark on the place, you know." I nod to myself as my eyes return back on the road. "Maybe one day."

"Yeah, maybe one day," she echoes in agreement.

As we start the drive up into the hills, the view improves even more. Seeing little bits of the stunning vista below peeking between the tall trees lining the road.

"This is . . ." she starts but doesn't finish, getting distracted by the first view of the abbey.

We pull up to the parking lot located a little walk away from our final destination. The abbey is a sight to see all in itself. The pale stone-walled monastery is tucked in a little valley floor, nestled between mountains. But the true beauty is hiding behind it.

We arrive just as the tour I booked starts. Walking hand in hand, we tour the grounds with a small group of tourists. It's been a few years since I last did a tour with Ma. It's one of her favorite things to do, especially during the summer.

Walking through the halls, you can't help but feel an overwhelming feeling of serenity and peace. In the nearly nine centuries it's been here, I'm sure these walls have seen a lot.

The tour guide does an exceptional job of guiding us through the history of the abbey, or at least I think he does. I'm too distracted by the stunning woman in the blue dress to pay any attention to the words coming out of his mouth. Watching her light up while the tour guide talks or as we get glimpses of the art within the abbey and little garden in the center is definitely a highlight of my day. And if she enjoys this, I can't wait until she sees what's just outside.

At the end of the tour, I guide Lindsay down the hall to the real reason we are here. Before stepping outside, I stop us from continuing down the path.

"I have a surprise, but you'll need to close your eyes until I say so. Can you do that?"

"Do you promise not to make me trip?"

I chuckle. "Cross my heart and hope to die." I mime the action while saying it.

She closes her eyes. "I'm trusting you." But she peeks out one eye. "Don't make me regret this."

"Never. And keep your eyes shut or you'll be punished," I tease, then clear my throat remembering where we are as I lead her outside.

It's summer so the sun sets later in the evening. It's not quite late enough for "golden hour" but we're getting close judging by where the sun is resting right above the surrounding mountains.

As I get us to the location with the best view, I step out of what will be her line of sight, enough so I'm not blocking her, but not too much so that I won't be able to enjoy her reaction.

"Okay. You can open your eyes now, *ma chére*."

CHAPTER TWENTY-THREE

LINDSAY

As I open my eyes, a flood of emotion hits me. So with tears slowly leaking out of my eyes, I take a deep breath, and attempt to soak up the majestic scene in front of me.

Small rolling mounds covered in a vibrant purple blanket, surrounded by lush green hills all highlighted by the angelic glow coming off the sun.

I take another deep breath in. Trying to just . . . be.

Absorbing all the shades of color surrounding me. Feeling the subtle wind blowing against my face. Smelling the relaxing scent of the lavender fields in front of me. Listening to the low chanting from the monastery behind me. Truly living in this moment and taking in as much as I can.

I'm not sure how long I stand there frozen in awe, but when I finally turn my watery gaze to Theo, he's already looking back at me with a soft smile gracing his face as the wind blows his waves.

He lifts his hand to gently swipe away my tears. His hand lingers on my face for a bit longer and I lean into the feel of his touch, grounding me during this experience.

"Thank you," I whisper to him, so soft I'm not sure he hears me. But as he nods his head, I know he did. Theo moves his hand to meet mine, guiding me off our current path toward a walkway closer to the lavender.

He places the small basket he's been carrying down under an olive tree. "We can walk the perimeter of the fields, but not in between the rows. Would you like some dinner first though?" he asks while motioning to the basket.

I nod, still unable to use words, and he sits down in the grass, dragging me down with him. I land on top of him in a fit of giggles, lightening the mood. Theo steals a kiss, which quickly becomes more passionate than it should. After reminding myself where we are, I stop us from going any further, adjusting myself so I'm in a seated position besides him. There aren't too many people walking around, but I'm sure someone saw us. I try not to let my anxiety of that fact bother me as Theo starts to unpack our dinner.

It's not so much dinner, more like a dressed up charcuterie board, made up of fruit and a selection of cheeses and meats. Oh, and what looks like a partial baguette. He takes out a jar of honey —from their hives I'm sure—and some sparkling water.

We eat in a calming quiet, enjoying the sounds of the lavender bushes blowing in the wind, their flowers brushing up against each other as well as the buzzing of the busy bees enjoying a break from the heat as the sun comes down. The people walking around the grounds are respectful and only talk in low tones, preserving the peace on the estate.

Nothing is said between us, but our actions are speaking loud enough. He's allowing me to sit in the comfort of our surroundings, truly enjoying the view around us as he makes little concoctions for us to eat. And though I normally would ask questions about what cheese or meat is being used, I'm enjoying the companionable silence between us. Plus, I can always just ask him what he packed once we get back to the hotel.

Being out here is surreal. I can't even begin to explain the overwhelming sense of tranquility. Everything seems slower and more purposeful. Nothing is taken for granted and the locals here are grateful for every minute of the calm. I could easily lose myself in people watching while enjoying the quality time with Theo next to me.

After finishing up the last of our dinner, we clean up our little picnic and wrap up our time at the abbey by taking a walk around the fields. The warm amber sky showcases the fields and surrounding hills in an ethereal light, making it look as if a layer of pixie dust was sprinkled all around us.

"We stick to the paths to help keep the foot traffic to a minimum, ensuring we do the most to preserve the beauty of the fields as well as keep the bees as undisturbed as possible," Theo explains as we make our way through the rows.

Like Theo's family, the abbey also harvests the lavender, honey, and beeswax to create a variety of items that they sell to help support them and the surrounding community.

After taking a few more photos, the sun starts falling behind the mountains surrounding us and we make our way back to the parking lot for the drive back to the hotel.

I sit quietly, still reflecting on everything I saw today for most of the drive back, and before I knew it, Theo shifts the car in park and turns it off.

As the car's headlights turn off, I notice just how dark it is outside. The stars and soft outdoor lights are the only lights around for miles. Turning to face each other, we both speak at the same time.

"Thank you—"

"Thanks—"

I look down sheepishly while he chuckles and runs his fingers through his hair. "Please, ladies first," he starts, gesturing to me.

"Thank you, Theo. Today was exactly what I didn't know I needed."

And it was. For someone as playful as Theo, he's been very intentional about showing me ways to actually enjoy life instead of just living it like it's another day to check off my to-do list.

It's so easy for me to keep my head down and stick to my

routine. Clearly, I've let life fly by while I've kept work at the forefront of my mind, instead of cherishing each day as the gift it is. In just a few days, he's opened my eyes on what a life outside the office could be.

Reaching over the center console, I grab his hands, making sure he sees my gratitude as genuine. "Thank you. Truly."

"You're most welcome, *ma chére.*" Theo adjusts our hands so he can squeeze mine in his. "Thank you for allowing me to show you that little slice of heaven."

He strokes his thumb back and forth across my knuckles. There's this sense of calm being around him. It's like a breath of fresh air, but at the same time it scares me. I feel almost out of control with how strong my feelings for Theo are. I mean, I leave in just a couple of nights. I can't get attached to him. This was—is—supposed to be just a fling.

I pull back, trying to keep some mask on so as to not completely ruin the moment, but Theo doesn't miss the change in my face. Clearing his throat he pulls his hands back and brushes them on his pants.

"Well, we've had an exciting day. I'm sure you want to get back to your room to sleep," he comments before getting out of the car.

He walks over to open my side then ushers me back to my room, not a word passing between us except goodnight. He ends the night with a kiss on the cheek like a perfect gentleman.

Only, I don't want him to be a gentleman.

Good going, Lindsay. God, of course I had to ruin a perfect day by freaking out.

Trying to distract myself from fixating on my mistake, I run through my nightly routine and text my family photos of the abbey. As I lie in bed, all the thoughts catch up with me and my mind spins out of control, replaying and analyzing everything I did wrong in the car. Wishing somehow I could change it.

CHAPTER TWENTY-FOUR

THEO

I'm not entirely sure what happened in the car when we got back, but I know something *did* happen. It was like a light switch went off. She tried to hide it. Tried to cover the way her face dropped before she painted her mask back on. Tried to conceal the way her body recoiled back like my touch burned her.

As much as I hated to do it, I walked her back to her room and left her there. I didn't want to overwhelm or smother her. She's clearly working through something, and I want to respect her space.

After unloading and cleaning up the picnic basket, I head off to the office to take care of anything I missed while I was out with Lindsay. A few calls came through about the wedding on Sunday. My parents said everything was already taken care of, and from the plans in front of me, everything looks like it *was*. That is, up until the groom's mom, Karen, started calling this week.

And yes, Karen is her actual name.

I don't know if she was like this for the weeks leading up to the wedding, but in the last forty-eight hours, I'm getting messages left and right with adjustments to things involving the ceremony and reception afterwards. It's not going to be a huge production, just ten people in total, but from all the work Ma put into planning, it will be classy and elegant.

I sip some wine and brainstorm ways to message her back. Ways that don't sound passive-aggressive.

> Dear Karen,
>
> After receiving your ~~eight~~ messages earlier today, I have reviewed your ~~absolutely ridiculous~~ concerns and ~~decided I don't care.~~ have come up with what I feel are ~~perfectly acceptable~~ creative solutions.
>
> Please review the attached plans and let me know if you have any comments or changes.
>
> ~~Regretfully,~~ Warmly,
> Theo

After typing up my email, I press send. This is one of my only concerns in going into the hospitality sector. I definitely need to work on my customer service before opening up a B&B of my own. I'm fine with those who are non-problematic, but the minute there's unnecessary drama? Forget it.

It's late and I'm exhausted by the time I get to my room. All I want to do is sleep, but my brain keeps running with thoughts of Lindsay.

Based on the moon light shining in my room, it must be the middle of the night when I hear a soft knock on my door. I grab my phone off the nightstand and see it's just after three in the morning.

One of the reasons I chose this suite—beside its proximity to

Lindsay's room—was how close it is to the kitchen, so if I ever slept in, Mateo's entrance would wake me up. He's not the quietest when he works, nevertheless, I'd take being woken up from his cooking over an alarm clock any day. But even three is too early for Mateo. Unless he's working on the wedding cake.

I spring out of bed, walk over to the door, and swing it open, finding Lindsay with her fist raised, about to knock again. She's in what looks to be a camisole and a matching pair of sleep shorts. Hair a little frazzled, but not bad for bedhead.

I rub the sleep away from my eyes, looking around the hall and finding nothing is out of sorts before asking, "Is everything okay?" I lazily prop myself up against the doorframe, waiting for her response.

"Um," she mumbles and lowers her head, then shakes it like she was about to say something but thought better. "You know what? I'm sorry to wake you. It's nothing." She turns and walks away. "Sorry again," she mutters and tosses her hand in the air, waving her apologies as she goes.

I chase after her. "Wait," I shout while grabbing her shoulder, causing her to jerk to a stop. "Talk to me Lindsay," I plead. "What's going on?"

She turns to me, brushing the hair out of her face. "Oh, it's nothing, really. Sorry for waking you."

"You said that already," I say, waking up a little more, which now lets me appreciate the glaring realization that she is not wearing a bra, and the thin tank is doing very little to hide that fact. "What's going on, Linds?"

"I just"—she exhales a large breath—"I feel like shit for ending things the way I did after the amazing day we had." She's fidgeting with the bottom of her sleep shirt now. "What I'm trying to say is, I'm sorry."

Looking up at me, her big eyes are filled with regret. God, they are beautiful. I've noticed sometimes they look more gray, while others more blue, depending on her mood or even what she's wearing. Right now, they are leaning heavily toward blue.

"Okay, well that's all, so I'm just going to . . ." her voice fades as she jabs her thumb over her shoulder and proceeds to walk back to her room.

"Hold on there, beautiful." I jog ahead of her, and see the shock on her face. "What? What did I just do?"

"No one has ever—" she starts but shakes her head, slipping that trusty mask back on again. "Nothing, I really should let you go back to bed."

"Tell you what," I say, blocking the stairway to her room. It may be immature, but I don't care. I'm not leaving this like earlier. "I promise to go back to bed, but only if *you* come with me."

"Theo," she complains. "You need your sleep. It's fine. I'll just see you in the morning."

With one swipe of my arm, I have her up and over my shoulder.

"Oh my god, Theo!" Her voice is shrill, but she doesn't fight it, that is until I give her ass a little squeeze.

"Let me ask you again, because maybe I wasn't clear enough," I say as I march back to my room with her over my shoulder like a sack of potatoes. "Will you *please* sleep in my bed with me for the very small remainder of the night?"

The door's still open as I walk us through the threshold.

"Ughhh," she whines and I slap her ass, just for good measure. "Fine! Okay! Are you happy no—" But the last word is interrupted by her squealing as I throw her down on my bed.

"Now don't get any ideas, *ma chére*." I wag my index finger at her. "I'm tired, and I know you're tired too from all that overthinking."

"I wasn't—"

"Ah, ah, ah." I turn off the light, and hop in beside her. "Sweet dreams, Lindsay."

There's a pause and then, "Theo?"

"Yes, Linds?"

"Thank you." She doesn't need to say what for.

I turn toward her and wrap my arm around her waist, pulling her close into my embrace while sneaking a kiss on the top of her head. "Goodnight, *ma chérie.*"

Finding my legs entangled between Lindsay's, I take a minute to enjoy the warmth of her soft body against mine. The sun is peeking in through the window, allowing an angelic glow to shine around Lindsay. With a kiss to the back of her head, I slide my legs out and reluctantly move my arm off her. I sneak out of bed and pull a shirt on, leaving to check if Mateo or Ettie is here yet.

I no more than close the door and turn around, only to be startled by Ettie standing there, arms crossed with a raised eyebrow.

"You close the door like that and I might think you have someone inside who you don't want waking up, Theo." She peers over my shoulder, even though the door is shut and she won't see anything. "Shall I assume that I can get an early start in cleaning *Madame Hartman's* room this morning?" How does she know these things?

"I guess you'll have to go upstairs to find out," I chirp, acting aloof while walking past her to the kitchen. I'm well aware she knows I'm full of shit. "Oh, and good morning, Ettie." I send a smile over her way but she waves me off before leaving to start her morning tasks.

"*Bonjour*, Mateo!"

"*Bonjour*," Mateo says, not even turning his head.

"Wow, a greeting this morning?" I bring my palm to my chest. "I'm truly touched, Mateo."

He just huffs in response. Mateo's deep in his routine, so I grab a few items for breakfast for Lindsay and me and quickly leave before disturbing him too much. "See you around lunchtime. Don't have too much fun today!"

Lindsay must be a deep sleeper, because I'm able to get back inside the room with a tray full of food, and set up the table for breakfast without her stirring.

I decide it's as good as any time to take a quick rinse off, but apparently that was loud enough to wake Lindsay. As I step out of the shower, I meet her stunned gaze.

Lindsay is standing there, mid-step, gawking at me while water runs down my body, and I can't help but smile.

"Good morning, *ma chérie.*"

CHAPTER TWENTY-FIVE

LINDSAY

Waking up to the sound of rain, I turn over, and see I'm alone in the bed. I slept with Theo last night. And slept in the actual sense of the word. I mean it was only for four hours, but still. I can't remember the last time I fell asleep with a man in my bed. Oh wait, yes I can. Never.

It entails a certain level of trust, one that I've just never felt with a partner before. And yes, I do realize that sex also entails trust, but I feel more in control with sex, whereas I'm in a more vulnerable state while sleeping. You never truly know what the other person is doing while you're passed out in bed next to them.

Standing up, I follow the scent of pastries and tea that Theo must've brought in. I hear the rain get louder the closer I get to the table. I turn as the rain stops, only Theo's very wet—very *naked*—body tells me it wasn't rain that I was hearing, but the shower.

It really is unfair how good looking he is, and with the water running down his stomach to the V between his hips, it's only adding to the mesmerizing view in front of me.

"Good morning, *ma chérie*."

Startling me, I look up to see him grabbing a towel. Shit, I probably have drool on my mouth. From sleep obviously. It has nothing to do with the naked man in front of me.

Oh, he's *definitely* putting on a show for me.

I'm practically gawking at him as he takes his time drying himself, twisting and turning to make sure nothing is left to my imagination. If he wants me to look, that's exactly what I'm going to do.

I notice the small dimples at the base of his back. The subtle scar he has on his waist. The defining lines of his calves as he turns. After a few more times of thoroughly checking him out, I'm finally able to form words. "You're good at that."

"Oh yeah?" he teases as he tousles his hair a bit with the towel, leaving himself completely exposed and giving me a full frontal view. "Maybe next time I can try it with you."

Did he just ask to take a shower with me? My body is feeling all sorts of hot right now. What was I doing before seeing Theo naked again?

"I brought some breakfast in. It's on the table."

Right . . . Breakfast. That's right. You're hungry.

Hungry for dick.

Shit. No, Lindsay. *Food*. You're hungry for food. Oh, but I do hope he brought some chocolate croissants.

One look at the table, I see that he has indeed brought those delicious, flakey pillows stuffed with chocolate. Definitely going home with an addiction to those bad boys, perhaps not the only addiction coming out of this trip.

I pour both Theo and me some tea, adding honey to both of our mugs before plating myself some fruit and a croissant. Breakfast is a little earlier this morning which I don't mind. Supposedly, I have a massage today, or at least that's what was in the information Fran gave me before I left. Though I haven't received any confirmation from Theo. Then again, I haven't really thought about it since being here.

For once, the days are just blending into one big lump. If I didn't have my phone, I'm pretty sure I would lose track of what day it is.

I can't believe I'm saying this, but it's been nice having this break from work. And I feel like I've done a pretty great job at not thinking about the office while being here. Well, other than when I checked my email at the airport. And when I texted Stephanie.

Fran kind of forced me to go cold turkey by revoking my access to the server. I've only used my phone for photos and talking with my family. Honestly, I thought I would get much more reading done, but a certain green-eyed devil has been stealing my attention.

I take a bite of the croissant as I see Theo walk toward me. "Thanks for getting breakfast," I say as he sneaks a kiss on the top of my head.

"You're welcome," he chirps as he takes his seat. "Thanks for sleeping with me last night." He's fighting for his life holding back the smile that's attempting to creep out as he grabs his cup, staring at me over the rim while sipping the hot tea. But that dimple of his gives him away.

"I actually found I didn't mind it so much." Trying to look unfazed by his double meaning, I steal another bite before adding, "Thankfully, you didn't snore."

"The same cannot be said about you, *ma chérie*."

My head turns so fast toward him, mouth gaping open. "You're lying!"

"Oh, I wish I were." Shrugging, he starts dishing himself some fruit. "Like a cute little bear." And he freaking boops me on the nose before taking a bite of his fruit.

"A bear?" Did I hear him right?

"What?" he says, finishing up the fruit in his mouth. "Bears snore."

"I know. I just can't believe you compared me to one." The complaint comes out a little more shrill than I intend it to.

"You would too if you heard yourself snore." The nerve of this man.

"Theo!" I shout incredulously and he just laughs, dropping his fork. His smile is so wide I can see all his teeth.

"Hey," he says, trying to compose himself. "I said a *cute* little bear."

"That does not negate the fact you called me a bear."

"Ah, ah." He wags his finger. "I said you *snore* like a—"

Shoving my hand over his mouth, I narrow my eyes at him. "Don't you *dare* repeat it for the third time," I warn and he fucking licks my hand. "Ewww," I whine and try acting like I'm grossed out, but end up in a fit of laughter with him.

I wipe my eyes and find him staring at me. "What?" I ask as I start wiping my mouth. "Do I have something on my face?" I'm sure I have smeared chocolate on my chin or some other embarrassing place.

"No, it's just—" He clears his throat. "You looked so happy just then."

"Oh." I look down and play with my fork and fruit on my plate.

"Don't do that."

"Do what?" I ask confused.

"Put the mask on," he breathes out. "Please don't put the mask back on, Linds."

Oh. That.

"That's what happened last night, too. Back when we were in the car."

"I'm sorry. I'm just not used to . . ." I shrug, I guess I have nothing to lose. "Showing emotion really. It's just easier that way."

"Easier for whom?"

"I don't know." I sigh. God, how did we get to this topic? "People I guess. You can't really control them. Emotions are big and take up a lot of room."

"That's kind of the point," he says before grabbing my hands. "It's okay to feel them. To share them. They aren't bad."

The sincerity in his eyes is endearing, and fuck if it doesn't make me want to break my walls right now. If only he knew he's already done a decent job at lowering them. More so than I've let anyone do in a long time.

"They make things messy. Plus," I add before grabbing another piece of croissant, "they can be a time-consuming bunch." I attempt a joke to break the tension, but he's not laughing, so I take a bite to avoid the awkwardness.

Reaching out, he swipes his thumb over my mouth, I guess I really do have chocolate on my face this time.

"I've got time." He smiles and raises his thumb, licking it clean before returning to his breakfast. "And I happen to like messy."

CHAPTER TWENTY-SIX

THEO

After breakfast, I walk Lindsay back to her room. As much as I'd like to spend more time with her, I have a few things that I need to attend to this morning. Plus, I'm sure she'd like some alone time. I feel like I've been her shadow these last few days.

To be quite frank, I'm addicted to spending time with her. Which is insane, because we haven't even known each other for a week. I can't believe she leaves in two nights. I'm trying not to think about that, but like it or not, there's an expiration date on us. One that's coming up quickly.

I feel like doing something extra special for her after her massage. Ma already planned it all, but I'm hoping to extend the relaxing afternoon into the evening. The plan is to set her up in another room for the massage, giving me ample time to set up her room for a surprise right after.

On my way to talk to Jean, our groundskeeper, I catch a glimpse of Lindsay in the pool. I guess she got the swimsuit that I asked Ettie to bring in from town.

It's nothing fancy. Just a simple, no frills, black two piece. It's not a string bikini, but then again, I did tell Ettie to pick something out that would make Lindsay comfortable. She looks at peace swimming around, moving through the water with grace while the sun beams down on her.

"You're drooling."

"Shit." I turn my head while wiping my mouth to find Ettie standing beside me. When did she get here?

"Language, Theo!" she scolds.

"Sorry, Ettie." Ruffling my hair, I turn fully to her. "Maybe don't go sneaking up on people if you don't like foul language."

It's like her superpower. Being anywhere and everywhere. She was always the one who caught me doing something I wasn't supposed to be doing when I was younger.

"Ah, but where's the fun in that?" Sending a wink my way, she starts walking away, but not without calling over her shoulder. "Looks like the swimsuit fits."

If there was any hope that she didn't know what, or *who*, I was looking at, that last comment burned it up in flames.

I get swamped handling more wedding drama, causing me to miss out on lunch with Lindsay yet again.

There's a storm that has already started and is forecasted to continue through Saturday night. Reports are saying that there will be lightning off and on, as well as some light rain.

"And what exactly are your plans if there's a downpour? I hope you don't expect us to traipse around the property, muddying our dresses and suits," Karen continues on as I zone out. She's been like this for the last ten minutes.

After a pause, I take my opening. "Karen, I understand you're worried about the weather, and I would like to do everything in my power to put your mind at ease." I roll my eyes at the ass-kissing I'm doing. "I think reserving an elegant clear tent may be—"

"Absolutely not! My son will not be getting married in some plastic tent. What kind of wedding do you think this is? Honestly, that's a terrible idea."

I palm my forehead as she criticizes my perfectly acceptable solution. How in the world did Ma deal with her for the last few months.

"What about the dining room?" I offer.

"What about it?"

"*If* it rains, we can fill the room with candles and the flowers that would've been outside, creating a romantic setting inside, away from the elements that we *can't* control."

"Well, it's at least better than the tacky garbage bag idea."

Really? Tacky garbage bag idea? I happen to think a clear tent would provide a creative solution to the rain problem. I could just see it now, candles and flowers decorating the covered area, rain pelting down on the plastic material. Sounds like a scene right out of a movie.

I say my goodbyes and draft a formal backup plan for Karen and email it to her, because apparently me communicating that we would shift everything inside wasn't confirmation enough for her.

By the time I finish everything, Lindsay's already busy with her massage, which is great timing because now I don't have to be nearly as sneaky.

I grab all the things I need for her surprise from the pile I hid by the front desk. A note tumbles out when I lift the basket up, of course it's from Ettie because nothing happens on the property without her knowing about it. She probably saw the little pile I stashed and drew her own conclusion on my plans.

Don't forget the champagne!
Enjoy!

-Ettie

I fold the note back up, and stuff it in my pocket, gathering up everything before walking to Lindsay's room. I knock just to be sure but when no answer comes, I open the door I know isn't locked. It's starting to sprinkle and my memory doesn't give justice to how amazing it is to be in this room.

It's easy to be fully immersed in the storm outside with how loud the rain beats against the skylights. Looking out the window over the bathtub, I catch a view of the water pouring down over the fields. The sky looks dark and ominous. So that, mixed with the current humidity, I'm guessing the lightning will start at any time.

I'm putting the finishing touches on the surprise when I hear the door open. I turn and immediately see Lindsay walking in.

Her hair is up in a messy bun, greasy from the oils from her massage. There's a little mark on her forehead where she must've been resting her head on the bed. She's wearing my sweats again so she must've changed into those after her swim. Something about that tugs at my heart, which is weird because it's just clothes. She probably didn't pack sweats and wanted to wear something comfortable for the massage. Shit, with how serious she takes work, she might not even own a pair of sweats.

Lindsay closes the door and her eyes immediately go to me. I'm standing frozen by the filled bathtub with bath salts in my hand. The room smells of lavender, not in an overpowering way but just strong enough to keep the relaxation going after her massage.

"Surprise." I smile and wave my arms around to the little setup I just finished, accidentally sprinkling a little bit of the salts on the tile around me. I quickly set the jar of salts down on the tub ledge.

There are various flowers around her room, all leading to the bathtub. When I called the florist for the flowers earlier this morning, she suggested white roses and some other ones that weren't too overpowering to make sure their scents weren't competing with the lavender scent from the bath oil and salts.

Candles of all sizes surround the tub, illuminating the space in a soft light as the dark sky outside provides an even moodier setting. I even hand dipped raspberries in chocolate earlier, remembering she has a strawberry allergy.

"What's this?" she asks, removing her shoes while she approaches the tub. "This is all for me?"

"*Oui, ma chérie.*" I pull the champagne out of the bucket, unwrap the foil, and pop the cork, allowing a little of the liquid to foam out. "Cheers to continuing your afternoon of relaxation."

CHAPTER TWENTY-SEVEN

LINDSAY

This is truly what dreams are made of, I think to myself as the Lizzie McGuire song plays in my head.

The flowers and candles. The bath with steam rising out of it, waiting and ready for me to get in and enjoy. The view outside of the lavender field and angry storm overhead. It looks like lightning will light up the sky at any moment.

"I don't know what to say," I note in awe before reaching out and dipping my fingers in the tub, feeling the hot water on my skin. "Thank you, Theo."

"Hope you enjoy it, Lindsay." He kisses the top of my head before walking to the door, and it's then I realize just how much I've missed him today. This might be the only time I see him for the rest of the day, since I'm not sure if I'll get to see him at dinner or not.

"Wait!" I shout, then internally cringe. That wasn't desperate at all, Lindsay. "I just mean—" Take a breath, Lindsay. He's not going to say no to getting in a bath with a naked woman. Feeling more confident, I relax my voice. "Want to join me?"

The shock he's feeling is clear on his face, but it quickly fades into something more sinful.

"I would never turn down a chance to get wet with you, Linds."

His mention of getting me wet pulls me back to when we first met at the airport. God, it seems like we've experienced so much since then.

"Do I get one of your famous strip teases again?" He's closer now, running his hands down my sides. "Or do I get to undress you this time?"

Fuck. Me.

Sneaking his hand under my shirt—well technically his shirt —he takes his time rolling the fabric up my body. When he reaches the bare skin of my breast, he lingers there. His thumb strokes right under my nipple, teasing me like the devil he is. My head rolls back with the simple touch and he takes the movement as an invitation to kiss my neck.

God, I'm officially a puddle. My muscles were already loose from the two hour massage I just received, so it's not taking much to warm me up. With a light squeeze around my ribcage, he continues to take my shirt off. Kissing me on my lips when the fabric finally lifts over my head.

While his hands move down to the waistband of my sweats, he lowers his mouth, sucking my breast while he pulls my pants off my hips. Without taking his mouth off of me, he lifts me up and sets me down on a folded towel resting on the edge of the tub.

He works the pants down one leg at a time, kissing a path on the inside of my thighs and calves while pulling the fabric off. I'm enthralled by his soft touches, each one making me giddy with anticipation for what he'll do next.

The thunder outside has started, and I can hear it booming in the background with flashes of light momentarily illuminating the sky moments after.

Before I can make mention of the storm, Theo lifts me up bridal style, and lowers me in the warm bath. My senses immediately go into overdrive. The warm water covering my already hot body is at war with the floral scent fighting to calm my racing heart. But it's not enough. I want—no—need Theo here, inside the bath with me.

"Are you coming—"

"Good things come to those who wait, *ma chérie.*"

That shuts me up. I don't have to wait long though.

There's no show this time. Theo's just as eager as I am, making quick work of pulling off his shirt. He only slows to grab a condom from his pocket before pulling the denim off his legs, swiftly securing the rubber around his already hardened cock. Theo looks up smirking at me while I move to the far end of the tub, allowing him space to get in.

Once submerged, he immediately pulls me to him so we're face to face, forcing my legs to wrap around his waist and making his hard length press against my opening.

"Oh, Theo," I moan as I shift my hips, working his tip over my already sensitive clit.

"Fuck, Linds," he groans as one hand settles on my hip, and the other digs into my hair, releasing it from my messy bun. His mouth finds purchase at the junction of my neck and shoulder, alternating between kissing and sucking.

The sensation makes me arch my back and push my breasts against the scruff of his facial hair all while another lightning strike lights up the field outside.

"If you wanted me to suck these perfect breasts, all you had to do was ask," he teases before doing just that. The sensation of his warm mouth pushes my need to the limit.

With one single shift of my hips, I'm riding his cock. "Fuck," I gasp out. "I forgot how thick you are." His husky chuckle against my nipple lets me know I just said that last comment out loud.

The thunder is booming loudly while I find my rhythm, working his cock in and out of me. As I make sure to grind my clit with each thrust of my hips, the water starts sloshing from side to side, some even falling over the edge of the tub and onto the tile floor.

"That's right *ma chérie*, you're taking me so well." The hand in my hair falls lower, roaming possessively down my neck, then following the indent from my spine down my back.

As another flash lights the sky, his hand continues lower and lower until it's underwater, cupping my ass. The shift causes his dick to push even deeper inside with each shift of my hips.

"Yes, like that. *Please*," I beg as I tilt my head back, reveling in the feel of him inside of me.

"You look so pretty begging, *ma chérie*," he praises while another rumble comes from outside.

God, this man.

"Theo, I'm—I—"

His hands grip me even tighter as my climax crescendos, and his curse tells me he wasn't far from finishing either.

I can't tell if I've temporarily lost vision or if another bolt of lightning just touched down. All I see for the seconds following is a bright flash of white light, illuminating not just the sky outside, but the room as well. I'm panting as I try to calm my heart when a loud crack follows the lightning strike. Suddenly, the power goes out.

"Shit," Theo curses under his breath. "I bet a strike hit a power pole. I better go check it out." He squeezes my ass before guiding me up and off of him. After a quick kiss on my head, he shimmies out of the tub.

Twice today I have had the privilege of seeing Theo's naked body, wet with water running down the chiseled lines of his chest and stomach. Really three times in the last forty-eight hours, if you include the pool, which I certainly do. It's a view I will never tire from seeing. Only this time, he's got this glow surrounding him from all the candles lighting up the dark room, highlighting every inch of his sculpted body.

"Stay here," Theo notes as he starts pulling up his denim. "I'll go check it out and see if anyone else is still here." He leaves before I step out of the tub to dry off and put clothes on.

After drying my hair, I notice the tray of chocolate dipped raspberries sitting by the champagne bucket. Not strawberries, but *raspberries*. The man dipped raspberries . . . for *me*.

Do you know how nice it is to feel like someone truly hears you? Someone who listens and is intentional? Showing they care, no matter how small the act?

I'm spiraling those thoughts for far too long until I realize, it's been a bit and Theo still hasn't come back to the room. It seems like the storm is picking up outside, too. I'm pretty sure a storm this size is bizarre for this time of the year, and it makes me a little nervous that he's been out in it for as long as he has.

He's probably just trying to fix the power, Lindsay.

Or maybe it took him a while to find a flashlight.

Or maybe he tripped and impaled himself and no one is out there with him and he's just laying there, bleeding out.

Wow. Okay, no. We aren't doing that. *Breathe in.*

He's probably helping Ettie or Mateo. *Breathe out.*

They normally leave around this time of day. *Breathe in.*

Yeah. He's definitely not laying dead in a rain puddle, because he was fixing the power, and got shocked only to be electrocuted when he fell down into said rain puddle where a power line has fallen, ending an electrical current into the water.

FUCKING BREATHE, LINDSAY!

I'm now pacing my room, hyperventilating about all the things that could be happening to Theo.

That's it. I can't sit here and do nothing.

Before I know it, I'm running outside in the pouring rain in nothing but my cami, a flimsy pair of sleep shorts, and my phone, because I need *some* sort of light source. No shoes because obviously who needs shoes when someone could be waiting for help because they were impaled by a tree that was struck down by lightning.

"Theo!" I call out, rushing around the gravel driveway between the family house and hotel. My feet are screaming at me from stepping on the small and jagged rocks, something I'm sure I'll pay for in the morning, but that's tomorrow's problem. "Theo?!" Where the fuck did he go?

I run around the hotel again and that's when I see him.

CHAPTER TWENTY-EIGHT

THEO

After the power went out, I run outside only to find Mateo attempting to jump his car. In a lightning storm nonetheless.

I shine my flashlight over to him. "What the fuck are you doing, Mateo?!"

He turns and shades his eyes from the bright light, waving at me to lower my flashlight.

"What's it look like I'm doing?" he shouts, then curses in French under his breath as he turns back to working under the hood.

"In case you didn't know, there's a lightning storm going on right now," I holler as I walk closer to him.

"No shit. Now if you help me, we can both be out of the rain a little faster." I scoff at his attitude. "And where's your shirt?"

I look down and realize in my haste to come find the problem with the power, I forgot to put a shirt on. "With everything going on, I hardly think that not wearing a shirt is the thing we should be focusing on."

"Speak for yourself. You're not the one who has to look at your naked chest," he huffs.

"Hold on." I turn and start jogging to the family house.

"Oh, so now you're leaving me?" he hollers.

"Don't get your panties in a twist!" I shout back. "And while you're at it, close the hood. You won't do anyone any good if you get hit by a strike." I hear a bang soon after, hoping that it was Mateo shutting the hood and not him getting hit by a rogue lightning strike. Stubborn bastard.

After running inside to grab Mom's car keys, I run back out and take the jumper cables from him.

"We'll handle your dead battery tomorrow," I say, dangling the keys in front of his palm, but pull back as he tries to grab them. "*After* the storm. Deal?"

He huffs, but nods, grabbing the keys before saying his goodbyes. He'll bring it back tomorrow, and by then, the worst of the storm should be over, allowing us to jump the car safely. And if not, he'll just borrow the car for another night.

With one problem solved, I walk over to the electrical box, and inspect it to make sure nothing is wrong. From what I can tell, everything seems to be in working order, so the storm must've hit one of the junction boxes on the outskirts of the property. If that's the case, that means we won't have power until tomorrow at the earliest.

Fumbling with my phone, I see that it still has service, so I report the outage as I do a quick walk around the estate making sure there's no damage to any of the trees.

It's completely pissing down now, warm rain soaking me to the bone. I walk to the driveway and hear who I think is Lindsay shouting my name.

"Theo!"

Turning the corner, I see her, hands cupped around her mouth from shouting my name. She's completely drenched. Her tank and shorts are so wet, they're practically painted onto her body. Before I know it, she's sprinting to me then jumping on me like a feral koala.

"Oh, thank god!" She kisses my cheeks. "Are you okay?" she

asks, giving me more kisses as I squeeze her closer. "Did something happen?" I'm leaning my head down to meet hers, noses touching as rain pours down.

"I was afraid you were out here dying in a ditch or something."

"Shhh," I console, brushing her wet hair out of her face. "I'm okay. Sorry to have worried you, *ma chérie.*" I kiss her again for reassurance. "Plus, we don't even have any ditches nearby." I'm attempting to bring her back to reality with a light-hearted joke, hoping to distract from her obvious spiral, but Lindsay doesn't laugh. In fact, I think she's crying.

"I'm sorry. You just hadn't come back yet and the storm. It was—" She's working herself up again. Her eyes have this panicked look to them. She's in fight or flight mode.

"Hey." I set her down and grab her face between my hands, lowering myself so we're eye to eye. "I'm right here. Look." I pull her hand over to my chest, running it around the skin there, assuring her I'm not hurt. "Everything is okay. I'm okay."

Crushing her back to me, she lets out a breath of air.

"I know I said I wanted to get you wet again, but this wasn't what I was expecting." I can't see her because she's still squeezed to my chest, but I feel the little pinch she gives me. "Come on." I chuckle as I pull away a bit. "Let's go get these clothes off, yeah?" Lindsay nods and we walk back hand in hand.

Attempting to avoid traipsing water all over the floors, Lindsay and I strip down by the back door. I grab a couple of pool towels, and we head back inside led by the light of her phone and my flashlight.

"Sorry about the power, but it should be back on tomorrow."

"It's not like it was *your* lightning rod that hit it."

I gasp and clutch my towel, acting appalled. "Did you just make a dick joke?"

Her laugh is free and unburdened, and I can't help but join along. "As much as I'd like to take credit, that pun was all accidental."

We're in nothing but towels as we walk down the hallway. Both soaking wet from the storm outside with no power on the whole estate, but somehow making the best of this moment.

"Want to grab some food before we head back to your room?"

"So bold of you to assume, Theo."

"Which part?" I tilt my head. "You're room? Because we both know neither of us is sleeping without the other tonight." I squeeze her hand in mine but continue with my teasing. "Or the part about food? Because I've heard your stomach growl three times since stepping inside." That's a lie. It's been more like five times.

Lindsay rolls her eyes but follows me into the kitchen. We try to get food that isn't in the refrigerator, doing our best to keep the food inside as cold as possible while the power is still out. Which means a lot of carbs, fruit, chocolate, and cured meats. Oh, and wine of course.

Walking into her room, I see the candles are still lit, so I turn off the flashlight opting for the softer light.

"I'm sorry. I didn't even think. I should've blown all these out before trying to find you."

I set our foraged dinner down and attempt to ground her. "Lindsay, everything is *fine*." With my hands grasping the sides of her head, I rub my thumbs back and forth on her temples. "No one is hurt. We are *both* safe. And there was definitely no fire caused by leaving the candles unattended."

She chuckles under her breath, relaxing a bit under my touch.

"Come on." I move my hands down to squeeze hers. "Deep breath in"—we both take one—"and deep breath out."

We repeat the process a couple more times, bringing her out of her spiral. But I want to make sure she truly gets out of that dark place.

"Now be a good girl and come." And by the shocked expression on her face, I'd say I did just that. "Come eat some sausage, that is," I clarify mischievously, holding up some of the cured meat we picked out from the kitchen.

"Yeah, because that made it less dirty," she grumbles as she takes a seat.

We spend the rest of the night eating and talking in bed about anything and everything, while listening to the rain pouring on and off outside.

"So you really never lived somewhere longer than a year?" Lindsay asks as she's cozied up against me.

At this point in the night, there are only a few candles left burning. The rest of them have burned themselves out.

"Nope. Never celebrated Christmas at the same house. I never celebrated my birthday with the same friends either. Downside of being a military brat."

Lindsay glides her fingers up and down my chest, making it easy to open up about a topic I so rarely discuss.

"It's part of the reason I got into the house-flipping business. Sure, I know a lot about fixing houses from spending my summers here. And don't get me wrong, that's helped a ton. But I love the idea of having a hand in creating a space where a family will be able to put down roots. A space where they can hopefully make memories of their own for years and years. Creating a place they can really call home, you know?"

She turns her head so she's looking up at me. Her icy eyes sparkle from the moonlight shining down from the skylights above the bed. "That's really beautiful, Theo."

I begin telling another story but a few minutes in, notice the subtle snore coming from Lindsay. The last thing I remember is me removing some chocolate out of her hand and tucking the blanket around her. I fall asleep shortly after, with nothing but the stars lighting the room, signaling the storm has cleared for the night.

CHAPTER TWENTY-NINE

LINDSAY

Last night was a whirlwind of emotions. I was so scared for Theo. Theo, a man I didn't even know a week ago. I guess all the forced proximity tropes I've read in the past really aren't all that far fetched.

I shift to get out of bed, but feel a hand gripping my hip, anchoring me in place.

"You are making it very hard," Theo's rasps, voice scratchy from sleep. He clears his throat. "To be a gentleman right now."

"Since when do you care about being a gentleman?" I tease, smirking to myself as Theo squeezes my hip as punishment.

I'm not sure of the time, but the sun is shining meaning there's a pause in the storm. Though I'm still not sure if the power has returned. I feel kisses on my shoulder and sink into the warmth from Theo's body as he gets closer. And that's when it dawns on me that we are both very much naked.

I feel the terry cloth material underneath me jogging my memory of last night's events. We must've shifted enough to unwrap our towels last night.

Shifting to face him, he quickly locks his leg around my hip and wraps both of his arms around me, forcing me even closer to his body.

"Hi," I squeak out.

"Good morning, *ma chérie.*" He punctuates his greeting with a sweet kiss on my head, then squeezes my ass. The move causes me to thrust my hips into his, making it impossible to ignore the way he's saluting me between his legs.

I thought I had been good, not being distracted when I woke up to his dick poking my lower back, but now that he's so close to where I want him, he's forcing my need to rise to a level where I'm aching for satisfaction.

Reaching down between our bodies, I do my best to stroke him while being smashed into him. Theo eases his hold on me, giving me more space to better service him. Shimmying lower, I palm his hips to get him on his back while I adjust my position.

I haven't given a blow job since my early college years, and even then, I never was one for oral sex. I would always get in my head too much about it, whether when giving or receiving it, to the point where I had never orgasmed while a guy went down on me. Well, up until Theo that is. Still blown away with his stunt in the pool.

And as far as giving it, I've been self-conscious ever since the first time I gave one. Immediately after the guy finished, he had the audacity to tell me he had better and that I should "loosen up." Not exactly what someone wants to hear. I mean hell, they don't call it a job for nothing.

Luckily, no one has said that since but then again, I now use it as a tool for foreplay and never rely on that act alone for a man to finish.

I play with Theo a little at first, stroking him in slow long pulls from base to tip as he folds his hands behind his head. Licking around his shaft, I make sure to spend a little extra time around that sensitive spot at the top. As I slowly start to take him into my mouth, I feel his thighs tensing up.

I've never been one to be able to take a whole dick inside of my mouth, and with Theo's size, I definitely would be gagging if I even attempted to try, so I rely on my hand to help out.

Not expecting the morning to start off like this, my hair isn't up, nor do I have a hairband easily accessible. But like hell am I stopping because of my hair getting in the way. I'll just have to deal with the curtain of hair surrounding me while I work my mouth up and down his shaft.

I grip him at his base and hollow my cheeks as I suck, providing as much suction as possible. He groans something in French under his breath, giving me more confidence and urging me on. I get into a groove of stroking him while sucking. Wetness gathers between my legs as I get aroused seeing how much he enjoys this.

There's a mess of saliva between us and my hair is just long enough to keep getting stuck to it. It's repeatedly causing me to reach up to move it over my shoulder, but with a few head bobs, it's back to falling down.

Just as I reach up to move it again, my hand meets Theo's as he wraps my hair around his fist, giving it a slight pull while also getting it out of my way.

His eyes meet mine when he says, "I'm not going to be able to hold on much longer, Linds."

With his encouragement—and assistance with my hair—I suck and stroke a little faster while using my now free hand to play with his balls.

While he's inside my mouth, I tease the underside of his tip with my tongue. I feel him tightening up, and though it's been a minute since I've done this, I know it's my signal that he's about to finish.

"Linds, I'm—" He gives my hair a quick tug. I think he's trying to warn me to take my mouth off of him, but I find I *want* him to finish in my mouth. "Lindsay!" he shouts as cum fills my mouth.

I attempt to swallow it down, trying not to choke while he finishes. Slowing my hand's pace, I don't completely stop as I ease him down from his orgasm. He shutters when I give him one final teasing lick, making sure not a single drop is wasted.

Popping my mouth off of him, I wipe my face with the back of my hand while keeping eye contact with Theo. He sits up, motioning with his hand to come over to him while a smirk takes over his face. I crawl over to him and straddle his waist, wrapping my arms around his neck. Theo runs his hand through my hair, kissing me with unwavering devotion.

"That was incredible, Lindsay," he praises in a whisper close to my lips. With blush igniting my cheeks, I kiss him, choosing that as my response instead of words.

With a quick squeeze of my ass and position change, I'm now on my back with him above me, caging me in. "I'm going to go grab some breakfast and check if the power is on. Don't move, and I'll reward you when I get back," he punctuates with a kiss.

"Hmm." I tap my bottom lip, "I'm not sure. How big is the reward?"

He leans in and nibbles my throat a little, then peppers my body with a trial of kisses. "Has anyone told you how funny you are?" he teases as he swipes his thumb over my hardened nipple before hopping out of bed.

I sit up in bed and wrap the fluffy comforter around my body, watching Theo pull up his pants. He kisses me once more before leaving the room. I immediately find I miss his presence.

Fuck. I'm in trouble.

CHAPTER THIRTY

THEO

"*Bonjour*, Mateo," I greet while putting together a tray for breakfast. "I see the power is back, thank fuck."

"Language, Theo!"

Shit! How does she do that? "Pardon, Ettie. I hadn't realized you were here with us."

"Haven't you learned by now? I'm everywhere," she taunts, wiggling her fingers like she's performing magic. "Mateo says the power was out last night from the storm? Were you and Lindsay okay throughout the night?" I know she's concerned, but I also realize she's probably trying to be nosy.

"Yes, thankfully after helping Mateo out, there were no other surprises. Also, Ma texted me an update early this morning about Grandpa. He's apparently recovering great and they should be back a little earlier than they expected."

"Ah, well that's good to hear." She turns to Mateo. "Seeing how it's Lindsay's last night with us Mateo, I think it would be a wonderful idea for you to make your lavender domes. If you have time of course." She adds the last part like she doesn't have him wrapped around her finger.

As far as I know, there has never been more than a professional relationship between the two of them, but I've always wondered.

Replaying what Ettie said, my mind whirls. It can't be Lindsay's last night already, can it?

"I have time, but I need more honey," Mateo comments without straying from his current task.

"Oh, I'm sure Theo can grab some from the bees after breakfast, right?" She turns to me expectantly. "Maybe even take Lindsay with you." God, she's good.

"Don't act like I don't know what you're doing, Ettie," I comment, heading out of the kitchen.

"I wouldn't want her to leave without sampling the goods. But then again," she pauses and looks at me conspiratorially. "Maybe she already has."

I turn my back to her, shaking my head while I walk away. I'm not about to confirm or deny that our guest for the week has most definitely sampled the goods, though feasted might be the better word.

"I didn't get to ask last night, but how was the massage?" I question before taking a bite of my omelet.

"It was really good," Lindsay answers as she finishes a bite of her chocolate croissant. "I think I even fell asleep at one point." She wipes her mouth before taking a sip of tea.

"I'll have to ask Juliette if you snored as loudly for her as you do for me." I chuckle, attempting to cover the sound by lifting up my mug, but her narrow gaze tells me I failed in disguising the sound. "You've got quite the pair of lungs on you, *ma chérie*."

She pinches my thigh under the table after that last comment.

"Ouch." I laugh, rubbing the not-so injured area. "I was talking about your snoring."

“Sure you were,” she quips as we start cleaning up the table.

“I’ve got to check on a few things in the office, but I should be back within an hour.” I pick up the tray full of dirty dishes.

“I’ll be waiting.” She attempts to kiss my check, but at the last moment, I turn so she kisses my lips.

“See you soon.”

After dropping off the dishes in the kitchen, I do a quick check of the hotel’s emails and voicemails. Thankfully, there were no pressing issues, and even more surprisingly, there haven't been any other calls about this weekend’s wedding, which gives Lindsay and me the morning to harvest honey.

On my way back to her room, I run into Ettie.

“Lindsay and I will be out by the bees if you need anything. Seems like it’ll be a quiet day, but holler if—”

She stops me by patting my shoulder. “We’re fine. You kids have your fun. Just tell Lindsay to be careful not to get stung.” She winks at me, double meaning clear in her tone. I shake my head and chuckle. “Now get out of here,” she says, shooing me away.

I knock when I arrive at Lindsay’s door, quickly getting greeted by a smiling Lindsay. She’s either super fast or she was waiting at the door for me. Something tells me it’s the latter. Or at least I like thinking that she’s eager to see me, even after being separated for only an hour.

“Hi,” she greets with a little wave then spins. “Is this okay?”

She’s wearing a deep green sundress. Similar to the one she wore at the abbey, but this one is sleeveless and a little shorter. Plus, there seems to be tiny polkadots sprinkling the dress. Definitely not an ideal honey harvesting outfit, but we’re going to be putting on a bee suit and veil, so it really doesn’t matter. Plus, she looks absolutely stunning in it. And if she takes that dress off now, I'll be after a different type of honey.

"Theo?" Her voice shakes me to the here and now, away from the intrusive dirty—and *sticky*—thoughts being curated in my head right now.

"Um," I chuckle at where my mind went. "Yeah. You look fantastic, but I need to add two more things to your outfit." I hold out my hand for her to grab, and we leave her room.

"I hadn't realized I would be covered head to toe." She looks herself over, inspecting the beekeeper suit. Frankly, I think she looks adorable, but I know no one really *likes* wearing this getup.

"We have to make sure that perfect body of yours doesn't get stung." I give her a little spank as I walk past her to gather our tools. "Plus, now we're matching."

"Lead the way, Beekeeper Theo."

The hive we're harvesting today isn't very far from the beekeeping shed. Once we reach it, I start the process off by applying some cool smoke to relax the bees, allowing us to grab the frames without disturbing them.

"You know, I first started doing this when I was a kid. Ever since then, I make it a point to do it every time I visit." Lindsay nods as I share, watching me spray the hives at a distance. Brushing off a few of the dazed bees, I start grabbing the frames and place them in the wagon.

"Did you want to grab some?"

"I think I'm better at supervising."

"Come on. At least pull one," I say, waving her over. "It's always fun when you get a little sticky."

"Only you would find a way to make harvesting honey, *of all things*, dirty."

Even through the beekeeping suit, I can see her rolling her eyes at me, but she relents and walks closer to the hive.

"Now they're heavier than they look because of the wax and honey," I warn, bringing her over to where I'm standing and fitting her body between my arms. "The key is to make sure to grab a frame that is fully capped—"

"What's that mean?" she asks, attempting to turn her head, but it only knocks into my suit. "Oops, sorry. I'm not used to wearing—"

"It takes some getting used to," I chuckle. "But capped means it's matured enough in the hive and has a protective seal over it, the creamy film on top. We also want to make sure we grab capped honey and not capped brood."

"What's brood? And how can someone tell the difference?"

"Inquisitive are we, *ma chérie*?" I taunt as I rub my gloves down her covered waist. Fuck, I'm even getting turned on from her being in a fucking beekeeping suit. "A brood is basically a baby bee. Most times the brood has a little bump or bubble appearance. Once you see a few of them, it can get pretty easy to tell the difference."

I pull a frame up from the box.

"See? This is exactly the kind of frame we want."

"Creamy but not bumpy. Got it." There's a pause before she adds, "Now would be a perfect time for a 'that's what she said' joke."

I chuckle as I grab another frame. We replace the wooden rectangles with clean and ready-to-use ones and then walk back to the shed with our ready-to-be-harvested frames.

"You can take your suit off now." I pull the top portion off before turning and facing her. "Though I find you just as sexy as a beekeeper."

"Pfft," she huffs while stripping off her beekeeping outfit. "I find that hard to believe."

"Oh, trust me. Something was *definitely* hard out there." I give her a pointed look only to look down at my crotch then back up to her, conveying my "see, look how hard my dick is" stare.

She just rolls her eyes while a little blush brightens her checks. "So what's next?"

"Now we extract the honey" I wave her over to where the next step happens. "We'll place the four frames into the extractor where it will spin the honey out. Once the frames have had ample time in the extractor, we strain and jar it." I point over to the multitude of sanitized ready-to-use glass jars on the counter. "Once all of that is finished, we spend some time making sure all of the equipment is cleaned and ready to go for the next harvest."

After we wait for the extractor to finish its job, we make quick work of jarring the honey.

"So, how'd I do for my first harvest?" Lindsay asks as she scrutinizes one of the jars of honey.

"I'm not sure . . ." I drag out as I rub my scruff and walk toward her. "I think I may need a taste test first." She gasps as I wrap both my arms around her.

"Theo! I almost dropped the jar!" she scolds, placing the jar down near the others. She snags a spoon and dips it in the glass container we used for the runoff and rubs a little over her lips.

I love it when she gets a streak of boldness. She's always sexy, but there's something about her being confident in taking control, her knowing what she wants and not being afraid to ask for it.

I move like a cobra snatching up my prey, kissing her while successfully covering both of our mouths with the sticky substance. Pulling away, I grab the spoon that still has honey all over it and bring it over to Lindsay's neck and chest.

Her dress is open just wide enough, allowing me to spread the honey without getting the messy substance on the green fabric. She gasps as the sticky liquid runs down her skin.

Putting the spoon down on the counter, I grip her waist as I start licking off the honey on her throat, slowly working my way down to the swells of her breasts. I move my other hand up to the nape of her neck, massaging it gently while I enjoy the feast before me. She moans while I lick the mess I've made off of her.

I start to gather the fabric of her dress into my fist, bringing it up to have the access to the real treat I'm craving. Reaching between her legs, a couple things happen at once.

Lindsay moans out my name—my new favorite sound—as she grips the edge of the counter, causing the spoon to fall, which leads to a louder than expected crash, all while I hear a mumbled "I'm so sorry."

The voice definitely wasn't Lindsay. And as I lift my head up, I realize the male voice sounded an awful lot like Jean. And that's when it hits me.

The crash wasn't from the spoon falling, but the shed door being slammed shut.

"I think we just got caught, *ma chérie.*"

Lindsay looks mortified. Her face red from embarrassment or maybe from having to stop what we were just getting started, I'm not sure.

After pulling her dress back down, I reach out for a rag I can use to clean her up. I run it under some water and clean the remaining honey off of her, though I'm confident I got it all before we were interrupted.

"After that taste test, I can without a doubt say that was the best honey I ever had," I note. My eyes are filled with lust as I lick a bit of remaining honey off the corner of my mouth. "I'm not sure if I'll ever be able to top it."

After kissing her one more time, I gather the jars of honey, and we make our way to the kitchen. I just know Mateo will work his magic with this harvest for dessert.

CHAPTER THIRTY-ONE

LINDSAY

After lunch, I left Theo so he could get some work done this afternoon.

There's a wedding party arriving tomorrow after I leave and the ceremony is on Sunday. It's so weird to be around a wedding and have zero hand in its preparations.

These last few days have gone by so fast, and part of me can't even imagine leaving right now, while the other part always knew there was an expiration date on this. It's helped that Theo hasn't mentioned me leaving either. I'm not sure whether he's caught up in our little bubble and living in the moment, or if he's not wanting to remind me that this will in fact end.

Tomorrow actually. This whole . . . whatever it is, it will end tomorrow. I guess I should start packing.

I never expected to come to France in the first place, but I'm pleasantly surprised how free I've been able to feel on a trip I had no hand in planning. Fully immersing myself in the experience that was handed to me was not something I thought I'd be able to do.

I mean even while here, Theo planned most of the activities we did. Were there things that went wrong, hell yes. Even the lightning storm brought back my past feelings from the crash and the helplessness I felt that day. But he never judged me or told me the oh so popular "just relax" that people normally give me.

God, I hate when people say that. You think I want to be the giant ball of anxiety? No. And trust me, if it was as simple as just telling myself to "relax," I would've conquered my anxiety a long time ago.

But Theo just held me and reassured me everything was truly alright during my panic attack. He provided me shelter from the storm, both from the one outside and the one in my head, allowing me time to come down from my spiral. All while reminding me that we were safe and out of harm's way.

I haven't felt that type of safety and security in a long time. Then again, it's not something I allow others to provide for me. I've always preferred to be the one in control myself, being the sole person to provide a level of security instead of depending on others. While the need for control may be my struggle, my sisters all have their own.

Taylor is a lot like me. Always stuffing her feelings away. She used to tell me it was easier to do that than to feel such intense emotions. Though *many* therapy sessions have told me the reasons why I shouldn't believe that, I still find myself doing the same thing. It's just easier that way. Plus, I don't need the distraction.

But on top of the compartmentalization, Taylor struggles with abandonment issues as well. However, I don't think she's let anyone else besides her childhood therapist and me know about that.

Tory is constantly trying to be the best role model for the three of us. Always trying to protect us from everything after the accident, even more so than a regular eldest daughter would be doing.

Then Emma has her fear of driving, though I hear Diego helped conqueror that a few weeks ago. I've always found it interesting how each of us sisters had the same event happen to us, but we all came out of it with different experiences and triggers.

The accident was the start of me taking back control. It's how I protect myself from getting hurt or disappointed or caught unprepared. I have a hard time depending on others for almost anything. I pride myself on getting where I've gotten in my career by my hard work alone.

I am meticulous and think through almost every scenario where something could go wrong, that way I'm always prepared. Whether it's having backup vendors for an event, extra supplies, or even something as small as carrying a tide-pen for accidental spills—which funnily enough I forgot the other day when Theo spilled his coffee on me. Though I'm not sure how much a Tide pen would've helped with a sixteen-ounce cup of iced-coffee.

But Theo . . . Somehow he wiggled his way inside the fortress I've built so tightly around myself. I wouldn't use the *L* word, it's way too soon for that, but it's the closest I've let someone get to it ever before.

My phone rings, interrupting my internal word vomit. I look and see it's Fran calling. Something must be really wrong if she's calling me on the trip that she forced me to go on because I needed a "better work-life balance."

"Hello, Fran. Is everything alright?"

"Oh yes! I'm so sorry to interrupt what I hope has been a relaxing and self-centering trip, so I'll make this quick. Cynthia" —her assistant—"said she received an email notification that your flight got canceled tomorrow morning, but that the airline is working on rebooking you a new flight for Sunday. Please feel free to stay another night on us, so you don't need to worry about finding last minute lodging somewhere else."

I pause my packing and take a seat on my bed. "Oh, okay. Thank you for notifying me of the change. Will Cynthia be texting me with the new flight information or should I just be checking the app throughout the day for an update?"

"I'm assuming she'll text you when they rebook you, but

knowing what I know about you, you'll also be updating the app constantly." She's not wrong. Though I won't lie, checking the app hasn't exactly been my top priority. I hadn't even thought about checking if the flight was running on time before I started parking.

"Okay. Thanks for the heads up, Fran."

"You're welcome, and I'm sorry for the delay. Enjoy your extra night!"

I say my goodbyes and end the call. I guess I didn't need to pack just yet, but at least it's basically done. Glancing around the room, I take mental note of the items still out and my eyes freeze on the amazing bathtub.

I have a couple of hours until dinner, so why shouldn't I take advantage of this tub one more time? After starting the water, I grab my e-reader and hop in once the tub is filled, immediately diving into my mafia romance.

It's ironic to be reading this book right now. It has a female lead who is normally reserved because of her past, but the main love interest is opening her world up with experiences she wouldn't normally do.

Of course there's more sex going on than what I've experi— wait. Now that I think about it, Theo and I actually have had a lot of hot spicy moments over these last few days. Like the stuff made of romance novel dreams. Though I do wish we weren't interrupted with the honey. I can only imagine how far that would've gotten. He is, by far, the best I've had in all departments, like no comparison at all. So inventive and it's only been a few days.

I mentally chide myself.

And that's all you're going to get, Lindsay.

At least I got gifted this extra night. I should probably find Theo and let him know. I know he's busy with the wedding, so if I want to make the most of my time with him, I could use my extra day to help him with all the preparations. Plus, depending on the time of my flight on Sunday, maybe even help him with the ceremony.

After reading a couple chapters, I dry myself off and put on some clothes.

Stepping into the hallway, I run into Ettie.

"Oh hello, dear. Looking for someone?"

"Hello, Ettie. Do you know if Theo is still in the office?"

"I'm not sure, but he wasn't in the kitchen when I left, so he's either in the office or getting the outside ready for this weekend."

"Okay. Thanks, Ettie."

"Have fun!" She knowingly grins and walks off.

Of course she's aware of Theo and me. I'm sure she's seen him sneaking out of my room or us together at one of the breakfasts. And even if she hadn't, I'm sure Jean has already told her and Mateo. Then again, we weren't really hiding it were we?

As I approach the office, I knock causing the door to open. I take a peek and see that Theo's inside. He's on the phone with his back turned to the door so he must've not heard me knocking.

Assuming just that, I spin to leave. I don't want to disturb Theo when he's clearly busy, but his whisper-shout stops me in my tracks.

"Don't go."

I turn and see a soft smile gracing his stunning face with warmth in his emerald eyes. I mouth "okay" and pull out a chair, but he waves his hand, motioning me to come closer.

Theo rests his phone on his shoulder and grabs my waist, hoisting me onto his lap.

Straddling him, I wrap my hands around the nape of his neck and play with his hair while he finishes his call. From the sound of it, it's someone from the wedding. He made a comment about the mother of the groom being a little difficult, so perhaps it's her.

I've definitely dealt with my fair share of difficult clients over the years. It's an unfortunate part of the business, but I find those clients make you even more grateful for the calm and joyous ones. Plus, with a bit of practice, you tend to learn how to handle the high maintenance ones.

He's still on the call when he pulls down the strap of my dress and starts kissing the column of my neck.

God, I don't know what it is about that spot, but it immediately melts me into a puddle whenever he gives it any sort of attention. Responding to whoever he's talking to, his voice rumbles on my skin. He's not even saying words, just sounds of agreement. I'm definitely distracting him at this point.

I pull back a little, allowing him to focus on the call, but he uses that change of position to kiss and suck the swells of my breasts, pulling the dress down even farther. *Fuck me*, I mentally groan. I'm half tempted just to grab the phone and end the call right now.

As I'm half undressed and still sitting on his lap, Theo continues teasing me all while somehow coherent enough to still be listening to the call.

You know what? Fuck it. Two can play this game.

I kiss his cheek and wiggle out of his lap. Reaching for my other strap, I pull it down causing my dress to fall into a puddle of fabric on the floor. Sliding off my shoes, I step out of fabric and am left in my black lace bra with a matching thong. I make a show of walking around the desk and locking the office door.

No interruptions this time.

Reaching Theo's chair, I sit my ass on the desk in front of him and cross my legs, splaying my arms behind me which showcases my breasts as they take center stage. I'm definitely sitting on paperwork right now, and normally, I would respect someone's work space. After all, I'd have a shit-fit if someone messed up the paperwork on *my* desk—then again my desk is never this messy. But he's the one who started this game. I'm just seeing how far he's willing to take it, sort of like a sexy game of chicken.

All I keep thinking is how this has to be the most vulnerable position I've put myself in. I've placed my body out on the desk as my own personal offering to him. I feel so out of control, yet the most in control I've ever been. In fact, that's how I'd describe my whole relationship with Theo.

Relationship? Is that what we're going to call it now? Lindsay, come on—I lose my train of thought as Theo pulls my legs apart.

Tangling my thong straps in his fingers, he lifts my hips up off the desk to pull my panties off, leaving me in nothing but my bra.

"What are you doing to me, *ma chérie*?" he mumbles so quietly I almost don't hear him.

Kissing the inside of my thigh, he works his hands closer to where I need him. He's still balancing the phone on his shoulder when he strokes his thumb lightly between the apex of my thighs. I roll my head back, enjoying the feel of him. When he reaches my opening, I let out a soft moan. He quickly moves his hand up and teasingly pinches my clit in punishment, which only causes me to moan louder. I'm expecting another pinch as my punishment, but am surprised when he stands up and stuffs something in my mouth.

What is it? It's fabric of some sort. But I quickly lose interest when I feel Theo's hands gripping my hips, fingertips digging into my ass cheeks, and his breath on my clit. Oh my god. Is he going to eat me out while on the phone with this poor person?

The feel of his tongue on me is answer enough as I instantly lose the ability to care. He shoves two fingers inside of me while continuing to lick the sensitive spot above. I whimper as he pulls his head away, but immediately groan around the ball of fabric in my mouth as I fall back into bliss, relishing the feel of his other hand taking over for his mouth.

"Yes, I understand, Mrs. Turlock."

I lift my head up just enough to see the irritation on his face, but he quickly replaces it with a look that promises ruination once he sees me staring at him. He picks up speed with his thumb while using the distraction to add another finger inside of me. The pressure building mixed with his thumb's rhythm is enough to get me to the edge of completion, but his mouth on my thigh is the final sensation that pushes me over.

I'm panting through my release and around the fabric stuffed in my mouth while he slows his movements, easing me down from my climax.

Finally coming out of my euphoric haze, Theo says, "Mrs. Turlock, I assure you everything is being handled, and I would like to continue to reassure you, but an urgent matter just came on"—he clears his throat—"across my desk."

Theo has the balls to wink at me, smirking during the whole exchange and making me drop my jaw which then causes the mysterious fabric to fall out of my mouth.

"I look forward to seeing you and your family tomorrow. Have a safe flight!"

Dropping his phone on the desk, he stands up and grips my waist, hoisting me up to stand in front of him. "That was a very naughty thing you just did, *ma chérie*." He spins me so I'm facing the desk and spanks my ass, just enough to sting but definitely not hard enough to leave a mark. "Now bend over like a good girl, and get that pretty ass up for me."

CHAPTER THIRTY-TWO

THEO

Well, fuck me. Lindsay knew exactly what she was doing when she stripped down in front of me. I tried my best to be professional while I spoke to Karen for what feels like the fiftieth time this week, but seeing Lindsay in nothing but her lacy, poor excuse for a bra and thong, I couldn't hold back any longer.

Making her come while on the phone with a client I've had nothing but problems with probably wasn't one of my most brilliant ideas, but it gave me the motivation I needed to end the call. One of which was going absolutely nowhere.

I can't help myself around Lindsay. The magnetic pull of her has me in constant need to be near her. Touch her. Kiss her. Make her mine.

Gliding my hand from her shoulder blades down to her lower back, I unhook her bra while lightly pushing her down into position. The lace falls down her arms, landing in a puddle on the desk. And now with her ass presented to me as the juiciest peach, I have the need to lean in and snag a bite.

Lindsay lets out a yelp while pushing her ass out farther. I smack it again, quickly replacing my hand with my lips soon after to soothe the burn.

While I unbuckle my pants with one hand, I pull the foil wrapper I'm getting used to carrying out of my pocket. After not having one that first night, I vowed to never go without one around her again.

I lean down close to her ear while stroking myself over the rubber, tsking as I shake my head in mock disapproval. "That was a very"—I nibble on her ear—"*very* naughty thing you did."

She moans while arching her back, shifting her weight onto her elbows. I rub my hands down her sides, one parking on her left hip and the other exploring further. Of course, she's already soaking, her body begging for me.

Lining up my dick to her opening, I murmur softly in her ear, "Think you can keep quiet this time, *ma chérie*?"

Her answer is a vigorous nod of her head, so without any more teasing, I fill her to the hilt, both of us groaning at the sensation.

"Shhh," I hush before I lick two fingers and glide them around her clit as she whimpers. "You don't want to be interrupted again, do you?"

The hand on her waist migrates up to her breast in slow, feather light touches only to stop when my fingers reach her hard nipple. I playfully roll it between the pads of my two fingers and repeat the same motion with my other hand, only between her legs. The movement causes her to clench on my dick as I thrust into her.

"Oh, Theo!" she shouts out and I bring my other hand up to pinch both of her nipples as punishment for her outburst. But I quickly reward her with kisses down her back while thrusting deeper as I massage her breasts.

"Yes! Fuck yes!" She tightens while moaning curses as she comes undone.

"Such a filthy mouth." I bring a hand down lower to tease her, knowing full well how sensitive she is from coming.

"Theo! You can't—" she pants and wiggles her ass against me. "Fuck, I'm going to—" Her head drops forward as she comes again, pulsing around me. She's so fucking tight that I have to move my hand to her hip, gripping her hard as I finish.

After we both calm our breathing, I slowly pull out of her and quickly discard the condom. Wrapping my arms around her, I bring her up to me, peppering kisses on her neck and shoulder as our breathing levels out.

"That was—"

"Phenomenal," I finish for her before kissing her cheek.

The phone rings, but one glance at the caller ID tells me all I need to know about the call, making it easy to let it go to voicemail. Lindsay, however, rushes to get herself back into the clothes piled on the floor.

"I should go. Please," she motions to the phone. "Take it. I'm sure it's important. I'll leave."

I look her up and down. Her shoes are in her hands. Dress disheveled and hanging on her haphazardly while her hair looks like she was just properly fucked—or more appropriately looks like she just came three times. Which is one-hundred-percent accurate. Her cheeks are still flushed from said orgasms.

"What? Is there something on my face?" she asks. She brushes her fingers over her face before looking down at her dress, straightening the fabric with the hand holding her shoes.

"Nothing is on your face. I was just admiring your beauty."

I walk over to her and run my fingers through her auburn hair, combing it back. She truly is the most gorgeous woman, especially as more blush creeps into her cheeks after what I just said. She seems to be uncomfortable whenever I compliment her, leading me to believe she doesn't get them often, which is preposterous.

"Theo?"

"Yes?"

"I, um, forgot to mention this before we, um—"

"Fucked?"

"Well, yes." She chuckles and pushes my chest away, but I'm quick to move my hands to her waist to not allow her to go any farther. "My flight tomorrow got canceled. I haven't received my new flight information yet, but I should be leaving on Sunday. I know the wedding party arrives tomorrow, but is there any chance I can extend my stay one more night?"

"Oh, um—"

"I'll even help out with preparations, and of course, you can charge me whatever rate you want. I mean, I guess I'm not paying, my company is, but . . . " she adds, clearly nervous based on her rambling.

I'm thrilled to not have to say goodbye yet but all of the rooms are booked for the wedding.

"If not, I guess I can always get a hotel near the airport for one night." She takes my silence as a no. "You know what, I'll do that. Just forget I asked, okay?" She's not mad, just consumed in a scenario she's conjured in her head.

"Wait, no. Lindsay, stop." I look into her eyes and emphasize taking in a deep breath. "Breathe."

She reluctantly follows.

"Good. Now out." I mimic the motion alongside her. "Now, one more time."

Seemingly calm, or at least calmer, I continue with my own train of thought, only out loud to keep Lindsay from spiraling again.

"Now, let's try this again. Tomorrow night, we are fully booked with the party." I pause and give her a sympathetic look when I see she's biting her lip as she looks down, obviously defeated. "But"—that perks her back up—"you can always stay in the family house with me. I can take the couch and you can take my bed."

"Theo, that is very kind of you, but I couldn't possibly ask you to sleep on the couch."

"You're not asking. I'm offering." I pull her closer and kiss her on the top of her head. "And if you're so uncomfortable with it, I can always sleep in my bed." I lean into her ear and whisper, "With you." I pinch her ass only for her to playfully swat it away.

"Let's just see how the day goes. Maybe a night on the couch will do you some good," she huffs.

The phone rings again, but this time Lindsay hands it to me, accepting the call before I can send it to voicemail. I roll my eyes at her, dramatically shrugging as I answer. "*Bonjour—*"

Before I can even finish my greeting, Karen is rattling off more demands for this weekend. Lindsay kisses me on my cheek and mouths, "I'll see you at dinner," before walking out of the office, leaving me to another grueling call about last minute changes.

CHAPTER THIRTY-THREE

LINDSAY

When I reach my room, I use the time to text my family about the extra night. While texting them, I get a text from Cynthia with the new flight itinerary.

> CYNTHIA:
>
> Here are your new flight times:
>
> MRS-CDG - 8:30PM -10PM
>
> CDG-RDU - 1:25PM - 4:10PM
>
> I'm so sorry for the long layover but that's the next flight they had available. You'll arrive in Raleigh Monday late afternoon.
>
> Please let me know if you have any questions or issues.

Ugh. That's fifteen hours I have to wait around in Paris. Maybe I'll get a hotel room, or one of those sleeping pods at the airport. I know I've researched those for a few guests doing international travel for their weddings. I guess I could even take a train and see some sights in the morning before the flight home.

My phone vibrates in my palm, and I see it's Emma and Tory texting in the sisters' chat.

TORY:

Is it a good thing or a bad thing you have an extra day?

EMMA:

Yeah, how's 'pool sex' and 'best orgasm of your life' guy?

LINDSAY:

He has a name.

TORY:

So you're still hooking up with him?

LINDSAY:

. . .

EMMA:

It's definitely a good thing that she's staying another night.

LINDSAY:

But the hotel is booked out, so I have to stay in his room.

EMMA:

Aw, it's your very own one-bed trope.

Leave it to Emma to put a romantic spin to it. I only have myself to blame.

When I was in college, she stumbled upon my stash of romance books. She was a bit young to start reading them, but I promised her once she got out of high school, she could *borrow* any book she was interested in reading. But you know how baby sisters are, and before I knew it, she had stolen almost all my favorite books. When I was boxing up my room for my new apartment at the time, I found I was missing a chunk of my library. The first place I looked was Emma's room. Lo and behold, she had been hoarding them like a squirrel with nuts preparing for winter.

LINDSAY:

No, he's sleeping on the couch.

TAYLOR:

Sure he is.

Of course she'd join the chat with a sarcastic text.

EMMA:

Until you have a nightmare and he has to soothe you.

OR!!!

Or the heat goes out and you have to cuddle for warmth!

TORY:

Emma you read too many romance books.

EMMA:

No such thing.

LINDSAY:

Well there was a storm and the power did actually go out the other night.

EMMA:

••

LINDSAY:

But to answer your first question Tory, yes.

I'm happy to be staying another night, but I fear it just drags out the inevitable.

EMMA:

Been there. Done that.

If you want it to work, you should go for it. Do what you do best, Linds.

Pull a you and take control of the situation!

We love you!

TORY:

Love you, sis.

TAYLOR:

Enjoy your last two nights.

LINDSAY:

Thanks ladies.

With nothing left to do, I take a shower and get myself ready for the rest of the night.

I would use my dress from earlier but there's a few drops of honey from our, um, tasting. Instead, I choose to dress up a little and grab one of the dresses I haven't worn yet. It's a rich sage color with sleeves that reach the mid upper arm. The dress is fitted with a ruched bust with buttons down the back. On me, the gown hits mid-calf with a thigh high slit on the left side.

With no curling iron at my disposal, I do my best to work my magic with the blow dryer and brush. After adding a little blush and lipstick, I strap on my sandals. Not the dressiest shoes but they go fine with my dress. Plus, they're all I have except tennis shoes or the work flats I wore at the airport.

Still having a little time, I decide to take a walk down to the lavender fields. As I stroll the grounds, I feel the warmth from the afternoon sun, but there's a small breeze blowing, not so powerful to mess up my hair but enough to provide a break from the heat. It's so peaceful out here. Quiet and calm. Honestly, it really does make for the perfect place to relax.

I remain still in the moment. Breathing in long inhales of the relaxing scent. Letting it take over my every sense while I close my eyes and just *be*.

I'm not sure how long I stand there, but I'm startled by Theo's hands sliding around my waist. He leans his chin on my shoulder and gazes out to the field with me. His chest is pressed against my back, raising and falling in sync with mine. Neither one of us speaks as we're both perfectly content in hearing nothing but the slight sounds of bees buzzing around the purple flowers.

We stand there for what feels like hours before he squeezes me while giving a sweet kiss to my cheek. "Dinner is ready, *ma chérie*," he whispers softly in my ear.

I nuzzle into him then start to turn in his arms. "I'm not sure I'm ready to leave yet."

He softens his expression and rubs his thumbs in soothing circles on my lower back in answer. He knows it's not the leaving for dinner I'm talking about.

"Come on." He rubs his palm up my back, following the line of tiny buttons. "Let's enjoy dinner first and then we can worry about what happens after. Yeah?"

"Okay," I agree before he leads us back to the estate, but we don't go inside.

As we turn the corner to the patio, I spy what I assume to be our dinner table for the night, dressed in front of the pool. It's covered in white and cream linens with a beautiful bouquet of various flowers at the center. Though the sun is still hanging in the sky, I can see a glow of light illuminating the pool from all the floating candles. They highlight the colorful flowers bobbing along its shimmering surface. It's absolutely enchanting. I think I actually have an image just like this on one of my Pinterest boards.

The heat has started to die down and the shadow from the house provides some shade, creating another barrier from the sun.

"You did all of this?" I ask, utterly shocked with the otherworldly sight surrounding me.

"I had some help with the setup. While I was the brains, Ettie and Jean helped me with the setup."

"But why?"

"Well, I was expecting it to be your last night and wanted to create something memorable for your time here with us." He rubs his thumb over the back of my hand and turns to me. "Your time with *me*."

"It's—" I take a deep breath. It's the nicest thing anyone has ever done for me. It's so thoughtful and a complete surprise. And I hate surprises. But I will definitely make an exception for this. With my line of work, I've seen some pretty spectacular setups, but this takes first place. "Thank you. This was very thoughtful of you." I squeeze his hand before I add, "And Ettie and Jean. I'll have to thank them both tomorrow."

"I think Jean was willing to do anything after your little peep show this morning." He smirks proudly with his dimple on full display.

"Hey!" I shout as I pinch his waist as he twists his body, trying and failing to avoid my fingers. "The only reason for said 'peep show' was you and your need to taste my honey."

Theo wraps me up in his arms and kisses my chest, right where said honey was poured. "Your *honey*, huh?" He continues his kissing, squeezing my waist and crushing me into his body.

"You know what I mean," I scold but it comes out breathy.

He lifts his head and gives me another squeeze before backing away. "Come on. Let's go eat before I devour something other than dinner."

I bite my lip as my blushing heats my face, following him to the beautiful table before us.

CHAPTER THIRTY-FOUR

LINDSAY

"So," I start before patting my mouth, making sure I don't have food on my lips. "When you aren't being a super-duper handy-man with flipping houses, what do you do?"

He clears his throat. "I, ah, volunteer my time helping those in need with small repairs around their houses."

I scoff. "You do not."

He gasps in mock offense. "Yes, I do!"

I shake my head. "No. You can't."

"And why not?" He eyes me suspiciously while he waits for my response.

"Because if you do that—the whole super-nice-guy-with-a-big-heart thing—it just makes it all that much harder to . . ."

"To . . ." He waves his arm, motioning me to continue with my thought.

"It makes it all the more difficult to leave you," I rush out, sighing when I realize how childish that sounds.

"Oh, *ma chérie*," he starts, but I hold up my hand to stop him. I don't want his pity.

"Can we just go back to talking about . . . *anything* else?" He gives me a soft smile with kind eyes. "Please?"

We go back to talking about his skillset. From the sound of it, there isn't much Theo can't do and if he hasn't done a job before, he has no reservations about diving head first and learning how to tackle it.

"At first it was hard, growing up with unconventional summers. Leaving the States as soon as school got out, only to return a few days before school was in session. But the time spent around my family and the knowledge gained in helping around the estate was invaluable."

I nod.

"Hell, that's inspired my dream to one day open my own B&B stateside."

"With a beehive out back, I assume." I chuckle.

"I wouldn't have it any other way," he says grinning. "But what about you? Any core memories that lead you to the life you live now?" He's joking with me but I can't help but be transported back in time. Flashbacks of the car crash that forever changed our family.

"You could say that," I say before taking a bite of dinner. But the food now tastes bland.

"Lindsay?" Though I hear Theo's voice, I'm still stuck with the image of me waiting outside of Mom's crashed car, waiting for someone to help her, all while taking turns with Taylor to sooth little Emma.

"Hmm?" I ask absentmindedly.

"Where'd you just go?"

"What?" I shake my head. "Oh, sorry. Got caught up in a memory."

I feel Theo's hand on mine before I hear him. "You don't have to keep it to yourself, you know. If you want to share, I'm here."

"Oh, no. I don't want to dull the mood." I pull my hand free of his to pat my face with the napkin, attempting to distract myself enough to not break down.

"I'm not going anywhere, Linds."

But you *are*, I want to protest.

My eyes meet his and god, no matter the reality of our time left, I feel so safe in this little bubble we've created. I take a sip of water to clear my throat before I tell him about that dreaded day.

"I was eleven. It was a scary time, filled with uncertainty. All of us sisters have our own views on what happened that day, and the months that followed.

"Mom was driving us home from school one day, and we were nearly to the house when a car came rushing from the other direction, swerving all over the road. It all happened so fast, but from what I can remember, Mom tried to veer left to miss the other car."

Somehow my hand ends up in Theo's grasp again and his thumb rubbing soothing circles on the top of my hand, coaxing me to continue with my story.

"Before we knew it, she had lost control. The car ran straight into the ditch that ran parallel with the road. Mom hit her head so hard, it knocked her out. I knew something was wrong when she wouldn't wake up."

Theo whispers something under his breath a lot like "Jesus Christ, Linds."

"Luckily, all of us kids were wearing our seatbelts. The airbags actually did more damage than the crash itself. Tory was quick to act. After attempting to wake Mom up with no luck, she decided it was time to get help.

"The car was leaning at a pretty steep incline, so before she left, she helped unstrap Taylor, Emma, and me, situating us next to the trunk of the vehicle where we'd wait for help. We had no cell phones back then, so the only way to get help was her walking to the nearest house and asking them to call for help."

"What happened to your mom, Linds?" he asks with sorrow thick in his voice.

"Oh, she's fine now," I reassure. "There was no way to tell how long we waited for Tory to come back, or how long Mom was out, but that was the longest wait in my life. Emma was crying for most of it."

Every now and then I'll still hear a phantom cry and I swear it's Emma's cry from that day.

"Taylor and I both took turns trying to calm Emma down. Whenever I wasn't consoling her, I was checking on Mom. Her face was covered in blood, but her chest was still rising and falling, proving she was still breathing. Even at eleven, I knew that was a good sign, but I had no idea just how much damage the crash had actually done."

I pause, taking a break from telling a story I haven't had to tell in so long. Sure, the topic comes up from time to time in our family, but I never have to tell it detail by detail like I'm doing now. I guess I don't even have to do that. I could've just said the girls in the family had a bad car crash when I was younger. But I feel safe with Theo. Something I haven't felt in a long time.

I wipe a tear threatening to fall before I continue. "I hated being stuck. Hated having to wait and depend on others to show up when I needed them most. I had zero control on when help for Mom would arrive. I was doing everything I could in that moment, but it still wasn't enough."

Feeling my throat dry up, I try my best to push through the rest of the story.

"There wasn't a single car that passed us by while we were waiting for Tory's return with help. But once she did come back, an ambulance was quick to arrive shortly after. Then Dad in his own truck."

I close my eyes and it's like a movie of that day playing in my mind. I can vividly see Dad's truck speeding down the road. See him rushing out of the vehicle leaving the door wide open as he runs to Mom.

"The look on Dad's face while they got Mom situated in the ambulance will forever haunt my dreams."

"You did good, girls. Mom will be okay. Let's get in the truck and follow her to the hospital."

"It wasn't until Mom finished her scans that we found out she had internal bleeding from one of the three ribs that broke and punctured her lung. All of us girls were lucky to walk away with only a few minor cuts and bruises. Mom had a long recovery after that, affecting our family in so many ways. Some of which have had lasting effects."

My eyes are still closed, not wanting to open them in fear of what will fall out when I do. Even though I can't see, I feel Theo come closer to me. His hand moves from mine to wrap around my back, the other arm quick to join.

"Ever since then, I've found it very difficult to put myself in situations where I won't be in control," I confess. A statement I haven't said to anyone but my therapists. "And even then, I still obsess over every single thing that could go wrong. I fear for the day something goes wrong again and I'm caught unprepared and helpless while I wait for someone else to fix the problem."

I feel Theo's head on my shoulder as his embrace gets tighter. "I'm so sorry you and your sisters had to experience that at such a young age. I can only imagine how scary that was."

I take a breath, feeling a weight lifted off my shoulders. "You know, I never really talked about it with anyone besides my family and professionals before. I just kind of—"

"Internalized it?" Theo finishes.

I blink my eyes open and turn my head, finding Theo's sparkling eyes. It looks like I'm not the only one with misty eyes here.

"Yeah. I mean, obviously it's clear that the trauma, if that's what you can call it, manifested in different ways for each of us. Tory still feels tremendous guilt for leaving all of us, Taylor hates emotions amongst other things, and Emma used to take any opportunity to not get in a car."

"And you"—he squeezes my hands—"bury yourself in work because it's an activity you deem safe. Your job is one you thrive in because you have almost complete control of how it gets executed for the client. And when it doesn't go as planned, you always have a backup plan. Even if things feel out of control, you find a way to take it back." He takes my silence as doubt. "Right? Tell me I'm wrong?"

I chuckle, but it's lacking a single drop of warmth. "I guess you got me all figured out then." I pull back, shaking my head.

I guess that *is* why I love my job. I still have to depend on others to show up and do their job. But I have the authority and power to call in a replacement or correct an issue before the client is aware.

Don't get me wrong, shit can and has hit the fan before, but never once has it been from something that I couldn't have planned for in advance. Hell, I even have a "worst case scenario" list in my notes apps for when the worst of the worst happens. I never want to be caught unprepared.

"I didn't mean to offend you, Lindsay. I only meant that I see you," Theo says softly. "Please," he reaches for my hand again and I let him take it. "I'm sorry." He brings my hand up and kisses the back of it. "Let me make it up to you with dessert."

"I guess I can't leave without at least having a little taste." My smile is subtle, but it's enough to make Theo grin right back.

"Trust me, you'll be licking your plate clean with this one."

He clears the table and I take the opportunity to gaze around us. The sun has finally started to set and the glow from the candles in and around the pool sets such a dreamy landscape. After putting the used dishes on the rolling tray, Theo places two plates down on the table. One for him and one for me.

Looking down, I see the dish has a creamy purple dome in the center with little gelatin and what looks to be white chocolate bees decorating the rim. A mold of honeycomb sits proudly on top of the dome. The plate is so beautiful I almost don't want to ruin it by eating it. Almost.

I take my fork and load it up, making sure to get every layer of the mousse-based dessert. When the dessert hits my tongue, my taste buds explode with flavor.

The creaminess from the mousse balances out the lavender,

while the honey is the perfect complement to the flavor profile on the dish before me. There's even a crunch from the bottom layer. I'm not sure what flavor I'm picking up from it, but the texture gives a nice break to the smoothness of the mousse.

"Oh my god. This is amazing," I praise, only to immediately shove another bite of the dessert in my mouth. I'm not sure how I'll live without it when I go back home.

"I know. It truly is the best dessert. Mateo is a mastermind." He's eating his slower, savoring the purple treat while I continue to devour mine. "Although, I think this may be the best one he's made." A wolfish smile appears on Theo's face before he adds, "And to think, it's all thanks to your . . . honey." I lower my head, blushing and giggling before taking another bite.

CHAPTER THIRTY-FIVE

THEO

Tonight was amazing. From the decorations, to the dinner, and to the dessert. Plus being able to share this time with Lindsay made it all absolute perfection. I'm beyond thankful I get one more night with her, but I need to figure out a way to keep whatever *this* is going.

We both flew over from Raleigh. Is it hopeful thinking she's from the surrounding area? I guess I can just ask. She's already been so open with me tonight. Man, to have to deal with such a traumatic event when you're a child, how could it *not* have a lasting effect?

As I start cleaning up the table, I casually ask, "Do you have your new flight information yet?"

She nods. "My flight out of Marseille isn't until eight-thirty Sunday night. I know you and the rest of the staff will be busy with the reception, so I'll call a taxi or something."

"Eight-thirty? That seems late. I'm guessing you have a long layover in Paris then? Unless, you're flying through another airport. I know London has some early morning flights," I say, sitting back down and refilling our wine glasses.

"Yeah, it's through Paris. The app says it's about a fifteen-hour layover. I was thinking about renting a sleeping pod."

"You could even sneak out to the city and visit a few spots if you move quickly enough around the city."

"I was thinking about that, but I think I'd be stressing too much about making sure I get back in time. I'll save the sight-seeing for when I have more time to really see it all."

I nod. She brings up a good point. No one should ever feel like they have to rush their experience with Paris.

"But someday I'll see it. Do it right. Really experience the Eiffel Tower."

"Was that an innuendo for a threesome, Lindsay?" I ask incredulously.

"Definitely not." She chuckles. "Just the thought of it makes me sweat."

"Good to know, because I have zero intentions of ever sharing you with anyone, *ma chérie*."

I pull her in for a kiss, but this one has a slight touch of possessiveness to it, especially when I nip at her lower lip.

As I finish clearing the table, she clears her throat.

"Anyways . . . my last flight to Raleigh doesn't leave Paris until the early afternoon so I'll have plenty of time to grab some gifts for my family."

So her last stop *is* Raleigh. I can't be *that* lucky, can I?

"Do you have much of a drive after you land?" Please, say no. Please, say no.

"Not too bad, my apartment is only about a twenty-minute drive east of the airport."

Oh fuck yeah! Game ON!

It is indeed my lucky day. She's got to live somewhere downtown. I don't want to come on too strong though. Especially not when I'm barely holding myself back with how excited I am knowing that there's a real chance of continuing this once I get stateside. Whenever that will be.

I know Ma said they'd be back sooner than they originally

thought, but that doesn't mean I can just rush right out as soon as they arrive. There will definitely be an adjustment period, one where I'm needed to help out with the new workload. But when I *can* leave . . .

But how could I ask Lindsay to wait for me. Sure, I have a rough ballpark of when I'm coming back, but things could change. Ma said I would most likely be needed for the rest of summer, so maybe five or six more weeks.

But tons of people do long distance relationships. Especially with the technology we have nowadays, and six hours for a time change isn't so bad. I can call her around noon my time when she wakes up, or maybe even when I go to bed and it's late afternoon for her.

And I can only imagine how good the phone sex with Lindsay would be. Fuck. Watching her touch herself while talking to me with that filthy mouth of hers, I'm getting hard just thinking about it.

"Theo?" Lindsay's voice wakes me from my momentary daydream of fucking my hand while watching her come over video call.

"Hmm? I'm sorry, my head was somewhere else."

"Were you ready to go to bed?" she asks with a coy smile.

"Oh." I must've zoned out longer than I thought, unless she chugged her glass of wine. "Yes. Your room again tonight?" She smiles and nods. "Why don't you head up and I'll take care of the cleanup."

"Oh, I don't mind—"

"It is my pleasure to serve you, *ma chérie*. Please," I stand and hold out my hand to help her up. "I'll only be a few minutes longer."

"If you insist." She kisses my cheek. "But I really don't—"

I interrupt that train of thought with a kiss to her lips. After all, it's hard to talk when your mouth is busy.

Pulling out of our embrace, I squeeze her ass. "Now go and get comfortable. I'll be right up."

Lindsay lets out a little grunt and reluctantly starts heading inside. I playfully smack her ass to keep her moving forward. She turns and scrunches her nose at me.

"I promise to make it worth your while," I taunt and that seems to get her moving, leaving me alone with my thoughts.

It takes me far longer than it should to clean up the patio. Luckily when Jean set this up, he was nice enough to offer to gather the used candles tomorrow morning as long as I blew them all out. Which seems easy enough, but the ones in the pool are a bit tricky to get to. So much so, I'm half tempted to just let them burn themselves out. I mean chlorine isn't flammable, so what's the worst that could happen? But I quickly scratch that idea when I remember the pool net. Work smarter, not harder.

Afterwards, I make sure all the dishes we used are loaded in the dishwasher and head up to Lindsay's room. I feel my phone buzz in my pocket, pausing me mid-step. Pulling out my phone, Ma's face lights up the screen.

"Hi, Ma."

"*Mon fils*!" she greets. "Grandpa is doing better than expected. If tomorrow continues to go well, Dad might be able to drive home on Sunday for the wedding.

"Amazing news! Just have Dad text if he's able to come. Are you doing alright?"

"Oh, everything is just fine. I just can't wait to go home and sleep in my own bed. You know how miserable these hospital pull outs are," she huffs. "How's Miss Hartman?"

"She's amaz—" I stop myself before I go anything further. "She's doing great. But her flight got pushed back to Sunday."

"Oh no! Well, I hope you helped her find a hotel for that additional night."

"I took care of it." Which isn't a lie, I did *technically* take care of it.

"Glad to hear. Listen, I have to go, the nurse just got here. I'll talk to you soon."

"B—" A click tells me she hung up before I even finished the word. Tucking my phone back into my pocket, I make my way up to Lindsay's room.

I don't even knock before entering the room, which in hindsight is rude, but I have tunnel vision right now. After finishing those dishes, I'm like a hound on the hunt.

Only this hound found his beautiful prey passed out on her bed, hands tucked under her head with her knees pulled up to her stomach. She must've been tired from the day and just crashed. She looks so peaceful lying there on top of the comforter.

Deciding to not disturb her, I clean myself up and strip down to just my boxers in the bathroom. Shimmying into the bed with my best impression of a stealthy James Bond, I lie on my side facing her back. It's warm enough tonight that we don't need the blanket.

Though I know I'm trying not to wake her, I can't help but reach my arms around her. I pull her flush against my chest and steal a kiss to the back of her head. Lindsay stirs a little, but not enough to wake her.

I take a few breaths, relaxing into her while inhaling her scent, which now smells oddly like home. It's probably because she is using the lavender soap Ma makes. Even so, the scent is fitting for her.

I love how perfectly she fits in my arms, like we were made to do just this. I fall asleep soon after, dreaming about a future with her that now doesn't seem so far-fetched.

CHAPTER THIRTY-SIX

LINDSAY

Waking up in bed alone was not what I imagined would happen after such an amazing night with Theo, but here I am. I could've sworn I felt Theo sneak in last night, but his side isn't even warm.

There's a lot going on around the estate today, and I'm sure Ettie would appreciate me vacating the room as soon as possible, allowing her more time to clean the room for the wedding party.

I do my morning routine, making sure to pack my toiletries when I finish using them, then packing up any loose items I find around the room as I go. Doing a sweep of the sitting area, I spot a breakfast tray on my table that I must've missed.

So I wasn't imagining things; Theo *was* here at some point.

I let my tea steep while I do my final check to make sure I didn't forget anything. After feeling confident I packed everything, I take a brief break to enjoy my chocolate croissant and fruit. While moving one of my plates, I find a small note card hidden by the fruit plate.

You looked so peaceful sleeping this morning, I

couldn't disturb you. Come find me as soon as you're finished with breakfast.
-Theo

Sipping my tea, I think about all that happened this week. Theo played a huge part in my enjoyment, in more than one way. It wasn't just the mind-blowing sex, although that alone would make this the best trip ever.

No, I feel like I have a Theo shaped hole in the walls I've built around myself. This trip really forced me to slow down. Really experience the moment you're given.

I pretty much lived this trip on a day by day basis, never giving too much thought on what I was doing the next day. Just going along with wherever the day, or Theo, took me. It's only now that the end of my trip has come, I'm starting to plan things out.

Obviously I need to plan for transportation to the airport, allowing time for checking in. God only knows how long the line at security will be. I also need to see if I can borrow the hotel's printer to print out my new itinerary. I always like having a hard copy with me, just in case.

But as I think that, I'm not sure I want my life to always revolve around the negative "what-ifs" of the world anymore, constantly prepared for what unfortunate events may or may not happen. Sure, there should be some level of preparedness. And of course, things in life should follow some type of schedule. Meetings and project deadlines being a couple of them. But maybe there's something to be said for allowing myself time in the day to relax. Find time to do what feels right in the moment without the fear of me feeling like I'm losing control.

I have a week, if not longer, when I get home where I still won't be able to go to work. Hopefully, it will give me time to settle into this new mindset before starting work again.

As I finish my breakfast, I tidy up the table as much as possible, stacking the dishes up neatly on the tray. I look around the suite one more time, snag another photo of the view from the window above the bath, and walk out, bags in hand only to find Ettie on my way to the entry.

"Here, let me help you with those."

"Oh, no. It's really no trouble. Do you happen to know where it would be okay to store these? Or should I just wheel them over to the family house now?"

There's a split second where I swear I see shock in Ettie's face, but she hides it quickly, replacing it with a sweet smile.

"Just behind the desk is fine, dear." Her smile turns knowing. "He's just outside."

A blush rises to my cheeks, knowing I don't even have to ask who the "he" is she's referring to. "Thank you, Ettie."

She nods as I walk outside, but before I do I remember the printer.

"Ettie?"

"Yes, dear?"

"Do you think it'll be possible to print something?" I ask.

"Sure." She grabs something off the front desk and walks it over to me. "Just email it to the hotel's email listed here"—she hands me a business card—"and I'm sure Theo can print it for you."

"Great! Thanks, Ettie."

She waves before I turn back around and head outside. I quickly send an email asking Theo to please print the attached screenshot of the new itinerary to the email listed on the card before searching for him in the back of the estate.

Immediately, I find him directing people carrying linens and dish rentals. He must hear my footsteps on the gravel because he turns to me with a heart-melting smile that lights up his entire face. Theo greets me with a passion filled kiss, one hand in my hair and the other squeezing my waist.

"Good morning, *ma chérie*." He leans his forehead on mine. "How did you sleep?"

"Like the dead. I'm sorry I fell asleep before you came."

"Mmm," he murmurs. "Trust me, I am, too." He lets out a husky chuckle as he kisses my forehead.

"Before you came *upstairs*," I clarify, rolling my eyes, but continue sheepishly. "Though I'm also sorry about not doing the other as well."

"It's okay. I could tell from your bear-like snoring that you needed the rest." I lightly smack his upper arm making him let out a little laugh. "Sorry, a *cute* bear."

"We've talked about this. It's not the cuteness of the bear, but the bear comparison itself." I attempt to speak sternly, but lose my composure as he starts to laugh.

He grabs my hand, leading me away from the group of vendors. "Come on, Fluffy. We've got a lot of things to do today."

"I'm not sure how I feel about that nickname either."

"You don't like Fluffy?" He "hmms" as he scratches his stubble. "How about Furry?"

"Oh my god, definitely not Furry. I don't think any woman wants to be called Furry. Can't we just go back to *ma chérie* or *chère*? Or whatever it is you call me?"

"Well," he wraps his arm around my waist, pulling me closer to his side. "Those have the same, yet different meanings. *Ma chère* can be a more formal way to say 'my dear,' though some may use it while being sarcastic."

He eyes me and I get the sense he has done exactly that with me at some point.

"While *ma chérie* is more intimate, one used between parent and child. Or even a romantic partner." He kisses my neck before adding, "It means 'my darling' or 'dearest one.'"

I'm pretty sure he's used both with me, but I'm not sure when the change happened. Or maybe I'm just hearing him wrong? Maybe it's only been the first one, *ma chère*, and there isn't any endearment behind it at all. Maybe I'm just making the whole thing up in my head? We both know this will end tomorrow. Why would he call me something that by his definition is so intimate?

"Theo? Are you out here?" Ettie's voice interrupts my internal spiral.

"We're over here!" Theo shouts back then kisses my cheek. "Just so we're clear," he says leaning down to whisper in my ear, "I now only use *ma chérie* when talking to you."

And now I'm covered in goose bumps. It's like he knew exactly where my mind went. I release a breath, not realizing I was holding it in.

Clearly we're both feeling something for each other. And while that's great and all, there's no way for us to continue. I don't even know where he lives. I mean he was on my flight over, so maybe he lives in Raleigh, too? But seriously, what's the probability of that? The world can't be *that* small, can it? And even if that was the case, he's still here for god knows how long, helping out his family.

"Someone from the wedding party called and said their plane got delayed. They'll be arriving later tonight. She said they may even miss dinner altogether."

"Okay, thanks, Ettie. I'll be sure to let Mateo know."

"Already did. I was just informing you. Need anything right now?"

"No, but thanks for the offer. I think Lindsay and I have it under control out here."

"Looks like it." Ettie grins like a cat that caught the canary. "You know where to find me if you change your mind."

"Will do! Thanks again, Ettie," he chirps and she waves him off as she walks back into the hotel.

"Exactly what *are* we going to be doing today?" I ask, lifting my eyebrow.

"The florist had a family issue come up, so I told her as long as she could have someone deliver the flowers, we could handle the arrangements."

I have made more than a few floral arrangements in my line of work. Whether it be because the bride didn't like the flowers used, or we needed more because of last minute guests. You tend to get creative in order to avoid any potential meltdowns.

"Sounds good. Have the flowers been delivered yet?" I say looking around, not seeing a trace of a floral delivery.

"They dropped them off earlier this morning in the dining room. But you were probably snoring so loudly you didn't hear them."

"Ha, ha. Very funny," I deadpan.

Theo chuckles at my expense while waving me on. "Come on."

Walking into the dining room, I feel transported into a fairytale. The room is filled to the brim with all sorts of roses, sprigs of baby's breath, and various greenery. The roses vary in colors and size. There are a decent amount of white roses, but a spectrum of pinks, ranging from soft baby pink to a warm mauve color. It's literally a dream being surrounded by all of this.

"So," Theo claps before explaining the goal for this project. "We need one bouquet, one boutonniere, and two wrist-corsages. All of the remaining flowers can be made into various arrangement sizes. We just need three that look similar for the dinner tables."

I'm already mentally creating arrangements from the selection before us. "Sounds easy enough."

CHAPTER THIRTY-SEVEN

THEO

It in fact was *not* easy enough.

Very quickly, Lindsay and I found that the roses hadn't been stripped of thorns, causing both of us to prick our fingers multiple times.

"Maybe scissors might help? We could attempt dethorning these before arranging them," Lindsay suggests.

"You know what, I bet Jean might have something in the shed that might help. I'll be right back."

Walking outside, I'm quick to spot Jean helping place the arbor.

"Jean!" I holler. "Do you have anything that could help take thorns off of roses?"

"Check the shed!" he shouts back. "There should be a few pairs of garden strippers. Just return them when you're done!"

I wave and thank him before searching the shed. Sure enough, two pairs are sitting right on top of a workbench. If only everything was that easy to find.

"Ready to strip?" I announce as I enter the dining room.

I hear someone clear their throat, but it takes a minute before

I realize who it came from. "Oh, sorry Mateo. I didn't know you were in here."

"Mhmm," he huffs while stomping out of the room.

"Thanks for the ideas, Mateo!" Lindsay shouts as he leaves.

"Mateo gave you ideas? On *flowers*?" I say incredulously, doubt clear on my face.

"Many actually."

"He actually *talked* to you?"

She laughs like it's no big deal. "Yes, Theo. Mateo talked about all the different ways we could make arrangements with the various sizes of vases here. He also gave me some tips on making flowers last longer. He's really a sweet man."

"Mateo? The man that was just in here?" I ask, pointing to the door he just disappeared behind. "Mateo the Grouch?"

She lightly shoves my shoulder at that last jab.

"Come on, we have flowers to strip." She grabs a pair of strippers out of my hands and starts to go to town on the roses.

The garden tools really pay off with the amount of roses we had to get through. Although, about half way through stripping the copious amounts of roses, we realize we don't need to strip the roses in the arrangements, just the ones being handled.

"Wow. I'm impressed. Not only do these look stunning, you made these *fast*," I praise.

"It's not my first rodeo."

"You don't say," I tease with a knowing look.

She rolls her eyes and acts unimpressed. But I know my eyes aren't playing jokes on me when I see the slight blush rising on the apples of her cheeks.

After completing all the arrangements, we sneak off to the kitchen and grab a bite to eat, all while trying not to bother Mateo while he works his magic with the wedding cake.

"So what else needs to be done?" Lindsay asks as I plate our lunch.

Ma had a sketch made up of where the ceremony and reception

are supposed to be, making setup less stressful. "The main thing is that they want the ceremony to have the lavender fields in the background. Jean already moved the arch over to the grass surrounding the field earlier this morning, so I'll just need to wrap roses around it early tomorrow, that way they won't wilt sitting out in the heat today."

"Sounds good. And what about the reception? Where's that happening?"

"We'll use the greenbelt between the pool and gravel walkway for the reception," I add before sitting down at the island.

Thankfully everything that needed to be delivered arrived earlier this morning, so setting up the tables and chairs should be a piece of cake, especially for only being a group of ten.

We were supposed to get another storm, but so far there's not a cloud in sight. If it does get stormy, we'll just follow the plan I had to meticulously map out for the groom's mother.

With everything going on today, I almost forgot to move Lindsay over to the family house.

"Are your bags in your room or did you already move them out?" I ask before biting into my *croque monsieur*; the cheese is melted to perfection today.

"I moved them this morning behind the desk in the entry. Want me to move them to your house?" she asks before taking a bite of the sandwich. A cheese string dangles from her mouth and crumbs drop everywhere.

"Don't worry. I'll get them. I'd like to show you the house so you know where you're staying tonight. But after, feel free to go relax, whether by the pool, in the hotel, or the family house."

"I don't—helping. You have—to do."

Honestly, I only catch every other word from her response. I'm so distracted watching her use her tongue to swipe at the bread crumbs on her lip, leaving them glossy and tempting me to take a taste.

"So is this a *croque monsieur* or *croque madame*?"

I startle and clear my throat. "*Croque monsieur*. The difference is *croque madame* has a fried egg on top. Sometimes poached."

"An egg for the woman. How fitting." She swipes her thumb across her bottom lip, catching all the leftover crumbs she missed with her tongue. "Which one do you prefer?"

"Depends on my mood. Either way is delicious." I snag another bite and finish chewing before I continue. "I will say, if the egg is nice and runny, it creates the perfect pairing with the crunch of the bread."

"I'll have to try one someday."

"Maybe I can—" But I get interrupted before I can finish my thought.

"Theo?" Ettie's voice travels through the kitchen.

"In here," I shout back.

"Oh good!" She pops in a second later. "I'm glad I found you two. A weather advisory was just sent out about tonight's storm. If I were you, I'd hold off on setting the tables and chairs up until tomorrow morning. Want me to have Jean cover the arch with a tarp?"

"Yes, that would be great. Thanks, Ettie."

"No problem. I just hope we don't lose power again. I don't think the group coming in will be as"—she eyes both Lindsay and me—"*flexible* as Miss Hartman was when the power was knocked out earlier this week."

I bite the inside of my cheek, attempting to hold back my laugh. However, a little laugh sneaks out when I say, "I believe your assessment would be correct with that one." I squeeze Lindsay's thigh, causing her to drop her fork. It makes a loud crashing sound as it hits the ground.

"Sorry about that," Lindsay huffs, biting her lip while she reaches down to get the fork.

"Don't worry, dear. I know Theo is probably wreaking havoc under the table."

I gasp and clutch one hand over my heart. The same hand that was doing just that. "Pardon me? How could you say such a thing?"

"Oh please." Ettie waves me off. "You've been chasing this poor girl all week."

"I second that."

Fuck, I forgot Mateo was in here. He's always so quiet and of course he would take this opportunity to use his rarely heard voice in support of Ettie's *assessment*.

"No one asked you, Mateo."

"You're in *my* space, so you don't have to ask me anything. If I have an opinion, I get to share it. And if you don't like it, you can leave my kitchen," Mateo states while pointing to me with his frosting covered spatula.

I throw my hands up, feigning innocence. You know for a man wielding a rubber utensil covered in what looks to be Pepto-Bismol pink frosting, he sure is intimidating.

"Okay, you two. Play nice," Ettie pipes in, rescuing me from Mateo's menacing stare.

I guess he does have a point. After all, it is *his* space. It's not like he can take all the cake stuff into another room because he's annoyed with us talking.

Meanwhile, Lindsay is content eating her sandwich. I thought this would make her uncomfortable, but she seems to be entertained by it. Her eyes just volley between Mateo, Ettie, and me.

I bring my empty plate over to the sink, near Mateo. "You know I love you Mateo, right?"

He side-eyes me and huffs an exhausted exhale. "You just love me for my cooking."

"Well, that sure helps." I punctuate my statement with a pat on his back. "But seriously, thank you for all you do."

"Who else would put up with your shi—antics?" If Ettie wasn't in the room, I'm willing to bet he was going to say shit.

"Ettie loves them, don't you, Ettie?" I toss the question over my shoulder, not needing to see the smile she's trying to hide.

"Keep telling yourself that!" she chirps before leaving the kitchen.

I look over and see Lindsay has finished her plate, so I grab it and clean up any leftover mess we created. "We'll leave you to it, Mateo. Shout if you need anything."

"I won't."

God, he's such a grouch.

"But thank you," he adds a little softer.

But a grouch you can't help but love. And shit is he a mad scientist in the kitchen. Some of the recipes he creates . . . man. If I could only cook with a fraction of his skill, I'm not sure I'd ever eat out again.

Take-out food that is.

After moving Lindsay's luggage, I give her a quick tour of the family house. It's nothing huge, but it's special nonetheless.

Walking into the house, I point out the living room and show Lindsay the kitchen in the back, while Grandpa's bedroom and the extra bath is hidden behind the stairs. His room moved to the bottom floor a few years back, that way he doesn't have to use the stairs.

"If you follow me, I'll show you my room." I take her hand in mine and lead her up the steps.

"Oh, Theo. You're so forward," Lindsay teases.

Ma and Dad sleep upstairs, and my room is up there, too. Whenever I visit, we do have to share the one bathroom upstairs, which is one of the reasons Ma puts me in the hotel if there's room.

There are a lot of memories in this home, all from spending my summers here with Ma and my grandparents. Dad would visit too, just not for the whole summer like us because of his job. But ever since he retired, he's loved spending his days here.

Because Ma does a lot of the prep work for the bath products here in the house, it has a permanent woodsy yet floral aroma from all the lavender she processes. To this day, I can't smell anything lavender without immediately getting transported back here.

"I know it's not nearly on the same level as the room you've been staying in back at the hotel, but I hope it'll do for one night." I wave her into my simplistic bedroom.

"It's got a bed and that's all I really need." She pops up on her toes to kiss my cheek. "Thank you, Theo."

"Well, feel free to make yourself at home. There are a few snacks in the fridge if you get hungry but otherwise, I'll come and get you for dinner when it's time." I give her a small kiss on her lips, feeling her palms sneak their way onto my chest.

"Are you sure I can't help in any way?" she asks, running her hand down my front, but I snag her hands in mine before they can tempt me to stay.

"Everything is under control. Plus, you heard Ettie. The storm is halting most of the setup until tomorrow anyways. I'm just going to be double checking everything around the hotel before the party arrives later tonight."

"Okay, if you insist."

"I do." I bring her hand up to my mouth and place a kiss on the back of it. "Grab your book and go relax." I sneak another kiss then walk out of the room, only stopping to shout over my shoulder once I get to the stairs. "I'd love a demonstration on what you've learned later tonight."

I can't see her face, but knowing her, I'm sure she's blushing like a nun in a sex store.

CHAPTER THIRTY-EIGHT

LINDSAY

I can't help but feel guilty for not helping Theo with all of tomorrow's preparations. I know he has help, and he did say he couldn't do much more than what we've already done because of the potential storm, but still. I am not used to sitting around, *relaxing*, while others work and prepare for an event.

It's still pretty hot outside but as much as I'd enjoy sitting by the pool, I don't want to get in everyone's way. I decide to grab my e-reader and cozy up in Theo's bed. The temptation to snoop around his room is strong, but I talk myself out of it once I'd snuggled in the surprisingly fluffy comforter. He probably doesn't even have anything juicy hiding in here since he only visits.

The bed isn't huge, probably a full size mattress, but it's comfortable. It's faint but the linens smell like Theo, warm honey with the comforting scent of lavender. But that should be obvious since it is *Theo's* bed.

Okay. Reading. I'm here to read, not inhale Theo's sheets like some creeper.

I'm about seventy percent through my book. The male main character is morally grey, which of course he is since he's in the mafia. Someone just captured the love interest and he's on the chase to get her back, threatening bodily harm to anyone who dares to stand in his way.

I'm a sucker for a good "touch her and die" trope, which probably explains my gravitation to stalker and mafia romance books right now. But there are a few dark romantasy books I favor, too.

Who am I kidding? If it's got romance in it, I'll read it.

A couple hours later, the book concludes with him rescuing the woman he loves and killing the man who took her, as well as anyone else involved. There's of course a hot and spicy scene, making it end in a literal bang. It isn't anything too different from scenes I've read in the past. But it does involve some light bondage play, making me curious what Theo would do if I tied his arms up. Or if I'd like *Theo* to tie *me* up.

My initial thought would be no, because of the loss of control. But after a long while of pondering that idea, I come to the conclusion that maybe trying it with someone I feel safe with might have a different effect.

I hear the front door open and footsteps up the stairs follow soon after.

"Well, don't you look right at home." Speak of the devil.

Theo's smile is full as he crosses his arms and props himself up against the doorframe. I think he's enjoying the view of me in his bed.

"It's quite comfy," I say while patting the cloud-like comforter. I always feel the need to have some sort of blanket, even if it's hotter than hell outside.

Theo walks over and sits on the side of the bed. "You get to finish?"

I'm fully aware of his games now, so I send him a knowing shake of my head.

"What?" He tries to act innocent, but his smirk gives it away. "I meant, did you finish your *book*?" Theo leans over and rubs his hand up my thigh, stopping near my hip. "That book is clearly a bad influence on you." He kisses me, running his other hand through my hair, making me lean against the headboard for support. "You should keep reading it," he whispers against my skin and I can *feel* him smirk.

God, his kisses are addictive. I lose sight of the world around us every time his lips meet mine, or any part of my body for that matter. It's like we're in our own little bubble, and the rest of the world doesn't matter. Sheltered from the reality that awaits us.

Theo moves his hand up my waist, exploring lazily as he moves it closer to my breast. When he reaches his desired destination, he palms me through the cotton material, causing my flimsy bra strap to fall off my shoulder. He takes his time as he slowly brings his lips to my neck then down my chest.

"Oh, Theo," I moan under my breath.

He uses it as encouragement, pulling down the straps of my dress causing my bra to follow suit as he continues his worship. Once there are no more barriers, he works wonders teasing my nipples with quick sucks and little nibbles. I'm about to beg for more when I feel one of his hands sneaking up my dress. I moan as his knuckles graze over the lace covering right where I want him.

"So fucking wet—"

"Theo? You in here, Son?"

Son?

Fuck! Is Theo's dad here?

We both freeze on the bed like two teenagers getting caught by their parents who were supposed to be away. Well, I guess that assessment is actually spot on, only we're both consenting adults and we aren't doing anything wrong. But I'd really appreciate having my breasts covered the first time I meet Theo's dad.

We hear footsteps coming up the stairs and I scramble to pull up my bra and dress while shaking my leg, reminding Theo that he still has his hand up my dress.

"Theo?" his dad calls again.

That seems to wake Theo up. He immediately stands up, straightening his shirt while finger combing his hair. I don't remember running my hands through it, but the disheveled state it's in tells a different story.

"Theodore?" His dad peeks in around the door frame. "Ah, Theo!" he greets. He starts walking toward Theo but stops in his tracks when he sees I'm *also* in the room. "Oh, shit. I'm sorry. I didn't mean to interrupt"—he motions over to us—"whatever *this* is."

"Hey, *Dad*." Theo chuckles awkwardly. "What are you doing home? I thought Ma said you would text?"

"I came home to help you with the wedding tomorrow. Your mom was going to come too, but she wasn't quite ready to leave Grandpa." He glances around the room, clearly not sure what to do. "Obviously now I see I should've called," he starts to chuckle and Theo joins in.

"Yeah, a heads up would've been nice." His dad hugs him while patting Theo on the back. "But nonetheless, I'm happy to see you, Dad." Theo turns and reaches his hand out to help me out of bed. "Dad, this is Lindsay. Lindsay, this is my dad, Will Johnson."

"Pleasure meeting you, sir," I greet, not sure if I should reach out and shake his hand or not. Honestly, I'm not fully confident in my clothes' ability to stay in place right now. I got dressed so fast that I fear moving my arm will cause the top of my dress to fall off. And I definitely don't want to pull a "Janet Jackson."

"Lindsay? Like Miss Hartman, Lindsay?" Will asks suspiciously.

Theo glances at me mischievously as he says, "One and the same."

"I hope your stay has been—" Will clears his throat.

"Enjoyable? Exhilarating? Dare I even say"—Theo bites his lip, attempting to hide his smile—"pleasurable?"

My face flushes at the insinuation, and I'm quick to lower my head in my palms. "Oh my god," I mutter through gritted teeth.

"Hey now, you're making the poor miss blush. No need to feel embarrassed, dear. Though I *am* surprised to find a woman in his room. He's never had one over before. In fact, I can't remember the last time he's even *talked* about a woman." Interesting.

"Yeah, well her flight got delayed another day. And since the hotel was rented out, I offered her my bed for the night instead of making her stay at a hotel by the airport."

"How nice to offer her your bed while you sleep on the couch," Will comments with a knowing look.

I look to Theo and find him sporting a closed-lip smile. "Of course. I was actually coming to get Lindsay for dinner, want to join us, Dad?"

"Aren't the guests expected to be here soon?"

"No. They called a little bit ago saying their flight got delayed. So they won't get in for another couple of hours."

"Then dinner sounds great." Will claps his hands together before heading out. "I'll meet you over there. Pleasure meeting you, Miss Hartman." Will waves and walks down the hall to his room.

I immediately turn to Theo once Will is out of earshot. "*Pleasurable*? Are you *trying* to kill me with that one?"

Theo chuckles. "What? Was your trip to the abbey not enjoyable? You want to tell me that riding a bike for the first time wasn't exhilarating? Or that our time harvesting the honey wasn't —" I shoot out my hand to cover his mouth before he continues.

"Don't even *think* about finishing that sentence. Your dad could still be downstairs." Narrowing my eyes, I lower my hand, exposing his roguish smile.

"How about I finish something else?" he teases with a wag of his eyebrows.

Fuck me. I bite my lip and take a good long look up and down his body. Yes, please.

I mean no. Shit. We're supposed to be meeting his dad for dinner any minute. Could you imagine, *"Hi, Will. Sorry we're late. I can't keep my hands off your son."*

"Theo, we can't," I admit, shaking the mental image of me

shoving Theo back on the bed, hiking up my dress, and taking a ride on Theo's rock hard—

I feel Theo's hand on mine, pulling me to reality.

"If your Dad arrives before us, he'll know something's up." Theo smirks, his dimple out in full force and it dawns on me what I just said. "God, you have such a filthy mind." I blush as I playfully swat him away. But his mind wasn't far off from mine.

"I learn from the best." He steals a kiss and pulls me out of the room. "Come on. We don't want Dad to think you can't keep your hands off of me." I shake my head while smiling ear to ear.

CHAPTER THIRTY-NINE

THEO

Well there goes tonight's plans to steal one, or more, orgasms from Lindsay. Dad showed up like the cockblocker he is and threw my plans to feast on Lindsay out the windows. My fingers were so close, I could feel how wet she was through her underwear.

Don't get me wrong. I'm happy to see Dad, but why couldn't he have shown up an hour or so later. Or even tomorrow so I could enjoy my last night with Lindsay. Just the two of us. In my bed. Naked.

No. It won't be our last night because I'll figure out a way for us to continue this somehow.

We talk with Dad over dinner about topics spanning from his childhood in Tennessee to him meeting Ma and their adventures going back and forth between the states and Europe.

"We moved around a lot when Theo was young. Hell, the estate here is probably closer to home than any other places he's lived," Dad admits.

I brush a thumb over my bottom lip, trying to think about anything else other than the only thing I truly wish I had. A place to call home.

"But all those summers here provided some great work experience for the job he has now, isn't that right, Son?" Dad pats my back, clearly waiting for some sort of response.

"Yup. Sure did." It comes out clipped, a little of my melancholy slipping out. "It also made it easier to move from house to house like I do with all of my flips." Lindsay's eyes meet mine, communicating a silent understanding.

"Well, it sounds like y'all did a great job raising him," Lindsay chimes in.

"I can't take any of the credit, Miss Hartman. My Little Flower did a fine job at raising him."

"I'm sorry, *Little Flower*?" Lindsay asks.

"That's his nickname for Ma," I explain.

"That's sweet." A warm smile appears on Lindsay's face.

"So, Miss Hartman, why'd you choose our little slice of heaven to spend your holiday at?"

"Lindsay, please," she gently corrects. "Actually, I was put on sabbatical. The company thought it'd been too long since I took a vacation or sick day so they forced my hand," she chuckles, but it's more forced than natural. "They sent me here on a paid vacation in hopes to kick my sabbatical off on the right foot. The goal is to achieve a better 'work-life balance' as they say it."

It's not the first time I've heard of corporations stressing the importance of a work-life balance, but I've never heard of a company giving an employee an all expenses paid trip to help achieve that.

"Sounds like you deserved a break, dear," Dad comments.

"I guess that's one way of looking at it, Mr. Johnson."

"Oh, please. Call me Will, Miss Hartman." Dad gives Lindsay a knowing look across the table.

And she returns it right back. "Only if you call me Lindsay, Mr. Johnson."

"That sounds like a deal," Dad chuckles. "So did it work?"

"Did what work?" she questions.

"The trip? Do you feel more relaxed than when you first got here?"

I turn expectantly to her and find her eyes waiting for mine.

"Yes," she admits while staring at me. "I would say this was a successful vacation." I sneak my hand to her thigh and give it a quick squeeze.

Dad clears his throat then pats his leg as he glances at his watch. "Well, if you don't need anything more from me, I'm going to head back to the house and get ready for bed." He stands up and Lindsay and I follow suit.

"Now? It's so early." It's only around seven. Hell, the sun hasn't even set.

"It's been a long week and I can't wait to get back to my own bed. But come get me if you need any help with check-in for the wedding party tonight."

"Sounds good, Dad. See you tomorrow morning."

"Night, Theo." Dad pats my back before he turns to Lindsay. "Pleasure meeting you, Miss Lindsay." Dad smirks at Lindsay, knowing he found a work-around. He reaches out his hand to grasp Lindsay's.

She shakes his hand with a warm smile. "Nice meeting you, too."

"Behave yourself, Theo," he commands with a stern look before leaving us for the night. As soon as the door closes, I turn to face Lindsay with a mischievous look on my face.

"Now that is *definitely* not the face of someone who just agreed with his Dad that he'd behave himself," Lindsay notes.

"Did you actually *hear* me agree though, *ma chérie*?" I tilt my head and stroke the scruff on my chin. "No, I don't believe you did." I move to wrap my arms around her waist, using one of my hands to palm her ass. "Plus, how can I behave with the most beautiful woman in my arms?" I prove my point by kissing her senselessly, bringing her even closer into my embrace.

Unfortunately, the damn phone rings and ruins the moment. Impeccable timing as always. I would normally send it to voicemail given the time of day, but it's probably the wedding party calling that they have arrived in Marseille.

Reluctantly, I reach for the phone. "*Bonsoir—*" A voice I am oh so familiar with interrupts my greeting.

"Yes, we've just landed."

"So glad to hear that, Karen. I hope your flights here were smooth."

"It would've been better if we arrived *on time* but seeing as you had no hand in the delay of our flights, I guess discussing it with you is fruitless."

"Yes, well I do apologize for the delay. Jeromy will be waiting with a sign in baggage claim. He will assist all of you and your luggage to the vehicles."

"Hopefully he isn't too hard to find."

"If you run into any problems, please don't"—actually, please do—"hesitate to call. I hope to see you in a couple of hours. Safe travels."

I hang up before she has the chance to respond. Based on our previous hundred phone calls this week, if I give her any opening, she'll take it and run.

"The group just landed so they should be here in less than two hours."

"What can I help you with?" Lindsay asks, always so quick to offer.

"I just need to tidy this room up and do a final check that the keys are all straightened away. Ettie, Mateo, and Jean all helped out tremendously earlier today. Mateo even made little snack trays waiting in each room since they missed dinner."

"That was very thoughtful, and now you don't need to worry about them being hangry. Let me help you clean this up then." She starts clearing the table with me before we walk the dishes back to the kitchen.

"I can load the dishwasher while you go and check the keys," she offers.

"Absolutely not." I chuckle, attempting to load the dishwasher.

"Absolutely *yes*," she mocks as she grabs the plate out of my hand. "Now go." It's her turn to be playful as she slaps my ass, encouraging me to leave the kitchen.

"Fine. But I'll be back," I promise before leaving.

"You better." She gives me a saucy wink from over her shoulder. I like that I'm seeing more and more of this side of Lindsay.

Walking by a few windows, it's still bright outside. It doesn't look like the storm will happen, but I'll wait to set up the tables and chairs until tomorrow morning just in case.

Because the wedding party is made up of a group of ten, and we were sure they'd bring multiple pieces of luggage, we arranged for a private transfer to pick them up from the airport later tonight. I'll have to be available around nine o'clock to check everyone in, but I'll hold off on the hotel tour until the next day. If they even want a tour that is.

After my final checks, there's about thirty minutes to spare as I meet back up with Lindsay in the kitchen. By the looks of things, she went above and beyond by not only cleaning up our plates but the rest of the kitchen as well.

"Wow. Someone used some elbow grease in here," I praise looking around the kitchen.

"I didn't want Mateo walking in tomorrow and finding his workspace a mess."

"Well, I'm sure Mateo will be very grateful for your efforts," I note as I cage her up against the sink.

"Theo," Lindsay warns while pushing my chest back a little. "The group will be here soon."

I lean in, kissing the spot where her shoulder meets her neck. "By my count," I kiss her on her collarbone. "We have around half an hour for"—I work my way up her neck, licking and kissing—"*other* activities." I lift my head back up and wag my eyebrows while gripping her waist.

We start kissing, hands roaming each other's body, only

breaking to catch our breath. But we don't get very far because a loud rumble outside steals our attention.

Lindsay and I pause to turn our focus out the window.

"You heard that too, right?" she questions with an edge of worry in her voice. The sky looks a little brown and ominous as clouds start to make their way closer.

"Looks like it's going to storm after all," I observe.

"Is there anything that needs to get moved inside?"

"No, I held off on setting up everything. Well, everything *but* the arch by the lavender. Jean covered it with the tarp, so unless the wind knocks it off, it'll be fine." Really, if the arch *does* get wet, it gets wet at this point. There aren't any flowers on it yet, so regardless, it's still going to be usable tomorrow.

"Does this mean the ceremony and reception have to be inside? Or do you have a tent or something for a backup plan?" I chuckle when she mentions the tent.

"I tried to talk them into a tent, but they said it was 'tacky.'" I hold up my hands miming quotations. "If we get a decent amount of rain, they'll have no choice but to move it all inside. But if it's just a quick shower, it should dry out in time for the ceremony. Plus, we could always set the tables up over the gravel to avoid the mud."

I peer outside again and see the sky light up with another lightning strike.

"My biggest concern is the power going off again. I thought we had a generator, but I couldn't find it when we lost power a couple nights ago." Has it only been a couple of nights since that kiss in the rain?

"I'm sure your dad knows where it is. You could always just —" A horn interrupts Lindsay's sentence. "I guess your guests are here a little earlier than expected. Do you need me to stick around and help with anything?"

"Absolutely not. You've already helped so much. If you give me a minute to greet them, I'll come right back to walk you back to the house." I give her a kiss, and speed out of the kitchen to greet the oncoming storm.

CHAPTER FORTY

THEO

I was not "right back." I should've known that Karen would demand my immediate attention. After informing everyone of their room assignments and handing out keys, I rushed back to the kitchen and found Lindsay gnawing off a piece of a baguette.

"I'm so sorry. That took entirely too long."

"It's okay. I get it. Bread?" She motions the long loaf over to me.

I chuckle. "No, I'm all good for the night. But thanks for the offer."

"Everyone in their rooms?"

"Well, not everyone." I walk closer to her spot on the island. "You see, I have this one guest that needs a bit of *extra* attention."

"Oh, let me guess." She uses the baguette to tap her chin like she's deep in thought. "Karen."

"Oh no, no, no, *ma chérie*." I disarm the baguette from her. "This particular client requires something special. Something only *I* can provide," I taunt as I wrap my arms around her.

"Oh," Lindsay's eyes brighten as she catches on. "And what kind of *service* does this client require?"

I run my hands up and down her arms. "A special . . . *je ne sais quoi*."

"Doesn't that mean you don't really know?" she asks incredulously.

"I thought you didn't speak French?" I pinch her ass.

"Ouch!" she whines as she rubs her ass.

"Don't worry. I'll kiss it better." I kneel to do just that as the door to the kitchen opens.

"Jesus, Son!" Dad's voice causes me to immediately stand back up.

"Again Dad? *Seriously*? Do you have a radar for this?"

"At least it was me and not one of the guests. Maybe ya should stop attempting things like that in public spaces," he scolds, but it's lighthearted.

"My room wasn't public," I note pointedly.

"No, but the door was open."

"You"—I protest pointing my figure at him, not raising my voice but still trying to prove my point—"weren't even supposed to be home."

"Anyways . . ." He fails at the not-so subtle topic. "I came here because I woke up to the storm. I wanted to make sure ya knew where the generator was."

"Actually, I don't. We lost power for a bit earlier this week and I tried looking for it, but came up empty."

So what if he's being super helpful right now? He's still a giant cockblock.

"I'll show ya and then we can all retire for the night. Lindsay probably is getting tired." He shoots her a closed lip, sympathetic smile. "Plus you'll need some extra time to set up the bedding on the couch downstairs."

It's almost cute how much he thinks I won't be sleeping in the same bed as Lindsay. I'm a thirty-year-old man, but I'll keep it PG. Dad's only down the hall and I can keep it in my pants for one night.

At least I think I can.

Maybe if I just cover her mouth. No, that won't work. My bed squeaks something fierce.

Maybe the floor? Yeah, put some pillows down and it'll be great.

Or better yet, the shower. I could sneak in under the guise of showing her how to turn on the shower. Hey, showers in Europe can be difficult to use. It's a totally plausible reason. Plus, even Dad knows it takes forever for the family house's water to warm up. Maybe I could even blame the length of time it takes us on showing her all the different spray settings. I obviously have to demonstrate how to properly use each setting. I'm only being a welcoming host. And Dad prides himself on raising a gentleman.

Maybe the last six-ish hours have proved otherwise with him catching us, or really me, in some rather compromising positions. But everyone's clothes were on. At least, they were when he got within eyeshot.

"Theo, ya paying any attention to what I just said?" Lindsay squeezes my hand, making sure I hear Dad. I think he said something about the generator but I'm not sure.

"Yeah. Sorry, Dad."

"He was just letting you know how to turn on the generator. Also, that it only powers the refrigerator and the guest rooms." Of course she was paying attention to Dad.

"That's right, Miss Lindsay. At least *someone* was listening," he huffs.

We reach the generator just as the rain starts to pick up. The lightning doesn't seem so bad right now, but I know that can change at a moment's notice. After Dad shows me how to work the generator, we head back to the family house right as the rain starts dumping. We all rush inside and brush off some of the water covering us.

"Well you kids have a good night. I'll see *you* in the morning, Theo." Dad's tone is tight but then softens when he adds, "Please feel free to sleep in, Lindsay. We appreciate your help, but you are still our guest."

"Thank you, Mr—Will. Thank you, Will."

Dad smiles at us and heads up the stairs. "Oh and Theo," I turn and meet his intimidating stare. "I expect to see you on the couch when I wake up in the morning." He takes a few steps. "Or when I wake up for one of my midnight water breaks."

Rolling my eyes I motion a thumbs up while shouting out, "Sounds good, Dad."

Lindsay leans in close to me so only I hear her when she whispers, "He really wants you on the couch, huh?"

"He's just never had to 'lay down the law' so to speak." I turn and face her. "Come on, let's get you out of these wet clothes." I insist as I tug her toward the stairs, remembering the plan I cooked up earlier. "Do you want to take a shower before getting ready for bed?"

"Oh," Lindsay ponders the option.

Please say yes. Please say yes.

"No, I think I'm alright. I'll just run a towel through my hair when I brush my teeth." Damn. "But I'll take one in the morning."

That's perfectly fine for her, but that doesn't help me. I'll be busting my ass early tomorrow for the party. Pillow fort on the floor it is.

"Sounds good. I'll probably be out of the house before then."

I open the door to my room, motioning Lindsay inside. Down the hall, I spot Dad's closed door. He's probably not asleep yet, but he never said *when* I had to be on the couch, just that I needed to be there when he gets his water.

"Sounds good." She reaches in her bag, grabbing what I'm assuming are her pajamas and her toiletries. She spins toward me with her hands full. "Bathroom?"

"Oh, right. Follow me."

I show her to the bathroom and do the gentleman thing, give her privacy. I use the time to throw a blanket and pillow on the couch downstairs, giving the appearance someone is sleeping there. Then after marching back upstairs, I grab some pajama bottoms and take off the wet clothes clinging to me. I absolutely hate the smell and feel of wet fabric.

I lay out my clothes to get them somewhat dry by the morning but I know I'll end up throwing them in the wash tomorrow as soon as I get a break from everything.

Rain patters the roof while thunder rattles the house with the occasional flash of lightning. The storm would've wreaked havoc on the decorations if they were outside. It's mildly windy, just enough to make the trees hit against the windows every so often.

Making my way into the bed, I hear the bathroom door close. Lindsay appears shortly after, immediately putting her toiletries bag back into her luggage.

"I hung my clothes up in the bathroom so they could dry a little before packing them up tomorrow."

"If they're still wet in the morning, we can put them in the wash with mine before you leave."

"Oh, that would be great. I hate the smell of wet clothes." I chuckle under my breath. Great minds . . .

"Me too, Linds. Now get in bed." I pull the comforter back, patting the exposed bed.

"But your Dad—" she protests.

"Is probably asleep by now." I motion my finger for her to come closer, but she doesn't move. She just stands frozen, chewing on her bottom lip. "Fine," I move my hand over my heart before pledging, "I promise to keep things PG and to move to the couch before he wakes." She narrows her eyes at me, folding her arms over her chest, making her tits even more tempting. "What?"

"I think you have a skewed understanding of a PG rating. Your PG rating is a little behind the times, more like a rating from the eighties."

"What does that mean?" I question, not completely sure where she's going with that.

"You know. Like how some of the most popular movies were rated PG but they still said fuck or have some nudity or crude jokes."

I scoot over to the edge of the bed, placing my hands on her hips. "Give me an example."

"Well, Beetlejuice is a great one. It has multiple crude jokes, crotch grabbing, and even air-humping."

"Air-humping?" I clutch my imaginary pearls. "Dear lord, someone alert the church elders."

Lindsay shakes her head while chuckling. "You wanted an example."

"You're right, you're right." I pull her between my legs. "But in my opinion, if something happens under the sheets, where no one can see, is it really breaking any rules?" I pinch her ass and grab the back of her thighs, lifting her on top of me as I fall back onto the mattress.

Lindsay lets out a loud squeal.

"Shhh. I thought the point was to *not* wake my dad."

She laughs free and without remorse. "I'm sorry." Her attempt at a whisper is weak at best. "I promise, I'll be quiet."

"Very well then." Rolling her on her back, I cage her underneath me. "Where were we?"

She giggles as I pepper her chest and neck in kisses. She wraps her legs around my hips, causing my lower body to rub against hers. My arousal is clear, especially in these thin ass pajama bottoms. Her shorts have ridden up so much so they are basically just underwear at this point. And as I move my hands up and inside the cotton fabric, I pause my kissing.

I don't feel anything. No cotton or lace, not even string. Nothing.

Fuck me. She's not wearing any underwear.

Lindsay props herself on her elbows. "Is everything okay?"

"I guess you have a thing for going commando around me." I grip her waistband and slowly pull her sleep shorts down, making sure to tease her with my finger tips while working the fabric down her legs.

My eyes take their time roaming the masterpiece that is her body. She's gloriously bare from the waist down as I press my palms to the inside of her thighs, spreading her wide open for me. Fuck, her skin is so soft against my callused hands.

I swipe my thumb across her clit causing her to jolt, which then makes the bed squeak, but I'm quick to soothe her with a lazy swipe of my tongue.

She runs her fingers through my hair, guiding me where she wants me. "Oh, Theo."

I lift my head up, playful mischief clear in my eyes. "I've already shown you I'm not afraid to stuff that delicious mouth of yours."

"Mmm," she moans. "I find I'm not opposed to the idea."

Fuck, well if she's offering . . . I shift our bodies to do just that, not caring how loud the bed squeaks from my movement. But as I get us into position, the power goes out.

The universe is truly getting off on edging me today.

"Shit," I mutter, shaking my head. "I'm sorry, Linds. I gotta go turn the generator on for the hotel."

I hop off the bed and throw a shirt on. "Get some rest," I say as I kiss her forehead. "The power won't come back on in this house, but it shouldn't get too hot. Feel free to open the window if you need some cool air though."

"Okay."

I stall at the door, not wanting to leave this moment. "I'm not sure how long it'll take, but I'll come back as soon as I can."

"Just be safe." Lindsay sighs before I head down the stairs.

CHAPTER FORTY-ONE

LINDSAY

I wake with no sign of Theo.

Scratch that. There's a chocolate croissant and thermos on the nightstand with what looks to be a note stuck to the side of it.

Last night when the power went out, it was like a bucket of cold water got thrown over us, for the *third* time that day. Apparently yesterday was *not* the day for fornicating.

I will say, seeing Theo in nothing but cotton grey pajamas bottoms was a treat. The grey sweatpant effect is definitely a thing. Very little was left to the imagination with those pants. Plus, I could feel *everything* when he hovered over me, kissing me with the passion I've felt from no man but him.

Popping a bite of flaky goodness into my mouth, I come to the conclusion I'm really going to miss these babies.

Smearing chocolate on the edge of the paper, I grab the green sticky note, reading it as I eat.

I left early to set up for the wedding.
Come find me after you finish.

-Theo

I chuckle while shaking my head. Theo and his innuendos.

Checking my phone, I find no missed messages from my family so I open the airline's app to check that my flight is running on-time. Unfortunately, it is.

After I finish my breakfast, I walk to the bathroom and notice the power is back on, so I take a quick shower. I make one more effort to look around for anything I might have missed and zip up my bags. The house is quiet as I move my luggage close to the front door, but as I peek outside, I see tons of movement.

Theo and his dad look like they are in a deep conversation, with who I'm assuming is Karen. She keeps pointing to the grass and stomping her foot. I'm guessing she's not happy about the mud. Oh, and now she's waving to the gravel. Maybe she's just not happy about *any* of it.

Theo spots me and waves, smiling big and warm. I make my way over to them as Karen storms off.

"What was that about?" I nod my head in Karen's direction.

"She doesn't want the reception tables in the mud, but hates 'the look' of the gravel."

"Whatever that means," Will adds.

"And now the dining room isn't an 'appropriate' substitution," Theo frustratedly adds.

"Doesn't one of the rooms have a deck?" I ask.

"Yes," Will draws.

"Okay. Is it big enough to fit a dinner setup for ten?"

"I'm not sure." Theo tilts his head, clearly mentally mapping it out. "But I think it could work."

"Great! Let's go check it out. If it seems like it could, you can take that idea to Karen and see if that will be to her liking," I offer as a solution.

Turns out, it's plenty big enough and Karen is happy enough to agree to move the dinner on the patio. I help Theo and his dad set up the table and chairs in the new location, then start bringing out the linens and floral arrangements.

I take a step back and take in the new layout. "You'll need more candles out here too since you won't have any direct lights in this area of the property," I suggest. Plus, candles only add to the mood.

"Good idea. I'll have Ettie bring some out," Theo adds as he places the last arrangement. We all stand back and admire the transformed deck. "This looks perfect. Thanks for the idea, Linds." He leans in and steals a quick kiss on my cheek.

"Not a problem. It's literally my job back at home."

"I can see why you're so good at it. You definitely made the vision come to life," Will commends with a pat on my back.

"Thanks, Will. I do take a lot of pride in my job so I appreciate the compliment. I've learned you always have to have a backup plan for those rainy days."

"Quite literally in this case," Will adds while chuckling. "I should probably check in with the rest of the team. Ya know, make sure they're doing okay. I'll see ya both inside soon, yeah?"

"Yup. We'll be right behind you, Dad. Thanks for your help setting all this up."

"I should be thanking you, Son." Will grips Theo's shoulder during the heartfelt moment. "Your ma and I appreciate you coming out here and helping us out."

Theo turns his head to me, one corner of his mouth peaking up. "I think it's worked out in my favor." He snags my hand and gives it a light squeeze.

"See you kids inside," Will says before turning the corner of the building, leaving Theo and me alone.

Or what I thought was alone until I saw a face through the sliding door of the room's patio that we commandeered.

"Looks like we got a Peeping Tom over there." Theo nods his head in the direction of the door.

"I don't think they were peeping on us as much as they were peeping on our decorating skills."

"I don't know. I think I saw some wandering eyes," Theo teases as he wraps his arms around me.

"Uh huh. Sure." I laugh and turn to follow Will. "Let's go before I get you in trouble with your dad."

"You are definitely worth the wrath of my father. But I'm not sure if I like people having a front row seat of you screaming my name. But let's find out." He squeezes my ass and jogs ahead of me.

"Theo!" I whine, trying to hold back my laugh but I'm entirely unsuccessful in doing so.

He turns around, continuing his jog only backwards. "Turns out, I don't mind it."

I shake my head, continuing my laughing as I follow him inside.

Surprisingly, the ceremony went smoothly. The bride and groom looked beautiful as I snuck a glance at them before they headed off to the field for their vows. I even saw a smile on Karen's face at one point.

Theo had gotten creative and used some clear tarp to cover the grass aisle and spot in front of the arch, that way the bride's dress didn't get all muddy. But it ended up being a perfect day for a wedding. Since the storm passed early this morning, it left the sky perfectly clear and the heat wasn't too bad for it being in mid-summer. And given how beautiful everything looked, I'm sure the photographer captured some absolutely stunning photos.

Theo was super busy most of the afternoon, but stole a moment with me in between the ceremony and dinner. One more interaction before I have to leave. Like *leave* leave. Like say one final goodbye to Theo.

Saying bye to this little bubble we created for the week. Saying bye to the only freeing experience I've had in god knows how long.

"Hey, where'd you go?" Theo interrupts my spiral while I wait with my bags for my airport pickup.

"Huh? Oh." I shake my head, attempting to clear my mind. "It's nothing," I sigh and take another deep breath.

"It doesn't *look* like nothing."

I should just tell him. Tell him I'm not ready to say goodbye. That I'm not ready to go back to the life I was living last week. Not ready to leave *this*.

But do I tell him any of that? Nope.

"Just doing a mental catalog and making sure I have everything ready before I get picked up."

"Oh, right." Theo shifts from one leg to the other. "Almost forgot that was happening tonight."

"Yeah. Actually, they should be here any minute." I look over my shoulder, hearing tires coming up the driveway. "Looks like you found me just in time."

"Linds, I—"

"Theo don't." I place my palm on his chest. "It's okay, you don't have to say anything. We always knew this had an expiration date anyways. I just got caught up in the lavender haze of it all."

"Wait, no. That's not—"

"Theo?! Can we get your help with the food?" Will's hollering interrupts what I assume was going to be some pity "we can make it work" offer from Theo just as my transfer to the airport pulls up besides me.

Or maybe not, given the regret filled stare aimed my way. Fuck, I don't know what to do with this.

There's a brief pause where we look into each other's eyes and I think maybe, just maybe he'll say something more. But we get interrupted again. Guess that's the theme of this trip.

"Theo! We kinda need your help now!" Will shouts again with more urgency as I start walking toward the car.

"I'll be right there, Dad!" I hear his steps jogging up behind me. Grabbing my hand, Theo spins me to face him. "Lindsay, wait. I don't want you to leave thinking that's all we were. At least, it wasn't that for me."

I don't have the mental capacity to have this conversation. Especially when I know I'll spend the next thirty-ish hours psychoanalyzing this very moment while I travel home. Alone.

And then I'm sure I'll continue overthinking once I get back to my apartment. Alone.

No, I need to take back control in this situation. So, I do the one thing that will end his protests. I kiss him.

I don't mean a quick peck on the lips. Or even a brief makeout session. No. I kiss him and make sure it's a kiss that will have a lasting effect. Forever ingrained in his memory. Haunting him for years to come because that's all we'll ever be. A ghost of what could've been. The typical "right person, wrong time."

I pull away whispering, "Goodbye, Theo," and hop in the car as the driver loads my bag. As we pull away, I look out the window and see Theo standing there, fingers touching his lips. Absolutely frozen.

He stays like that until I reach the gates. He might've stayed longer, but I can't see because the hotel is behind me now. Out of sight, but definitely not out of mind.

CHAPTER FORTY-TWO

THEO

What the fuck just happened?

One minute I'm kissing Lindsay, and the next, she's in a car. A car taking her to the airport. Fuck, I don't even have her number.

Fuck fuck fuck.

How did I not even get her number? I guess it didn't even dawn on me since we didn't need to text or call while she was here. She was always just a quick walk or knock away.

How did I just fumble the best thing that ever happened to me so bad?

"Theo!" There's definitely more urgency behind Dad's voice.

"Yeah, sorry! I'm coming right now." I jog over to help with dinner.

Throughout my time serving the meal, I'm a mess. I drop a plate, luckily a finished one. I spill water on the table cloth. I even stepped on someone's gown. Not the bride's—or Karen's, thank god. After the cake is served, Dad pulls me off to the side.

"You did good, Son," he cheers as he pats my back.

"Everything looked great and went smoothly." Not everything.

"Thanks, Dad." I take a deep breath.

It's a little past nine and things are finally winding down. Half the group already went back to their rooms, Karen and her husband being among them. After a few glasses of champagne and a slice of cake, she thanked me for all my hard work. It may have come out a little slurred, but I'll take it. The other couples are sitting by the pool, drinking and talking. Leaving the patio clear of any guests.

Lindsay's flight should've left by now, but I can't get her out of my head. That can't be the last time we see each other.

"You bummed about Lindsay?" Sometimes I admire his ability to see through the bullshit.

"I didn't even ask for her number, Dad."

"But didn't your ma give it to you when you picked her up in Aix?"

Oh my god! He's right!

"Dad, you're a genius!" I say squeezing his shoulders then pulling out my phone to pull up her number.

"Okay, so you have her number. So what? You're just going to call her and . . ." He looks at me with wide, expecting eyes and an arched eyebrow.

"I don't know yet. She has a long travel day ahead of her. Maybe I'll just send a text to her, letting her know I'd love to call her when she gets home."

"How long is her layover again?"

"I think it's something ridiculous, like fifteen hours."

"That's right. I remember seeing that when I printed her itinerary earlier today."

Printing her itinerary? "What are you talking about, Dad?"

"She emailed something she needed to print out. I left it at the front desk around lunch." There's a pause as both of us digest the situation. "Why don't you—" Dad doesn't even have to finish his thought.

My face brightens up as realization dawns on me. "Thanks, Dad!" I beam as I pat him on the shoulder.

I start to head in the direction of the car, but realize I should help clean up as much as possible before I abandon Dad to do it all himself. I walk back to the dining tables and start cleaning up plates only for Dad to bark at me. "What the hell do you think you're doing, Son?"

"I'm not about to leave you with this mess of a place." I motion to said mess surrounding us. "I've got time."

"No, you don't." He grabs the dishes out of my hand. Quite aggressively if I do say so myself. "Go get your girl, Theo."

So that's what I do.

After a night of sleeping in my car in the Marseille parking lot, it's finally time to go through security for the first flight to Paris.

I drove as fast, and safely, as I could last night but it didn't matter. Turns out, Lindsay was booked on the last flight to Paris so there was absolutely no way I would've caught that flight. The best I could do was catch the six a.m. flight.

It shouldn't be an issue because she has such a lengthy layover. Dad had the great idea of reminding me to grab the copy of Lindsay's flight confirmation, that way I can find her based on what gates her flights go through.

I'm assuming she chose to stay in those sleeping pods since that's what we talked about. But if I don't find her, I'll make my way over to where her flight to North Carolina should be boarding.

Though I can always text her, I want to see her face when she realizes I flew here to . . . to what? Say goodbye again?

No. I need to work on that answer.

As I walk through security and then to a cafe near my gate, I can't help but fixate on what to say.

"You came!" I imagine her soft and cheery voice in my head.

"As will you if you—" No. A sex joke *cannot* be how I respond to that.

"I can't help it when it comes to you." Fuck. That's horrible Theo.

"You know I love a happy ending." Theo! Focus! No sexual references. This is serious.

Okay, maybe it's the prompt. How about if she were to greet, "You're here!"

"Of course I'd come." I slap my palm against my forehead as I walk out of the cafe with a chocolate croissant tucked away in a white take-out bag. God, why is this so hard for me?

That's what she—

Fuck!

This isn't helping. And why am I spiraling right now? I never spiral. I'm very much a "whatever happens, happens" kind of guy but here I am, obsessing over making sure my opening line to Lindsay is perfect.

Texting her first might be the best option after all. But I should wait until I'm actually *in* Paris, just in case something were to happen.

And man did something happen. We sat on the tarmac for an additional forty-five minutes before take-off, only to wait an additional thirty when we landed in Paris. Something about the gate not being available, but I'm not really sure. The muffled announcement from the captain made it so I could only catch every fourth word or so.

After a quick trip to the bathroom, I make my way to the sleeping pod area in the ginormous Paris airport. I stand near the entrance for a solid twenty minutes before I cave, deciding not to waste any more of our short time together.

THEO:

Where are you right now?

I need to see you again.

Shit, sorry. This is Theo by the way.

I immediately cringe at the string of texts I just sent.

THEO:

Not some random stalker.

And now that's four texts in a row. And I'm still left on "delivered."

THEO:

But I could be if you wanted.

A chase scene with you would be hot.

I'm sure you've read about those in one of your books. 😉

Okay. That's a little better. But still, that's one, two, three . . . *fuck*. Seven texts! Jesus, Theo. Dial it back.

Maybe I should just call.

Yeah. Calling isn't so bad. Plus, I'm sure we will look back at today some day in the future—far off future —and laugh.

I hit "dial" on my phone and pace while the phone sends me to voicemail. While waiting for Lindsay's voicemail to finish, I can't help noticing how professional it is. Very Lindsay.

"Please leave me a message with your name, number, and date of the event, and I'll get back to you as soon as possible. Thank you and have a terrific day."

The voicemail beeps right after giving me zero time to prepare for what I'll leave in her mailbox.

"Hi! Yes! Lindsay. You may remember me from our week in France? Or that guy who taught you how to ride a bike? Maybe even the guy who licked honey off of your—"

I stop my pacing when I get a very pointed glare from the man sitting in front of me. Maybe a commuter given his grey suit and polished loafers. Whatever reason he's here, he is definitely judging me right now.

"Anyways, where are you? Because I'm in Paris. The airport more specifically. I couldn't let that be my last time seeing you."

The line beeps signing the end of the allotted time for my message. I take a seat on a bench in the sea of chairs. In all the times I've flown this airport, there's never really been a time where it's felt this empty. Slower sure, but empty? No.

As I attempt to distract myself while I wait for Lindsay's returning call, or even text, I lose myself in picturing a future with her. Maybe it's not so far-fetched. We both deserve to be happy and what's a couple of weeks doing long-distance really matter in the grand scheme of things?

I look down at my phone and see only ten minutes have passed even though it feels like it's been more like thirty minutes since I've last called Lindsay. Even so, I decide to call her again.

"—have a terrific day." Her voice is melodic, a haunting reminder of all the good that happened this week. And if I don't see her again, it will plague my dreams knowing it will never happen again.

"Linds, I want to give us a shot. It's clear we have something rare, and I won't be able to live with myself if I let you go without at least seeing where this could go. And believe me, it's going places, *ma chérie*. Just please call me."

The line beeps again, letting me know my time is up.

I hunch over while dragging my palm down my face. I'm not giving up yet, but it's not looking good. Pulling out the chocolate treat I was saving for Lindsay, I start to comfort eat.

The croissants aren't nearly as good as the ones at my family's hotel. While Mateo's are moist and ever so flakey, these taste dried out and the chocolate to dough ratio is so wrong. But I suppose they'll do the job just fine this morning as I wallow in my self-pity, face buried into a sub-par bakery staple.

After finishing the lack-luster croissant, I call her once more, desperately hoping she'll pick up and she was just asleep this whole time because she slept past her alarm. But even as I try to pump myself up, I don't see that being the reason. No, the Lindsay I know would wake up naturally just before the alarm only to feel a bit victorious at being prepared, even in sleep, for beating the ringing of the alarm.

Her voice floods my ears once more. This time, I can pick up more from the brief voice message. She's clearly frazzled, so maybe she had to record this little snippet multiple times? Or maybe she was running late for a—no, Lindsay would never run late for a meeting or event. She's Lindsay.

I almost miss the beep before I get my last chance at reaching out and making my dream a reality.

"Lindsay, I'll wait for you. I promise I will. I just can't wait here. I'm going to be leaving Paris to go back to the hotel in the next couple of hours . . . but I'll be waiting, *ma chérie.*" My thumb hovers over the red button before I whisper out, "Please call."

CHAPTER FORTY-THREE

LINDSAY

A FEW HOURS PRIOR . . .

I land in Heathrow around eleven o'clock. That flight was awful. I sat next to the most obnoxious people ever. Not only were they loud—so much so that *everyone* could hear their conversation—but one of them took off their shoes and rested their feet on the arm rest of the seat in front of them. So gross.

I tried to tune them out with my headphones for the remainder of the flight. It worked up until the shoeless woman needed to use the bathroom, barefoot. I had to pretend like I didn't see that to stop me from obsessing over how dirty that woman's feet would be after her jaunt to the tiny airplane bathroom.

The only positive was that the kind desk agent was able to switch my flights. When I mentioned how long the layover was, and that my original flight had gotten canceled, she was super helpful in offering another flight itinerary with a much shorter layover. Three hours to be exact, instead of the fifteen plus in Paris.

By the time I got off the plane from Marseille, I had less than two hours to collect my bag, recheck it, and then wait in security before my next plane boarded.

Nervously shifting from left to right, I swiftly put my things in the grey container before the machine takes it, allowing me to walk through the metal detector.

As I walk up to the other side to retrieve my belongings, the belt suddenly halts, causing my phone to go flying out. Another second later, the machine starts back up again only for me to stand idly by, watching as my phone slips deeper and deeper into the crevice between the two rubber belts. I hear two cracks before realizing it's my phone making those sounds.

This has to be some crazy freak accident because no way in hell did I see this as a potential reason for missing a flight. But here we are.

I stand there frozen, not sure what to do as I hear a "Miss? Is this your phone?" I note that the voice has a very heavy English accent. That's about all I pay attention to as I stare at my crushed phone and start brainstorming all of the ways this will affect my next flight.

"Miss?" The voice is closer now. "Miss?! Are these your belongings?"

My brain is finally catching up to the situation in front of me right now and not the ones I've conjured up in my mind.

It's just a phone, Lindsay.

Phones can be replaced.

Easily replaced in fact.

Just *breathe*.

You have plenty of time to make it to your next flight.

"Yes. Sorry. That's my bag and *that's* my phone. Or at least, what's left of it."

"I'm sorry to say, Miss, but your phone was damaged during its security screening."

"Yes, I can see that," I note as I start to pick up my belongings out of the bin.

"If you want to speak to the supervisor on duty, I can get them." He hands my phone back to me in a plastic baggie. "Otherwise, all you'll need to do is file a claim online and that will get you on your way to potential compensation for these damages. Sorry for the inconvenience."

"Do you mind if I take a picture of your name badge for reference?" I say out of reflex but quickly remember I don't have a way to do that. "Sorry. I guess I can't do that," I add sarcastically as I look at what's left of my phone.

"You're not allowed to take photos in a secure area anyway, but if you write down my name, today's date, and time, they'll be able to find me. Plus, I'm going to file my own report with the supervisor right now, so by the time you get home and submit your claim, mine should already be in the system."

While I'm not the most satisfied by that answer, I guess it'll have to work. I mean what else could he do? Get me a new phone for the eight hour flight? Yeah, that's not going to happen.

"Alright. Well, thanks for the tip about the claim," I chirp with a wave as I walk away with my bags and whatever remains of my phone. There's absolutely no way of using this hunk of tin now.

Having to rely on the information provided, I hustle toward the nearest flight board and find where my flight is taking off.

After walking to my assigned gate, I look around for a desk agent at any of the surrounding gates, quickly finding a woman one gate over at a desk operated by the same airline.

I make my way over to her, and after making sure she's not on the phone, I ask my question. "Hi. Is there a chance you can reprint my boarding pass? My phone got smashed in security and I only had the mobile pass."

"Sure can do. Can I see your passport please? And where's your next flight headed?"

I pull the blue book out of my tote bag. "I'm flying to Raleigh soon," I add as I hand her my open passport. "Actually, the flight leaves in two hours."

She types something into her computer and then I hear the clicking of a printer. She smiles at me before handing me my new boarding ticket. "Was there anything else you needed?"

"A new phone?" I joke but her smile drops. "Kidding of course," I add with an awkward chuckle. "No, that will do it. Thank you so much."

She plasters on a smile, this one missing all the warmth from the one she greeted me with. "Enjoy your flight."

"So tell us *everything*," Emma starts from Taylor's phone.

Thankfully I was able to get a temporary flip phone from Walmart the same day I arrived back home, but I was told it would take some time to get a new phone with my original number.

"She"—Fran from work—"told me they wouldn't have the replacement phone until after I came back, which won't be until next week." I sigh.

"Well at least all of your stuff is saved in the cloud for now and you can just reload it once you get your new phone," Tory notes as we walk around the bridal shop.

"But enough about the phone. We want to know about the *man*." I pull the phone up so Emma can see my eyes as I roll them. "What? Who cares about the phone? It'll get replaced but it sounds like some magic was happening between you and . . . what was pool guy's name again?"

"His name is Theo," I huff.

"Okay, ladies. Here she comes," the sales associate says before Taylor walks out in her wedding gown.

We gather over to where a little pedestal is framed by three floor-to-ceiling mirrors as Taylor walks out of the dressing room. The gown is simplistic but jaw-droppingly beautiful, fitted to all her curves with a flare around her knees. The neckline is straight and the gown is made entirely up of a buttery satin. There are no embellishments to be found except the row of tiny fabric buttons running down her spine.

"So?" Taylor turns to face us after getting situated on the pedestal. It's just then I realize I haven't lifted the phone to show Emma the dress. "Do y'all like it?"

"Oh Taylor," Mom gets out before she starts crying.

"Taylor, it's *stunning*," Tory adds in awe.

"That dress is made for you," I comment.

"Jess better realize how fucking lucky he is," Emma shouts over the phone.

Taylor just rolls her eyes before turning to look at herself in the surrounding mirrors. "It really is a beautiful dress," she murmurs to herself as she straightens out the invisible wrinkle on her bodice.

Mom walks over to wrap her arms around Taylor. "And you make an absolutely breathtaking bride, sweetie."

Taylor leans her head down to rest on Mom's. "Thanks, Mom."

We all are quiet for a minute as we admire Taylor.

"Okay, but seriously," Taylor starts before turning to face us. "Would you tell us about Theo already?"

"Today is about you!" I insist.

She scoffs. "Fine. At brunch then?"

"Fine," I quip with a nod as she turns back and admires the dress again.

"Should we try a veil?" the associate asks as she approaches with two in her hands.

"Oh, no thank you," Taylor kindly rejects, then whispers in our direction, "I always thought those make people look like beekeepers."

I smile at the memory Taylor unknowingly brought to my mind.

"What even *is* the difference between a *croque monsieur* or *croque madame*?" Tory asks as we pursue the menu.

"Something with the eggs I think," Taylor notes.

"*Croque madame* has a fried egg on top. Sometimes poached," I add as I'm taken back to when I asked that very same question to Theo.

"Something you picked up on in France?" Mom asks.

"Something like that," I mumble thoughtfully before the waiter walks over and takes our order. Even with a sea separating us, I'm still seeing him everywhere I go.

"So did you at least get this 'Theo's' number?" Mom asks after she takes a sip from her tea.

"He texted from his cell when he picked me up. So it's not saved but should still be in my messages once I get my new phone all situated."

"And you really just . . . *left*?" Taylor asks.

"What else was I supposed to do?" We pause as the waiter brings us our brunch, thanking them as they leave. "Extend my stay? *Again*?" I take a sip from my mimosa. "Just to have to say goodbye all over again?"

The table goes silent.

"I don't even know where he lives," I admit bitterly. I'm kicking myself for not asking that.

"You said you met in the airport here, right?" I nod as Mom continues. "And not many people fly *into* Raleigh for an international flight. So there's a good chance he's from the surrounding area."

She has a point but before I explore that train of thought any more, Tory speaks up.

"But other than *him*,"—I internally chuckle at Tory's attempt to redirect—"did you love it?"

Thinking about last week, I sigh. "I really did. It opened my eyes on a lot of things. Speaking of which," I turn to Taylor. "I've decided it's time to go back to therapy for my anxiety."

"Good for you, sis!" Tory cheers as Mom gets misty-eyed while holding her hands in front of her mouth.

"Happy for you, Linds," Taylor adds sincerely.

"Thanks, ladies." I smile and my heart warms knowing all the support I have at this table. And I'm sure if Emma was here, she'd be rooting for me all the same.

"Will you go back to the office on Monday then?" Mom asks as she passes her credit card to the waiter.

"Yup. I told Fran about a few changes I want to make going forward and she was onboard with all of them."

"Sounds like you brought home a whole new Lindsay," Tory notes.

"Yeah," I sigh as we leave the restaurant, thinking about the one thing I *left* in France.

CHAPTER FORTY-FOUR

LINDSAY

Two weeks later . . .

"You've reached Lindsay Hartman," I say in greeting to the person on the other line as I sit up in bed.

"Lindsay?" Claire's shrill voice is so loud I have to pull the phone away from my ear.

She's new to our company, but not new to the industry. In the past, she's only had the role of assistant but now she's running the show.

During my first work week back, Fran and I agreed that a less hands-on position might work better for my skill set, as well as stress level. The hope is to shift my position to more of a coach than an actual planner. I'll help recruit new venues and vendors but I won't be involved in the planning side of things. My role would also entail being there for new planners in their first few weeks on the job. For now, I'm doing a little of both and Claire is my first mentee.

"We have a problem at the Kent wedding. They're all magenta."

"What's all magenta?" I ask as I rub the sleep from my eyes.

"The flowers! They were supposed to be lilac roses but instead everything is bright purple. It's like Barney threw up in here."

I'm a little surprised that someone in their twenties knows who Barney is, but I appreciate the reference all the same.

"Okay. First things first. Let's take a breath."

I do my best to breathe in and out in a dramatic fashion so Claire can copy me from over the phone. It's not until I hear her take a few deep breaths that I continue.

"Did you double check with the florist that they delivered to the correct venue?" I question as I walk over to my entry way to grab my laptop.

"Yes. We double checked the name, date, and location."

"I'm at home but let me pull up the file on my laptop to double check the order was placed correctly."

Opening my laptop on my counter, I make quick work of entering the company's terminal server and clicking the file labeled "Kent Wedding - July 2026."

"I'm looking at the florist's contract . . ."—I scan the document, trying to find the confirmation of the color of the roses—"Ah!" I cheer and point to my screen. "Yes. You did in fact order *lilac* roses."

"Okay. So now what?"

"Now you call the florists. See if—"

"They already told me they don't have any lilac roses. In fact, I called five other florists in the area and none of them have lilac or anything close."

"Okay. No problem." I search my brain for creative solutions I've used in the past, then park on the purple flower still haunting my dreams. "Did they have any white roses by chance?"

"White? But I need purple—"

I cut her off. "Just go with me. If they have white roses, we can pair those with lavender and at least they'll have the same color scheme."

"Okay, I'm following, just let me put you on speaker so I can write this down."

"Oh and double check that no one in the bridal party has a sensitivity to lavender. And insure the bride that there will be a partial refund of the flowers due to the mistake. We'll try to get a complete refund but I don't want you promising the bride that just in case we can't follow through."

"Okay. Thank you, Lindsay."

"No problem. You're doing great, Claire." I try my best to reassure her. "At the end of the day, the color of the flowers won't affect the couple getting married, and if it does, they should've never been getting married in the first place."

I hear her sigh before she thanks me again and hangs up.

Putting away my laptop, I make my way over to the bathroom and wash my face. I guess I'm up now, might as well make the most of my Saturday.

It's been refreshing to have my weekends to myself. I actually can't think of a time where I wasn't stressing over work or school on the weekend. Last weekend, I did a 'read and rot' session for both days. This weekend, I want to check out this new cafe that just opened down the street.

After exchanging my pajama set for a pair of shorts and tank top, I walk the two blocks to the little cafe. On my way, I pass a couple riding side-by-side on bikes.

Things like that have been happening non stop these last few weeks. It's like everywhere I turn, I'm reminded of my week in France.

When I received my replacement phone from Fran, I was finally able to reconnect with all the missed calls and texts. Imagine my surprise when some of them were from Theo.

After reading all his texts then listening to his pleading voicemails, I felt like complete shit for not replying to him. By the time I was finally able to get my phone up and running to listen to his messages, over a week had gone by.

Of course I wanted to text him or call him, but what would I even say? I've been contemplating that very thing for almost two weeks now. A horrible case of analysis paralysis. I can't help but go back and forth on what I should say to him. Poor thing probably thinks I just used him for a vacation hookup.

Well, I guess I did, at least at the beginning. But even today, I still feel like it was so much more. And there could be even more *if* I just get over myself and text him.

Approaching the cafe, I'm giddy with how adorable it is. Little cream planter boxes filled with yellow primroses line the pale pink painted picture windows. As I step inside, I can already tell I'm going to be coming here a lot more based on the various drinks and bakery items I see on the tables.

The walls are lined with thick pale pink and cream stripes paired with a light beige scalloped wainscoting on the bottom half. Marble tables paired with pink and cream wicker patio chairs fill the cafe, and almost every chair is occupied.

The line moves fairly quickly as I peruse the menu. Everything looks so delicious and I can't decide what I want.

"Hi, welcome to the Little Flower. What'll ya have?"

I smile at the name. I swear if I get one more sign, I'll text him. "Hi. This is my first time and I'm a bit overwhelmed with all the choices. What do you normally order?"

The woman behind the counter smiles. "On days I want to really spoil myself, I order our lavender honey latte with a chocolate croissant. I'm sure you'd love it."

I can't stop the chuckle that comes out. Of course she would. "That does sound up my alley. I'll take that please."

"And if for some reason you hate it, just come back and I'll get ya something else."

"Oh no, I'm sure it's exactly what I need." I scan my card and hit the twenty percent option. "Thanks for the push," I add before taking a seat at a nearly vacated table.

Looking at the number I've saved but never used, I contemplate what to type out.

LINDSAY:

I'm sorry it's taken me so long to

Nope. Hitting backspace, I clear the message. I don't want to start off with an excuse. I've had more than enough time to call or text him since I've gotten my replacement phone.

LINDSAY:

I can't stop thinking about you.

No, too desperate. I delete the line.

LINDSAY:

Hi

"Lindsay?" I look up after hearing a man call my name. "Lavender honey latte with a croissant?" He tips the plate and then corrects himself. "Sorry. With a *chocolate* croissant?"

I barely raise my hand. "That's me." But the move is enough to jostle my phone out of my hands. My cat-like reflexes catches it but at the cost of hitting send on my incomplete text message to Theo.

"Great catch," the waiter notes as he places my order down on the table.

"Thanks," I sigh, staring at the two letter word on my screen.

Monday morning and still no reply from Theo. It's not that I'm surprised at the lack of response, especially given how long I took to text him back. But I was hopeful for once in my life that someone would come through for me. Hell, this morning I even subconsciously put on the same blue dress I wore when we went to the lavender fields by the abbey, hoping it would bring me some luck. Silly, I know.

A knock at my office door brings my attention up off of my desk.

"Lindsay?"

"Good morning, Fran. How's your morning going?" I stand up and motion her to come and sit.

"Oh," she waves me off. "It's just fine. I just came in to tell you I have a vendor coming in later today, but I double booked. Would you mind running it?"

"Oh, sure. What time?"

She pulls her phone up, glancing at it before answering. "Two. It's an overseas vendor. Small boutique hotel that's interested in hosting more destination weddings. I already vetted them. Just need you to dot the i's and cross the t's."

"Sounds great. I'll be there." I nod.

"Perfect. Thanks!" Fran turns to leave but uses her hand to stop herself at the threshold. "I think you'll like this one." Her smile looks almost mischievous as she turns away again.

My phone rings, dragging me away from my current project. Looking at the number, it's someone from the front desk.

"Yes?"

"Hi Lindsay, your two o'clock is waiting in the conference room."

"Perfect. I'll head there now. Thank you."

I hang the phone up before gathering my notepad and a few new vendor forms.

Walking through the office, my mind wanders back to my unanswered text. Do I dare send a double text? I mean the guy did send seven texts. *Seven*! Who does that? I'll tell you who, a guy who looked at our relationship as something more than a vacation hook-up, that's who.

I round the corner and see a man already sitting in one of the oversized black roller chairs. His back is to the glass door so I can't see his face but based on how high his head is over the chair's back, I'd say he's around six-and-a-half feet tall.

"Sorry to keep you waiting," I announce as I walk into the room.

"Like I said before," the man stands up and his piercing green eyes are the first thing I see. "I'd always wait for you, *ma chérie.*"

CHAPTER FORTY-FIVE

THEO

"Theo," she whispers after seeing me.

"Hi," I say, mimicking the same two letter response from her text.

I hadn't wanted to respond to it because I was about to fly out when the message came through. But my smile was so big that my cheeks hurt when I saw that text message from her. Even if it was just a one-word text.

I won't lie. There was a part of me that had second thoughts on flying out. Not about what I feel for Lindsay, but whether or not she'd appreciate the gesture or if she'd think I was some sort of stalker.

"Hi," she repeats, still frozen by the door. And though I don't want to rush this reunion, I can't wait any longer to have her in my arms.

Making my way over to her, I wrap my arms around her body, picking Lindsay up and spinning us around in the conference room as she links her arms around my neck.

"Miss me?" I whisper in her ear as I lower her back to the floor. "Because I've missed you." I kiss her cheek before pulling away to glimpse the face I've yearned for these past few weeks.

We stare into each other's eyes, soaking in the moment of us finally being together again. But it's hard to resist the pull of Lindsay so I push her up against the glass, not giving a fuck who sees as I kiss her with all the built up emotion from our time spent apart. One of my hands grip the base of her head while the other is looped around her side, fingers gripping possessively into Lindsay's ass.

When I finally pull away, we're both breathless. "Fuck, I've missed you so much, Linds."

"I've missed you too, Theo. So, so much." She punctuates her sentence with another relaxed but quick kiss. "And I'm so sorry it took so long for me to text you back." She sighs as she brings her hand up to my cheek. "But what are you doing here? *How* are you here?"

"Well, after Dad boasted to Ma about you all but saving the wedding that weekend, she figured it might be a good idea to partner with your company to attract more attention for destination weddings." My fingers brush back a stray piece of hair that's blocking my view of the eyes that have been haunting me ever since she left. "And since Grandpa is recovering so quickly, I was able to make this an in-person meeting. I actually got your text right before I got on the plane."

I help her straighten out her dress before turning around to grab the little white bag off the table.

"Now, I didn't get much, but I was hoping three could tie you over for a bit."

"You didn't!" she exclaims as I hand her the little white doggie bag I picked up before my flight.

"Look for yourself." I taunt but my grin is filled with pure joy.

She peeks inside the bag and her smile lights up the whole room. Somehow it's even brighter now than I remember.

"I can't believe you did this." She leans in and steals a peck on my cheek. "Thank you."

"Anything for you, *ma chérie*," I say as I brush a strand of hair out of her face with all the tenderness I can muster. "Now, do you think there's a chance we can get out of here? I'm a patient man, Lindsay, and I'm trying my best to keep things present-day PG, but I'm not sure how much longer I can wait after seeing you."

"Oh." She looks me up and down, and now all I'm thinking about are my hands and mouth all over her body proving to her *exactly* how much I've missed her.

"Don't look at me like that or I'm going to need to do something about it right here and now," I threaten in a husky tone.

She clears her throat, "But seriously. Are you actually thinking about being a potential venue for our clients?"

"I mean if y'all think we're a good fit." I wink before adding, "but if you need a demonstration, I'd be happy to oblige, *ma chérie*."

"Mmm," she mumbles before licking her lips. "I think I might just take you up on that." She eyes me up and down. "Let me shut down my computer and I'm all yours."

"It fell *between* the belts? God, it's like a scene from a book," I comment while dishing Lindsay up another piece of pizza.

In order to maximize our time together, we opted for takeout for dinner. Before phoning in the order, Lindsay offered to cook, saying her pantry and fridge were filled with fresh ingredients, but I wanted to make things as simple as possible for her tonight.

Apparently she wants to cook more, something I hope I can assist her with in the not so distant future. I'd love to make a mess with her in the kitchen.

"I know! Can you believe it? And by the time I got my new phone all situated, I felt like shit for how much time passed without a single response from me." She rubs the cornmeal dust from the crust between her fingers before adding, "And honestly,

I feel a little embarrassed with how long it took to finally text you."

I reach over the pizza box and grab her hand. "Hey. I'm here now, aren't I?"

"Yeah." She nods. "And how *are* you here? I thought you were supposed to stay the whole summer?"

"Like I said, Grandpa was moving around better than they projected." I shift my hips on the little pillow I'm using as a chair for the picnic we've created on Lindsay's living room floor. "Plus, the whole idea of bringing in more people for weddings really put a pep in Ma's step."

I chuckle thinking about how Ma practically begged me to leave. In her own words, "If you leave now, maybe I'll be planning your wedding, too."

"I'm happy to hear your family is doing so well, Theo."

I move the box out of the way and grab her chin, lifting it so I can look into her icy blue eyes. "Lindsay—"

Her eyes flash to mine, clearing my mind of what I was going to say next.

"You're really here." Her voice is soft, a barely there caress to my ears.

I lean in close, still holding her chin while I gently press my lips against hers, only to pull back just an inch. "I'm really here," I whisper against her mouth.

That seems to be all the proof Lindsay needs as she pushes me backwards on the floor and climbs on top of me.

"I'm so sorry I didn't reach out sooner, Theo. If I had known—"

I kiss her before she can get whatever excuse out of her mouth, because honestly, I don't care. I'm here. She's here. And we're both here *together*. That's all that matters to me.

She perks her head back up as her knees fall into place around my hips. "I mean, my sisters thought I should've called you immediately."

I sit back up while keeping her legs wrapped around me.

"Glad to know the sisters approve," I tease as I work kisses up her arm and to her neck.

"Oh, yes. Though I won't lie, Tory's on the fence." She leans her head back giving me better access to her neck.

"I'm sure I will win her over in no time. Especially now that I'm stateside." I sneak my hands under her blouse, feeling the subtle goose bumps rise on her skin. I tell myself it's because of my touch and not due to the slight breeze from the fan.

"And you're sure you're not moving any time soon?"

I stop my exploration. "Well I'll be moving out of my house soon, but only because I need to move on to another project. I'll still remain in Raleigh."

She sighs and I feel her physically relax at my words. "So whatever this is between us . . ."

"We have all the time to figure it out, *ma chérie*."

I strip off my shirt and start wrapping the cotton fabric around her wrists, forcing them behind her back. "But now that I have you"—I knot the fabric creating a makeshift pair of handcuffs—"I'm never letting you go again."

"Are you seriously tying me up right now?"

"You bet your fine ass I am." I flip her on her belly before grabbing her hips and raising them in the air. "Now," I start, admiring the view. "It's time for my dessert."

I lay so I'm facing the ceiling while I'm in between Lindsay's knees. Okay, so "facing the ceiling" is a bit of a stretch. I'm currently looking right at the lace covering Lindsay's pretty pussy.

Pulling her down to sit on my face, I wrap my arm around her thigh and proceed to tease her opening with one hand. I'm sure I look as gleeful as a pirate finding his long lost treasure—or for this scenario, his long lost booty.

I loop the dark lace with one finger, scooting it to the side to reveal her gloriously wet lips. You'd think it'd be darker with how her dress is covering my head, sheltering me from the bright light still emanating from the soon setting sun, but no. The cotton fabric of the dress is just light enough that the rays from that bright orange sky are still lighting my way.

Dragging my tongue flat against her center, I get my first taste of her since having her back in my arms. And fuck if I'm not greedy about it. My tongue takes its time as it moves from her needy opening to already swollen clit. I suck a bit before swirling my tongue around its tip, using the distraction to bring my fingers to her pussy.

"Fuck!" she shouts. "That feels—" She gasps as I sink two fingers in, continuing my tongue's rhythm right above.

Pulling away, I speak against her opening. "You know the French call an orgasm *la petite mort,"* I swirl my tongue around her clit before pulling back again, "which translates to 'little death.'" She rocks her hips back and forth while I continue thrusting my fingers in and out. "Tell me, *ma chérie,*" I taunt before flicking my tongue against her. "How many 'little deaths' should I give you tonight?"

My fingers and tongue move in unison to create the perfect amount of friction and pressure.

"Oh, Theo. Yes. Right there," she chants as her movements become less predictable.

Trusting she won't break out of my make-shift bindings, I move my other hand to her ass cheek and squeeze hard as she pushes down against my mouth.

A string of indiscernible curses come from Lindsay's mouth as I feel her clench around my now three fingers. She's making a fucking mess of my face and I'm eating up every second of it. Literally.

"I'm so close, Theo," she pants as her moves become more desperate, wiggling herself in whatever position she can in the hopes of finding her release.

Lindsay's core is squeezing my fingers so tight now that I can barely pump them in and out. Her body shutters against me and her release floods my face as she moans through her climax.

Staring up at her, I watch as she gyrates her hips from side to side. Her nipples are so hard they're visible through her dress's fabric as she arches her back. Both of her hands are still restrained as she rolls off to the side.

"That was—it was—" Words fail her as she attempts to catch her breath.

"Don't worry. We don't need words for this next part."

I move to pin her arms above her head as I use the other hand to start unbuttoning the front of her dress.

"You know, the last time you wore this dress was at the abbey."

"Mhmm." She nods.

I'm about halfway through the buttons when I add, "And just like then, I want to do unspeakable things to you, Lindsay." I've revealed the nude bra she's wearing underneath, the sheer fabric giving me a preview of her hard nipples waiting to be uncovered.

Before I unbutton any more, I kiss down her revealed center, following the line in between her breasts. "I want to show you *just* how devoted I am to you, *ma chérie*."

Her hands squirm in my grip. Once she realizes I have zero intention of letting her be in control right now, she relents.

"That's my girl," I praise as I pick back up where I left off, fingers working to undo each and every button until her body is fully revealed.

Once her dress is spread open, leaving her in only a nude bra and lacy brown underwear, I strip off my jeans. One-handed of course. I didn't want Lindsay to get any ideas about moving those greedy hands of hers.

Pulling out the condom I saved in my pocket just in case we found ourselves in this exact situation, I realize just how lucky I am that everything worked out today. A little better than I'd hoped if I'm being honest.

As my hands work back up her body, I stare at the swell of her breasts pulling tight against the confining fabric of her bra as Lindsay continues breathing hard. I slip my fingers through the thin fabric wrapped around her hips and bring it down her legs.

The lace is still drenched from her earlier release as I take them off, and my smile grows even more knowing I did that to her.

Stroking myself, I look down at Lindsay as her back arches off the floor and her eyes remain glued to my dick.

"See something you like?" I tease as I pull the rubber on.

She nods while licking her lips then thrusting her hips up and causing my tip to skim her entrance.

"Stop teasing," she whines as she repeats the motion.

Keeping her bound wrists firmly in one hand, I rake my fingers through her hair as I easily thrust inside.

My groans mix with her gasps as I sink deeper into her. "You are absolutely *dripping* for me, *ma chérie*."

The sound of skin hitting against each other echoes throughout Lindsay's living room as the warmth radiating off both of us creates an inferno that rivals the August heat outside.

"*Theo*," she whispers against my lips.

"I'm here, *ma chérie*. I'm right here." As our lips meet, our mouths open to each others' again.

I never thought I'd find someone I feel this deeply about, let alone so quickly. The few weeks we spent apart was absolute hell and one I don't ever plan on repeating.

Lindsay's breathing picks up, causing her to pull her head away from our kissing. Moving my mouth south, I drag down the sheer fabric of her bra with my teeth before licking and sucking on her left nipple.

Her locked hands beg to be untied, and with how good of a girl she's been, I decide to finally undo her bindings. In no time, her hands shoot up to find purchase in my hair as she moans out her pleasure.

"Oh my god! *Theo*!"

She spasms around my dick but I give her zero time for a break as I flip her back around so she's on all fours. Pulling her ass up in the air, I take a bite of my favorite meal before pushing in again. One of my hands grips her hip while the other explores the exposed skin and journeys to her clit. As soon as my index finger finds it, Lindsay pushes her ass even further into me.

"Oh you like that, huh?"

"Theo—I—I—can't," she stutters.

"Come on, Linds," I tease as my fingers gather the wetness between our bodies then goes back to swirling that sensitive spot. "We both know you have a few more left in you."

She whips her head around to try and look at me. "A *few*?!"

"One for now, and more for later." I pinch her clit causing her to gasp.

"You're going to pay for that, Theo."

"I'll happily get on my knees and grovel for you, *ma chérie*."

Two of my fingers work in tandem, rubbing against both sides of her clit as I increase my thrusting. She feels like a dream tightening around my shaft as we both get closer and closer to finding our release.

"Yes, Linds," I praise as my eyes roll back. "You're taking me so well."

Her scream reverberates against the four walls as she comes, taking me over the edge with her. My muscle-memory guides me through the final thrusts as I lose myself in the feeling of the two of us finishing together.

Bending down, I kiss the length of her spine before whispering, "Is it too soon to say I love you, Linds?" Her head tilts like she's not sure she heard me right. "Because I do."

"It is too soon." She pulls away before turning around on her knees to face me. "But I love you too, Theo."

We both grin with pure joy before clashing together again in an effort to get our hands and mouths on whatever parts of each other's bodies we can.

CHAPTER FORTY-SIX

THEO

A FEW WEEKS LATER . . .

The rest of August passed in a blur.

Early in September, the first few leaves are starting to turn, creating that picturesque fall setting. One of the reasons I love North Carolina is having all four seasons. I get to actually enjoy autumn instead of it instantly turning into winter like some of the other places I've lived.

Lindsay's currently away on Taylor's bachelorette party as I move into her apartment this weekend. My current house is in escrow and I was practically living over here anyways. I didn't have much to move so I was able to fit all my things in one trip. The most important necessity being my air-fryer of course. Matter of fact, I used that to heat up tonight's dinner, even though Lindsay has a perfectly good oven.

The sisters drove to the coast for the weekend to celebrate. Nothing too crazy. Just a nice quiet weekend, or at least that's what Lindsay's sister, Emma, promised before she left with Linds.

"Just a little bit of girl time. Nice dinners, brunches with mimosas, and of course some reading time as we relax on the beach. You know the drill," Emma teases before getting in the passenger seat.

"Oh, yes. I'm super familiar with 'girl time,'" I note with a playful eye roll. "Have fun and be safe ladies."

"I'll text you when we get there!" Lindsay shouts before driving off.

Emma flew out a few days before the girls' trip, so it was nice to finally meet her. Since she doesn't live in town, she's the only sister I haven't had the opportunity to really get to know.

All of the sisters are so unique in their own way, but when they're together, there's no doubt they're sisters. Not just their looks, but their mannerisms are so similar.

Lindsay and Taylor are starting to heal their relationship, too. While everything definitely isn't fixed just yet, it's nice to see them hanging out more often.

Taylor's wedding is next weekend and it's supposed to be a real classy one. But it does seem like the sisters all have their own reservations about it, ones they don't share with Taylor in order to avoid another fight.

Taylor looks to be mostly excited about it. I still haven't met the guy, which I find a little strange, but that'll change come the rehearsal dinner.

Work has been terrific. We acquired five more properties in the last few weeks and they should be ready for market around the holidays.

Life is good. Like *really* good. I feel a sense of belonging that I never really felt before. Moving around so much as a kid, hell even now as an adult with my job, I never felt like I had roots anywhere. The only place I really called home was the hotel. It's familiar and the only constant I've ever had in my life. Well, I guess that's not true now.

My phone dings and I check the screen to see it's Lindsay texting.

LINDSAY:

What are you wearing? 😉

So much for a quiet weekend.

THEO:

Your pink fluffy robe.

Hope you don't mind that I'm borrowing it.

I can't find the box with my pjs and it's just so soft against my skin.

LINDSAY:

Just don't forget about the matching slippers!

But seriously, how's it going over there?

THEO:

Fine. I'm basically all moved in.

Though I'd be better with you naked in bed next to me.

LINDSAY:

Poor Theo, can't go two nights without me?

THEO:

Why do you think I'm wearing the robe?

I'm going to miss my cute little bear snoring next to me. 🥺

LINDSAY:

Hey! You told me it was getting better.

It really has been. I wonder if reducing her stress levels helped with that. Or maybe all the sex we're having is tiring her out. Either way, I'm not complaining.

THEO:

You're right. It is.

Was dinner good?

LINDSAY:

Yeah, no drama. Everyone's mostly happy.

THEO:

Mostly?

LINDSAY:

Just normal cold feet. Taylor insists it was just the alcohol.

THEO:

Hmm.

Okay, I'll let you get back to it.

Goodnight! I love you!

LINDSAY:

I love you.

I'll text you tomorrow. Good night.

CHAPTER FORTY-SEVEN

LINDSAY

THE FOLLOWING WEEKEND . . .

The wedding venue is about an hour outside of town at a beautiful golf resort and hotel, so the wedding party has rooms booked for the entire weekend. Most of the guests are also staying over tonight so they can stay late at the reception without having to worry about driving home late, or drunk since there is of course an open bar.

I walk downstairs to peek at where the reception is being held and it's absolutely stunning. Almost everything is already decorated. In fact, the staff looks to be placing the final floral arrangements on the dining tables right now.

The ceremony is being held on one of the course's greens. It's not set up yet since the golf course is still open to players, but I can spot the arch. It's currently broken down in three pieces, already covered in one of the most beautiful floral arrangements I have ever seen. There are a variety of red roses, ranging from reddish pink to velvet red to scarlet with a few cream roses mixed in and plenty of greenery. It's gorgeous with a touch of moody.

Taylor's soon-to-be mother-in-law may be a little controlling, but she definitely has fabulous taste.

Strong arms wrap around my waist and the smell of lavender and honey fill my senses. Theo kisses the top of my hair while whispering, "Good morning, *ma chérie*."

I lean my head back onto his shoulder while enjoying the warmth from his chest up against my back. "Good morning."

"It's going to be a beautiful wedding."

Taking a deep breath, I attempt to hold my tongue. "I just hope Taylor's happy."

Theo kisses my head again and squeezes me tightly. "Me too, Linds. Me too." We stand still, enjoying the ambient sounds of people working the grounds in the early morning and the rustling of the trees from the slight breeze.

"Come on," he says, spinning me toward him. "Let's go get some breakfast before the chaos starts."

"Sounds good."

We walk hand in hand to the dining room as everyone is starting to trickle in, well everyone except the groom and his groomsmen. They left early to grab breakfast before they play a round of golf. Even with them missing, there are a ton of people. Some of the guests opted to spend the whole weekend here so a few of them are already down here.

"Thankfully ours will be a lot smaller," Theo whispers low enough that only I can hear.

I stop in my tracks and spin to face him. "What?"

He's grinning like the devil he is while that damn dimple makes an appearance. "What? You're telling me that with all the weddings you've planned, you haven't once thought about yours? About *ours*?"

Of course, I have but *we've* never talked about it. I'm caught off guard, but pure happiness takes over quickly because Theo thinks about our wedding. *Our* wedding. Him and me.

"Like you said, I'm surrounded by ideas. But it's nice to know you're thinking about it, too."

"I can't wait for you to share those ideas with me." He pulls my chair out and leans down for a quick kiss. "If you have time between breakfast and doing your makeup with the girls, I can show you a few ideas of my own for the wedding night."

"I heard that, Theo," Tory scolds from her place across the table.

"Good morning, Tory," Theo sing-songs. "So nice to see you."

"Uh huh," she huffs while arching her eyebrow. "And she most certainly doesn't have time for that. We are on a tight schedule today, so whatever you have planned will have to wait until tonight."

"But do keep in mind our room is next to yours," Emma chimes in as she takes her seat.

"And if you don't keep it down, we won't either," Diego adds as he pushes Emma's chair in.

"And *my* room is on the *other* side. Plus, I have a child in mine. Innocent ears and all," Tory adds.

"Mom, I'm an adult. I know what sex is." Haylee rolls her eyes as she pulls out a chair by Tory.

"That doesn't mean you need to hear your aunt *having it*." Tory is clearly taking this very seriously while Emma is losing control over her attempt at a stoic face.

"*Please*, mom. I've seen the things you type in the sister chat." That cracked Emma's composure and now all of us are laughing. I even see a slight smile from Tory.

"All right, all right. Let's just eat so we don't run behind on our 'tight schedule.'" I mime finger quotes on the last part. "Has anyone seen Taylor yet this morning?"

"No."

"Not yet."

"I texted her but no reply."

"Hmm. That's weird," I comment. That's so unlike her.

"How about we order for her and we can bring the plate up to the bridal suite after we finish eating. That way she doesn't have to do all this on an empty stomach," Tory offers.

"Yeah. That sounds good," I agree as the waiter appears, taking our breakfast orders.

After we finished our breakfast, there's still no word from Taylor. I kiss Theo goodbye while Tory grabs the to-go box full of Taylor's breakfast, and we ladies head off to Taylor's bridal suite.

Tory knocks on her door. "Taylor?"

We hear movement and the door opens a minute later. Instead of the beaming bride we're expecting to see, we're met with a wide-eyed, tight lipped Taylor.

She does *not* look good. Her hair's in a messy bun for fuck sakes. And while that may not seem like a red flag, for those who know Taylor, it is.

In the past five years, she's *never* worn a messy bun. Literally, this girl works out with her hair down, and somehow always ends them with flawless waves, not a hair out of place.

But right now, there are little pieces of hair framing her face as well as falling out of the scrunchie. Her eyes look a little puffy like she's been crying. She's wrapped up in the hotel's robe without a stitch of makeup on.

"Well come in if you must," Taylor huffs as she swings her arm inside the room.

Emma, Tory, and I all look at each other in silent understanding that there will indeed be no wedding today.

"Haylee, why don't you go take your shower and stuff."

"Oh . . . yeah . . . yeah. Okay, Mom. Sure thing," Haylee says before walking down the hall. And then it's just us sisters in the room.

"Please, oh please, tell me I can kick his ass?" Emma begs as soon as the door shuts.

Taylor huffs. "I don't want you to do anything. I guess part of me knew this was going to happen." She plops on her bed, folding her legs up under herself. "On the bright side, at least it happened *before* we got married."

"Oh, Tay." I sit down next to Taylor and rub her back as she cries into her hands. I can't imagine what is going through her head right now.

My phone dings and from where it's sitting on the bed, I see it's Theo so I hit ignore.

"It's fine. You can answer it. It's just Theo. He won't tell anyone," Taylor sniffs.

I trade places with Emma and take my call in the bathroom. Theo picks up on the first ring.

"Hey, Linds. Was Taylor okay? Need me to bring anything up? I know today's going to be busy for you ladies."

"Yeah, about that," I start, biting my lip before I continue. "It looks like our day just opened up."

"What? What does that mean?" He's surprised, which I get because I've barely had time to absorb it myself. Hell, I haven't even gotten the story of how the wedding got called off. Something tells me it was that asshole's fault though.

"The wedding's off, Theo."

EPILOGUE

LINDSAY

Several months later . . .

Theo snuck out early this morning, but he slipped a note in with my breakfast delivery.

Good morning, ma chérie.
I can't wait to make you my wife.
Meet me at the end of the aisle.
I'll be the roguishly handsome one at the end.
With all my love,
Theo

P.S. I've been told I need to hold off on wearing my "slutty little glasses" as you so like to call them. According to your niece, they don't

mix well with taking photos. But don't worry,
I'll wear them for our wedding night.

What a way to start the morning. How is this my life?

I can't believe it's been almost a year, down to the day, since that infamous first day where Theo spilled his coffee on me. If someone would've told me back then that I would return only a year later for my own wedding to said coffee-spiller, I would've laughed my ass off, telling them that there's a better chance of me learning to ride a bike. But here we are a year later, and both things are happily true.

After a week filled with amazing excursions with my family, it's nice to start a morning enjoying a laid-back breakfast with the girls.

"Did y'all close on that old house with all that acreage?" Tory asks as Emma hands me a mimosa.

"Right before we flew out here, we got the call that it's officially ours." The room fills with cheers before I clarify, "We're a couple years out from making our dream into a reality, but it's a step in the right direction."

"Damn right it is. You should be so proud, Linds," Emma notes.

"Yeah, being able to build a space where you both get to combine your dream jobs? That's truly amazing," Taylor praises.

The hope is being able to create a boutique inn with indoor and outdoor event space, merging each of our talents and creating something special to both of us. And of course, we'll be living on property in our own house, similar to what his family does here. But fixing the house we'll be living in is Theo's first priority with the property.

"I'm sure it'll be amazing after the renovation," Theo's mom, Annie, adds. She's been popping in and out all morning in between squeezing in some final touches for the wedding. I honestly couldn't have asked for a better mother-in-law.

"Obviously it'll be a great space for sister sleepovers," Emma notes.

"Hey!" Mom and Haylee whine in unison.

I walk over holding my mimosa in one hand as I bend down and kiss each of their heads. "Once it's up and running, y'all are always invited to stay."

"Thanks, sweetie." Mom's been in an especially good mood this trip.

One would think it's because she's happy I'm getting married but I really think it's due to the fact that she's been able to visit so many lavender farms this week. Well, that and has made a new friend with Annie.

She's been practically floating on cloud nine ever since our visit to the abbey earlier this week. Though I won't lie, the views were even more majestic than I remembered. Plus, Mom and Annie had their own mini-adventure a couple nights ago. Apparently they didn't come home until after midnight. I still have zero clue what those ladies were up to but they are quickly becoming best friends. Hell, Mom's even talking about making yearly trips out here.

We clean up what remains of breakfast before getting ourselves ready for the ceremony this afternoon.

"Are you excited for Paris?" Haylee asks as I start warming up the rollers.

"Beyond excited. Theo planned the whole trip so I can't wait to see what he has up his sleeve."

One of the reasons we had the whole family come so early is so that we could show them around Aix all before Theo and I leave on our honeymoon. And I'm finally going to be able to see Paris without feeling rushed, just like Theo promised.

"I know I've asked this before, but is there anything else the guys need help with before we start on hair and makeup?" I ask as I pull out my makeup bag.

"Absolutely not. The men have it all under control," Tory assures without batting an eye.

"I agree with Tory," Annie chirps.

We all spent yesterday setting up the tables and chairs as well as making all the floral arrangements. Ever since seeing the lavender fields on my first trip here, I just knew I wanted white roses with lavender sprigs mixed in for the bouquets. The only things left for the guys to do today should be decorating the tables and ensuring the arbor—

"Oh the arbor! Did Jean—"

Annie holds her hand up, attempting to calm my spiraling thoughts. "Jean just finished draping greenery and some lavender sprigs along the arbor. It's in position and ready to go along with the tent." Her tone is calm and reassuring as she walks over to me.

It's supposed to rain a little later in the day, so instead of moving dinner inside, Theo and I decided on renting one of those clear tents to cover the reception area.

"Thanks, Annie," I say, directing my attention to brushing out my hair.

"Of course, sweetie. I'll be back in a bit to bring some water and check to make sure you don't need anything else." She steals a hug and kiss on my cheek before whispering, "I can't wait to officially call you my daughter."

I fail to hold back the tears that start running down my face.

"Oh, now don't do that." She sighs as she pulls a handkerchief out and dabs my eyes. "We don't want puffy eyes for the pictures."

I laugh before nodding. She does have a point.

"Love you, Annie." My voice breaks as I say it.

"Love you, too." She kisses my head then goes to leave. "Let me know if you ladies need anything."

Theo's mom has been absolutely incredible throughout this whole planning process. No wonder the brides I send her way love her. I'm happy to finally be able to call her Mom after today.

The day passes quickly, filled with music, giggles, and plenty of champagne while we get ready for the ceremony. All of us ladies are bursting with joy, so carefree while we enjoy the day. I know I'll cherish these memories we're creating for the rest of my life. I start to get a little misty-eyed from thinking of it all as I put on my gown.

"Don't you dare ruin that makeup, Lindsay!" Tory scolds.

"Look up and dab the bottom of your eyelids. Helps to prevent the tears from falling," Taylor comments.

Annie peeks her head in briefly. "Alright ladies, time to zip up those dresses."

"I'll make sure they do!" Haylee quips.

She's been busy snapping photos throughout the chaos while we get ready. And she's super talented behind a camera. I can't wait to see where life takes her.

After everyone is laced and zipped, Dad sneaks in while Haylee snaps a few photos of us and with Mom.

"I think it's time we make our way out there, Linds," Tory interjects.

"We're so proud of you, Lindsay," Dad says with tears in his eyes. "And we love Theo, but if you don't want to walk down the aisle, we can stop all of this right—" I stop him by placing my hand on his.

"I love you, too, Dad, but you don't need to finish that sentence. I love Theo, and I very much want to marry him." I smile wide. "Like *today*. Right now actually. So let's go." I motion my head over to the door, excited to marry my husband.

"You heard her. Let's go!" Emma cheers, opening the door wide for us to follow behind.

I squeeze Dad's hand again. "Thanks, Dad."

"Of course, Lindsay. Now let's go get you married!"

Dad and I walk hand in hand to where our little ceremony is set up. As we approach the aisle, I get my first look at Theo on our wedding day.

He's smiling ear to ear as he waits for me to take those last few steps. It's probably the biggest smile I've ever seen from him. I can't help but return the smile, it only grows as he mouths, "I told you I'd wait."

And with that, I lose control over the tears as my heart bursts with happiness. But for Theo, I'd surrender all control.

BONUS EPILOGUE

THEO

After sneaking out earlier this morning, I went for a walk around the lavender fields. It's a little chillier than normal for a mid-summer day but I'm enjoying the break from the humidity.

"And what are you doing up so early?" I hear Ma's voice before I see her.

"I could ask you the same thing," I note before wrapping her in a hug.

"Well there seems to be a *very* important wedding happening today. One that's been in the making for the last year," she adds with a wink. "You aren't getting cold feet are you?"

"With Lindsay?" I scoff. "Never." We start walking down a row before I continue. "She'll be up soon and so will the sisters. I'm sure they'll enjoy having the morning to themselves."

That's the PG answer anyways. I had a sneaky suspicion that if I would've stayed in that bed any longer with Lindsay's deliciously naked body pressed up against me, we'd be having a late start to all the wedding festivities. And as much as I love distracting her, this is one day I want to make sure everything goes according to plan. But not all things are within our control.

"I looked at the weather forecast before heading out here and the rain is supposed to start around six tonight."

"Well it looks like you made a great call on the tent then," Ma praises as we turn down another row. As we stroll, I can't help but hope to have a similar setup with the lavender at our new property, once it's renovated of course. "You and the rest of the boys going to set it up after breakfast?"

"That's the plan. Everything else is ready for the ceremony."

"Theo." Mom stops and grabs my hand. "I'm so incredibly proud of the man you've become. And I'm so happy you've found Lindsay. It's clear that your heart seems to be at home with her."

"It really is, Ma." I wipe my eyes before adding, "Thanks for always being there to support me. You and Dad both."

"We love you so much." We hug then wipe our eyes. "Now stop frolicking in the flowers and let's get ready for your wedding," Ma teases as we head inside.

Everything feels like a dream as I watch my beautiful bride walk down the aisle to me. She's a precious gift I'll never deserve, but greedily take.

God, she is truly a vision in white and she's all mine. Lindsay's makeup is light, allowing her natural beauty to shine as well as all of her tiny freckles that pepper across her nose. Her hair is styled half-up with gentle curls, showing off her ever so sun-kissed shoulders, even with all the sunscreen she wears.

When she looks at me, she's absolutely beaming. Her wide smile is stretched from ear to ear and her icy blue eyes are still as haunting as the day we met.

Fate really did me a favor that day and every day since. For I have found my forever home in her and it's my favorite place to be.

ACKNOWLEDGMENTS

I would first like to start by thanking my husband. I am forever grateful for your love and support. You are my biggest cheerleader.

My two incredible daughters, I love and cherish you both more than words can ever describe. Thank you for all of your help in creating bonus cover designs and packing all of my orders. We have definitely made some of my favorite memories during those special moments.

My parents and two sisters, who I've spent a million and one hours yapping to about everything that goes into making a series. Thank you for listening to my rants and giving me support during this journey.

A special thank you to my outstanding editor, Amy Pritt. Throughout this process, you have pushed me to be a better writer and I am forever grateful for your honest critiques and kind praises.

I would also like to thank my Beta team. Bree, Dee, Jennifer, and Raquel, you all are such incredible human beings. I loved seeing your enthusiasm for Lindsay & Theo's story. Thank you for all of your notes and helpful comments as well as constant cheers along the way.

To my ARC readers. Thank you for volunteering your time to read Lavender Haze before it's published. With your help in spreading the news, more people are able to fall in love with the Hartman sisters, and their men of course.

And finally, I would like to acknowledge my deepest love and gratitude to all of my readers. Theo's slutty glasses are for you!

Ciao!

-A

www.ingramcontent.com/pod-product-compliance
Lightning Source LLC
LaVergne TN
LVHW091254150826
845673LV00006B/1414

* 9 7 9 8 9 9 4 4 3 0 4 4 6 *